Summer Holiday

PENNY SMITH

FOURTH ESTATE · *London*

First published in Great Britain in 2011 by
Fourth Estate
An imprint of HarperCollins*Publishers*
77–85 Fulham Palace Road
London W6 8JB
www.4thestate.co.uk

A catalogue record for this book is available from the British Library

ISBN 978-0-00-736073-4

Typeset in Minion by
G&M Designs Limited, Raunds, Northamptonshire
Printed in Great Britain by Clays Ltd, St Ives plc

Mixed Sources
Product group from well-managed
forests and other controlled sources
www.fsc.org Cert no. SW-COC-001806
© 1996 Forest Stewardship Council

FSC is a non-profit international organisation established to promote the
responsible management of the world's forests. Products carrying the FSC
label are independently certified to assure consumers that they come
from forests that are managed to meet the social, economic and
ecological needs of present and future generations.

Find out more about HarperCollins and the environment at
www.harpercollins.co.uk/green

To Rob, Hilary, the man from the Danish biscuit commercial and the wife of my dentist.

CHAPTER ONE

When Miranda Frayn was little, she'd wanted to be a vet, an astronaut or someone who got lots of free stickers and felt-tip pens.

At around twelve years old, she decided that being a vet was not a good job, since it seemed that all they did was put down hamsters, massage Minty, her Jack Russell, up her bottom, and get scratched by cats. Astronauts did not spend their days bouncing round the moon and far-flung planets, but instead did tedious experiments with seeds and rubbishy-looking rocks. She no longer wanted free stickers and felt-tip pens, but instead yearned to be famous and get married to Luke Skywalker or Han Solo.

With that in mind, she put her name forward for every school play and, by dint of hard work and the non-stop badgering of the drama teacher, managed, the year before she left, to achieve the giddy heights of Maria in *The Sound of Music*. The boy who wrote the review in the school magazine described her as radiant, moving – a star in the making. Miranda had discovered early that if you wanted something badly enough, you had to be prepared to kiss really unattractive people – sometimes more than once. If she had not virtually sucked his head off at the back of the cinema, he would have written a very different critique. He would have said that as a nun she was unconvincing, and as a singer she'd made his ears bleed. He would have said that she should take up any other career but acting.

But, once caught, the performing bug is difficult to shake off, and there are any number of people willing to take your money for everything from head shots to acting lessons.

Luckily for the viewing public, fledgling starlet Miranda Frayn fell in love and decided that what she really, really wanted to do was get married and have babies. In her dreams, she imagined combining a career in film with bringing up children, but MGM failed to come knocking at the house in Oxfordshire, and instead she trod the boards in amateur plays, where the costumes were creaky, the sets were wobbly, and there was always a sweaty man playing fourth lead who wanted to have an affair with her.

It was all so dispiriting that, eventually, Miranda settled on acting the part of the devoted wife and became a passionate advocate of scarf knitting. She would have liked to create something a little more advanced but, frankly, with two small children and a man who wore Savile Row suits and cashmere from Brora, that was never going to happen.

Nigel Blake, her husband, was everything she had wanted: smart, funny, handsome and rich. She hadn't realised she wanted rich but, increasingly, it was the only thing he still was. When she divorced him after two decades, having discovered his long standing shagfest, as she called it, with his secretary, she would have described him as fat, boorish and rich. Or Knobhead, for short. But he was the father of her two children, so she reserved such comments for evenings when she was out with friends and for phone calls with the man himself.

Meanwhile, she was living in London, back on the dating scene and hating it. It was like constantly seeing bad films. She had started off excited about the prospect and then, over two years, a sort of malaise had crept over the whole thing and she had stopped worrying about matching underwear – or even matching outerwear. And as for her friends' view of what constituted handsome …

Here she was, for example, on yet another night out with an allegedly suitable man. Passers-by glancing into the little restaurant would have seen a couple who had probably been married for an eternity – they weren't speaking.

Miranda was bored again. She imagined her date as an icon on her computer that she was deleting.

And while she was at it, she might delete some of her friends' numbers. How on earth they could think that this pompous tit was her cup of tea … And her steak was tough. Still, at least it was giving her teeth a workout.

'Sorry?' She raised her eyebrows at her dining partner.

'I asked if you wanted more wine.'

'No,' she responded baldly. 'Thank you,' she added. No point in adding rudeness to the patronising she had already been. Mind you, he deserved it. Right-wing. Fascist. Fat. Twat. She smiled as she thought it.

'What?' he asked suspiciously.

'Nothing. I was just thinking silly words. Rhyming words. How much better they are than when they're on their ownsome.'

'As in?' he queried, trying to get on to her wavelength, although he had almost given up. He was not a man who struggled to get women. He was rich and lived at a very expensive address in Mayfair.

Miranda knew, as she opened her mouth, that it was going to be a hopeless conversation. The man had no imagination, the verbal dexterity of a Clanger and she honestly couldn't be bothered to try to explain what she found amusing about rhyming words. And of course she couldn't articulate the words she'd come up with to describe him, so she had to make up two more. 'Numpty and flumpty,' she said, off the top of her head.

'Which means?'

'Nothing. It's the rhyme that amuses me.' Oh, God. Now she was going to have to explain. Or feign partial death and get out of this place.

'What – so Humpty Dumpty's funny?' He wrinkled his nose.

As if I'd done a trouser cough, she thought, and smirked.

'Is it?' he asked, mistaking – again – her expression.

'I think you either find words funny or you don't. Have you finished? Shall we get the bill?' He looked at his very expensive watch, clearly hoping she'd clocked its exclusivity. 'I know it's a bit early,' she added, 'but I've suddenly remembered I have a five o'clock start tomorrow, and perhaps tonight wasn't the best for organising a long dinner.'

'A five o'clock start? What for?' he asked.

'Erm. Flight. Early flight. Late booking. I needed to get away. Going to …' her eyes fell on the tablecloth '… the Czech Republic,' she said brightly. Like I care whether or not you believe me. She tried to look innocent and apologetic at the same time.

To give him his due, he asked promptly for the bill, then insisted on paying. That was the one good thing about the blind dates: they

4

hadn't cost her anything. But they were all bankers or company directors, so she felt guilt free. In fact, with the bankers, she was practically doing the country a service.

She was barely home and through the door before she was entirely disrobed and in front of the television. What a waste of an evening. What a waste of a lot of evenings.

Miranda realised she was accidentally watching the news and it was all too depressing. She clicked it off and wandered up to the bathroom to wash her face and moisturise. After she'd cleaned her teeth, she looked at herself in the mirror. Put her hands to either side of her face and pulled them back to see how she'd look with a face lift. Would she have the guts to let someone literally take off her face, trim the edges and hem it again to smooth out the wrinkles? At least her eyesight was starting to go a bit. It was a relief not to be able to see the crow's feet quite so clearly.

She sighed and padded through to the bedroom. Odd, she still couldn't get used to sleeping alone. For almost a quarter of a century, another body had slumbered beside hers, getting larger, taking up more space, and snoring louder as the years passed. It was such a luxury to do a starfish impression and not touch flesh.

Tomorrow is the day I take control, she thought. Life has got to perk up, big-time. She lay between the cotton sheets trying to decide what control needed to be taken.

Her friends would have described Miranda Blake first and foremost as a laugh. Pressed to expand, they would have said she was attractive, with a penchant for extremely high heels. Her parents would have described their daughter as wayward but tamed by a decent man, whom she had divorced for no good reason (after all, everyone has a little dalliance on the side). Miranda herself would have said she was all right, considering the alternatives. Everything was heading south and hairs were starting to sprout in strange places, but it could have been a lot worse. She had friends with prolapses, fallen arches, bad backs or bunions.

Early in their relationship, Nigel would have described her as a cracking bit of totty. The two had met at a party in Fulham where neither knew the host. Miranda was dressed for success in a little blue dress and very high black heels, which she found surprisingly easy to walk in. Nigel was wearing what she later came to describe as his out-of-hours uniform – a Pink's shirt and corduroy trousers with Gucci loafers. His thick brown hair fell in messy abandon to his shirt collar and his amber eyes looked admiringly into her sparkling blue ones as they shared the bottle of Château Latour he had brought, having mistakenly thought it was a dinner party.

He had looked around for a corkscrew and she had handed him one wordlessly – she'd been on the lookout for a semi-decent bottle since she'd arrived ten minutes earlier with a girlfriend. He had walked her home afterwards and they had kissed fervently on the doorstep of her minuscule studio flat. Within a year, they had married in a picturesque church in the Cotswolds and Miranda got pregnant on honeymoon. Lucy's birth was followed two years later by the arrival of Jack.

It wasn't until the children were on the verge of leaving home that Miranda realised she categorically loathed her husband. The sound of his key in the front door of the smart stuccoed building in fashionable Kensington filled her with a horrible *ennui*. It didn't help that he now resembled an overstuffed pork sausage. Maybe he had actually absorbed a whole other person. Watching him tie his shoelaces was a lesson in physics: how did he bend in the middle when the middle was so much bigger than either end?

When she'd brought up the subject of divorce he had been stunned. 'On what grounds?' he had demanded.

'My unreasonable behaviour? Your unreasonable behaviour? Bird molestation? Giraffe bothering? I don't really mind, but I do want a divorce,' she had said, in a reasonable tone.

'Are you having an affair?' His eyebrows had come together.

'No. And I assume you aren't?' she asked, her eyes on his paunch. When a paunch got that big, did it become a super-paunch?

He went pink around the ears, and it dawned on her, with a shock, that he *was*. And as the conversation (now a shouting conversation) continued, she discovered that it was of long standing and with his secretary. She remembered yelling at some stage that he was a cliché. It was strange that even though she wanted a divorce, wanted never to see Nigel step out of his trousers ever again, it was still awful.

It was the division of the spoils that did it. There were days when she had cried over the toaster for her lost dreams. The things they had bought together when she had imagined herself in love. But now she could see that that had been youthful folly, a combination of lust and laziness. Marrying Nigel had relieved her of the need to get a proper job.

Lucy blamed Miranda for breaking up a happy family. Jack had been upset but understanding.

After the decree absolute, Miranda had bought herself a house in Notting Hill and put the rest of the money in the bank. It wasn't a huge amount, but she had reckoned that, if she was careful, she could have a lovely break before she found employment.

The time had come. But what job?

I need a change of direction, Miranda thought, putting her toes out from under the duvet and wiggling them. Tomorrow I'll do something to facilitate finding a job. At least it'll be a change from thinking about sodding dates.

Eventually, as her mind wandered off to variations on a theme of sheep, she drifted into sleep.

The next morning she arose full of purpose. She had a shower, washed her hair and put on a conditioning treatment, then vigorously applied a body scrub, which smelt slightly off. Wrapped in a fluffy new towel – she had thrown out all those that might have touched Nigel – she plucked her eyebrows and moisturised, using industrial quantities of cream. She applied blow-drying serum to her mid-length red-gold hair, then hung upside down to do the roots, leaving the rest to curl naturally.

'Right,' she said, as she strode to the wardrobe. She took out a thin pink shirt and a pair of jeans cut off to the knee. Looking critically in the mirror, she was in two minds about whether she was mutton dressed as lamb since she could see her bra through the shirt. But without a husband or children to declare either way, she decided to go with it.

She breakfasted on two pieces of toast, one with marmalade and the other with Nutella, which looked a little funny – she'd probably bought it when Jack was about eight, and a lot of buttery crumbs had gone under the bridge since then.

With a cup of tea in hand, she opened her computer, checked her emails and hovered over the Google search space. What should she put? Maybe, she thought, I should get into the habit of having a job before actually applying for one. It was a bit scary, the idea of an interview. And she was a bit long in the tooth to be asking for work experience.

In the absence of anything springing to mind, she typed 'Constructive Things to Do' and clicked on the first result. A list of twenty-five possibilities popped up, including updating your MP3 player and throwing out clothes. Very therapeutic, but not what she was after.

Another suggested learning how to spin a pencil round your thumb. Not now. Although it would be a good trick – and certainly an advance on dating.

An hour later, Miranda had got herself on to a website advertising eco-produce. She went and made herself another cup of tea, and opened the kitchen cupboard to see if there was anything that might help it go down. There wasn't. That was the flip-side of living on your own – there was never a biscuit when you wanted one.

Back at the computer, she chose a different heading for Google: 'Constructive Things to Do In Your 40s'.

One word stuck out: 'Volunteering'.

'By Jove, I think she's got it,' she said, double-clicking on a link. By lunchtime Miranda Blake, divorcee, forty-three, had volunteered for canal clearing in the Cotswolds.

She printed off the list of suggested items to take with her, ticked off those she had, and ringed those she hadn't. What on earth was a 'wicking shirt' when it was at home? She Googled it. Oh, right, she thought. What we used to call Aertex when we were at school and forced to play hockey in inclement weather.

Her mobile phone rang. 'Hi, Lydia.'

'Miranda,' said Lydia, the wife of one of Nigel's friends. 'Wondered how the date with James went last night.'

'Erm. Fine. But I don't think he's right for me,' answered Miranda, suddenly remembering she had told James she would be on an early flight.

'Oh?'

'You know. Not really the same sense of humour. And things,' she ended lamely.

'Handsome, though,' stated Lydia, in her clipped way.

'Yes. Oh, yes. Definitely,' said Miranda, shaking her head vigorously even though Lydia couldn't see.

'And he's loaded.'

'Yes.' She had noticed his very expensive watch and the new Aston Martin.

'So, are you going on a second date?'

'Well … no,' said Miranda.

'But you'd be *perfect* together,' pronounced Lydia.

In what way? wondered Miranda. Perfect together as in chicken and Lego? 'Mm,' she said, debating where to go from here. 'Thing is, I don't think it would work. He's sort of similar to Nigel.'

'To Nigel?' Lydia almost shrieked.

'Banker. Square?' she essayed.

'Square?' repeated Lydia.

There was a silence while Miranda tried to form a sentence that wouldn't antagonise her friend. Or was she a friend? Would a proper friend have set her up with such a – such a muppet? 'I think what I'm looking for, Lydia, is a change,' she finally tried. 'Someone who isn't in the banking world, maybe. Someone to be silly with. Carefree with. A diversion.'

Lydia of the carefully styled coiffure was not having that. 'What you need is someone who is going to look after you. And that means a man with a solid career. Money in the bank. James ticks all the boxes – *and* he doesn't have any children to get in the way. As I told you, he's newly out of a long relationship with a concert pianist. Which means he *can* be arty. And so on and so forth.'

Really! How could she have a friend who would say 'and so on and so forth'? She typed into the computer: 'How to End a Friendship with Someone Dull'.

'Are you typing?' asked Lydia.

'No,' responded Miranda, swiftly, smiling to herself at the options listed. She would read them all later.

'I think he's worth a second stab.'

'Maybe you're right,' lied Miranda. 'Leave it with me and I'll have a little think.' Anything to end this conversation. 'Now,' she added, 'I have to sort myself out. I'm going on an expedition and I reckon I need some wicking shirts and a pair of gaiters. I'll speak to you later.'

'Shall I tell James to call you?'

'No. I'll call him myself. 'Bye.' Why had she said that? Damn. She pursed her lips, then sent a text: **James. Thanks for dinner. All the best, Miranda.** No self-important alpha male could possibly take that as anything but a brush-off. Particularly not when he found out from Lydia that she was definitely in town and not in the Czech Republic.

She grabbed her list and her bag and left the house with a spring in her step. It was a beautiful day and she decided to walk to Kensington instead of driving. After all, she was going to have to get used to being in the fresh air, and it wasn't always going to be this sunny.

CHAPTER TWO

On Saturday, having told nobody about her new career as an eco-bod, Miranda woke up to the alarm and wondered whether she should cancel. She'd bet loads of people did, what with one bronchitis or another. She lay in bed for a minute, luxuriating in the beauty of being alone under her king-size duvet. No man-smells here, she thought. If Nigel had been there, he would have farted, scratched his scrotum and demanded breakfast in bed. And possibly nudged her with his early-morning broom handle, emerging from below his distended stomach. Urgh. Just the thought of it got her out of bed.

She meandered over to the curtains and threw them back. Damn. Raining. Typical. Maybe she wouldn't bother to wash her hair, after all. She checked the time. An hour to get ready. She pottered into the bathroom and turned on the shower, catching sight of herself in the big mirror over the bathroom sink as she reached for her toothbrush.

Whoa. What was that? She peered closer. Bollocks. A spot at my age, she thought. That is just *so* unfair. And then she smiled at her reflection. She was sounding remarkably like her daughter going through puberty. The difference was that Miranda would leave the spot to do its own thing and not fiddle with it, unlike Lucy who would dig and squeeze until it virtually needed stitches and a few weeks to heal. It was amazing that Lucy's face had survived without a scar.

Miranda stepped into the shower – and couldn't get out again because of a severe bout of water-induced inertia. She was in the zone, just wanting to stand there for ever letting the water cascade down her back and creep round the front. What would snap her out of it? She had to make a move. Any move. A move that would break the spell. No. It wasn't going to happen. She'd be found on Wednesday by the cleaner. Blown up from water absorption and with five days' hair growth on her legs. Would there be maggots? Are there always maggots? 'Yuk,' she said, and reached for the shaver.

There was something wonderful about stepping out from a long shower into a warm mist, and it was even better not being able to see herself in the fogged-up mirror. She moisturised every available inch of skin, covered the spot with concealer, then hovered over the perfume. Was there any point? She sprayed some on the back of her neck.

She could just not turn up. Simply call in sick. How wonderfully naughty. Who would care? But she used to push the children into doing things they didn't want to and they usually came back saying it was the best day they'd ever had. She girded her loins and walked with purpose to the plastic carrier bag from which she had not yet unpacked the requisite items on the list.

My goodness, she thought, when she was dressed. I look like the sort of woman who's never heard of Brazilian waxing or eyebrow-plucking. In short ... a mad feminist. All men are bastards. I'll take them down with my sharp wit and disused tweezers.

She fluffed up the duvet, threw on the coverlet and the six cush-ions, then decided she had just enough time for a quick coffee.

Ten minutes later she was wondering why, with all her experience of life, she hadn't put a dash of cold water into it. The burnt roof of her mouth hurt. On the bright side, there would be that strangely enjoyable peeling away of the skin tomorrow.

The green Jaguar purred into life and she put the postcode into the sat-nav as she waited for the garage door to lift. She drove west towards Shepherd's Bush and the A40, searching for something to listen to on the radio, finally settling for XFM because it made her feel connected to Jack. Her adorable Jack. Nigel hadn't been able to make him conform and he was now wandering the world with a clutch of A levels and a backpack. She did worry about his future and, in a secret, locked-away bit of her brain, actu-ally wished he had gone into banking and done the hiking stuff later.

Lucy, mind you. Chip off the old block. Miranda tried out her singing voice along to some god-awful rackety piece of music.

The weather was getting worse. The rain was sluicing down as though a pipe had been uncorked. There was little traffic on the roads and she made it to the rendezvous within an hour, parking between a muddy old Fiat and a yellow VW Beetle. After she'd struggled into her brand-new, state-of-the-art Gore-Tex anorak, with zips under the armpits for letting off steam, she emerged from the car with a modicum of decorum and tiptoed to the boot in her trainers to get her wellingtons. Four people were watching her from under umbrellas. Their clothing looked like it had been stolen from a tip. They were filthy.

14

'Hi,' said Miranda, brightly, stuffing her new gloves into her jacket pocket.

The assembled group smiled and nodded, drinking tea from a flask and chatting about the work in hand. A man in a high-visibility jacket, with teeth that might have been thrown into his mouth by a blind parsnip-tosser, introduced himself as Will. 'We're basically going to be getting rid of the undergrowth and stuff on the towpaths so that the dredger can get through to clean out the canal,' he said. 'At the moment, as you can see …' he looked around and amended that '… as you can't see through this atrocious weather but I assure you is the case, the canal is all silted up and full of algae bloom and duckweed. The dredger can't do its work until we've done ours.' He waved a hand in the direction of the sky. 'Now, apparently the good folk at the Met Office are predicting that this rain is going to blow through pretty quickly. Since we're all here, with the exception of Alex, we may as well get cracking. At least nobody's cried off with the "flu".' He made quote marks in the air as though that was a usual excuse for someone not turning up. Miranda shook her head in disgust.

He walked towards the Land Rover and bent over, his large trousers gathering in an elephant's bottom of grey as he rummaged. 'I've got a collection of implements in here. Come and take your pick. Not literally.' He laughed – it was obviously a line he'd used before. Miranda smiled. Might as well show willing.

The others had obviously done this work before, since they showed no hesitation in lunging for the tools, leaving her with nothing but a pair of enormous leather gloves and the job of picking up litter. 'It's like being at home with children,' she commented to the woman in front of her. Her name was Teresa: she had hair like a newly shorn sheep and a wart near her nose.

'What? Walking along wearing protective gloves?' Teresa asked, with a confused expression.

'No, having to pick stuff up. All their toys and things. Socks. Although usually I didn't wear big leather gloves to do it. Do you have children?'

'Cats,' responded Teresa, briefly.

'Lovely. Hairy ones?'

'Yes. Well, one short-haired and two long-haired.'

'Rescue cats or pedigree?' Like she really cared.

'Rescue.'

'Lovely.' Bloody hell! She had to stop saying 'Lovely' – she was beginning to sound like a game-show host.

They stopped speaking as they reached the rest of the group.

'Here's where we left off last week.' Teresa nodded to a newly cut section on a bush.

Will was hunched over, talking to one of the men, but turned and said something to Teresa, who moved forwards, leaving Miranda standing alone. She sniffed the air appreciatively. The rain had stopped, leaving a damp, green smell. It reminded her of finding a little patch of camomile in the corner of the garden and lying on it to see how comfortable it was. When Nigel had found it, he had covered it with weed-killer.

'So, Miranda,' said Will, 'you've picked the short straw, and are doing the tidying up. It's one of the most important jobs, but also one of the most unloved as it plays havoc with your lower back.' He rubbed his own and grimaced, his lips slightly parted to reveal one of his yellowy parsnip teeth. 'I'd recommend that you stand up and stretch it out frequently or you'll wake up tomorrow unable to walk. And try not to get too close to the cutters – they can get a bit carried away, if you know what I mean.'

Miranda nodded, although she wasn't sure she *did* know what he meant. She added a smile, then turned quickly as loud running was heard through the gloom, followed by the sudden appearance of a superbly scruffy man with dreadlocks, wearing a jumper with so many holes that it resembled a string vest.

'Alex!' exclaimed Will, warmly, clasping his outstretched hand and clapping him on the shoulder. 'We were wondering where you'd got to. Thought you must have been struck down with summer flu or some other lurgy.'

'Camper van sprang a leak in the middle of the night. I've been doing emergency repairs. Couldn't leave until I'd made sure it was watertight. Don't want to get back and find all my Armani pumps wrecked, do I?'

'Ha-ha. No. You betcha you don't,' Will said jovially. He pointed a big square finger. 'I saved you a machete.'

'Can I have a machete?' asked Miranda, moving closer.

'Ha-ha!' He laughed again. 'No, I don't think so. Not on your first day.' He strode back to the Land Rover, his boots sliding on the muddy path.

'Alex,' said Alex, holding out his hand to Miranda.

'Miranda,' said Miranda, shaking it and looking into the greenest eyes she had ever seen. They were leaf green. Ireland green. Ridiculously green.

'First time, then.' He smiled down at her.

Miranda was tall, but he was taller still – and what her friends at school would have called 'well tasty'. Although she wasn't sure about the dreadlocks. Didn't you have to be seriously grubby to get them? Not wash for months? She sniffed cautiously. He didn't smell. 'Lovely fresh air, isn't it?' she exclaimed, to cover herself, and then answered his question: 'And, yes, it is my first time. I wanted to get out of the city and do something constructive.'

'Which city?'

'London.'

'Which part?'

'Notting Hill,' she said semi-apologetically. Ever since the film *Notting Hill*, she'd felt something akin to embarrassment about living in a place that was synonymous with a romantic comedy starring Hugh Grant and Julia Roberts.

'Nice,' he said, as he accepted the machete from Will. 'Shall we?'

'"Lead on, Macduff,"' she said, even though they were already where she needed to be to start picking up rubbish.

'"Out damned spot,"' he threw back, as he advanced into the undergrowth, the crotch of his baggy trousers catching on foliage and shooting raindrops in arcs.

Was he flirting, Miranda wondered. How lovely. That bloody word again. 'Lovely, lovely, lovely, lovely,' she said, under her breath, to use them all up. 'Lovely, luvverly. Luvverly bunch of coconuts. Oh, wouldn't it be lovely? And the new word of the day is …' she paused, putting a big lump of greenery into the bag '… gorgeous. Scrumptious. Handsome. Steady on, Miranda.' What was happening to her?

She gave herself a stern talking-to. 'I am a forty-three-year-old woman with two children, one of whom is probably about the same age as he is. It's disgusting. Nigel's eyes would literally come out of his head on stalks if he knew what I was thinking. No, not literally – particularly with all that lardy, piggy flesh holding them in.'

Her mind rambled on aimlessly as she bent to her task. She didn't notice the time slipping by because she had wandered into a rich seam in the creases of her brain and hopped incrementally to a reverie about Harrison Ford in *Raiders of the Lost Ark*. Then she stood up. 'Ow,' she squeaked. A searing pain had shot up her back and exploded tiny pinpoints of light through her retinas.

Will ambled back to check she was all right.

'Yes. And, yes, I know you told me to stand up and stretch, but I got into a rhythm and completely forgot,' she panted, rubbing the base of her spine.

'Stand with your feet apart and drop your body forwards from your hips,' he ordered. 'Go all floppy. Take the strain off your lumbar region.'

She hung forward and felt her anorak slip up past her nose, so that she was breathing into the zip and smelling something she couldn't quite put her finger on. Was it man-made-fibre scent? She suddenly realised what it was: the smell of hard work, alias sweat, and she had obviously forgotten to put on any deodorant. How very, very … in a weird way, almost pleasant. If acrid.

She stood up to get away from it.

'Feeling better?' asked Will.

'Yup,' she announced – although, actually, she felt a bit sick from standing up so fast. 'Onwards and upwards,' she said, with determination.

She reapplied herself to the task in hand, stretching every few minutes and admiring the clean and tidy state of the path. Well, tidy but muddy and a damn sight better than the view in front, with its branches and undergrowth melding together. She could just see Alex's dreadlocks whipping to and fro as he sliced the heads off unsuspecting plants.

It felt like days since she'd had her coffee.

She waved Will over.

'Problem?' he asked.

'Er, I hope not. I was suddenly overcome by a wave of hunger but I haven't brought a packed lunch with me. Which I seem to recall was on the list. A bothersome omission. Is there anywhere I could get something when we stop?'

'Yes – most of the regulars bring their own because they don't want what's on offer from the nearest shop. I'll warn you now, it ain't exciting. There might be a pie but it'll be more pastry than filling. And if the filling's meat, it might be a part of the animal you aren't familiar with.'

'A dollop of testicle, a dash of oink and an earlobe, eh? Beggars can't be choosers, as they say. That's what I'm going to have to do when we break. Which is when?'

Will checked his watch. 'Half an hour. Can you last that long?'

On cue, Miranda's stomach howled, like a small woodland creature in pain.

He laughed, and jerked his head upwards, revealing hairy nostrils. 'I'll take that as a no. If you could possibly hang on for a quarter of an hour, that would be better for us. We're dealing with a knotty branch and it would be nice if we could get that sorted before we have lunch.'

'I'll keep my stomach on a short leash, and tell it to pull its horns in, if that's not too much of a mixed metaphor,' she promised. She bent forward and pushed a great wodge of vegetation and sticks into her bag, suddenly noticing a stripy snail stuck to one of the leaves. She picked it off and it retreated quickly into its shell. She held it until it came out again, then gently touched one of its antennae. It retracted. She poked the other.

'Aw. Leave him alone,' said Alex, who had arrived at her side without her noticing, absorbed as she had been in the snail's defence mechanism.

She smiled and put the snail on the side of the path where they watched it unfurl from its shell and make off. 'Racing home to his wife and daughters,' she said. 'Or her husband and sons. Having said that, they're hermaphrodites, aren't they?'

'Yes, they are. And the way they mate isn't what you'd want to be doing if you were out on a date. They twist themselves round each other and cover themselves in frothy slime. Then they both set off to bury their eggs in a mulchy bit of ground. They cover them with mucus, soil and excrement, and about a month later, bingo, loads of tiny snails are ready to munch their way through your prized garden plants. Some snails live to fifteen and they're excellent fodder for birds, toads and snakes.'

'Snakes?' she queried.

'And that's all you've taken from that superbly informative lecture?' he said sadly, shaking his head.

'Of course not,' she told him, 'but I don't know why, I thought snakes went for fast food. Mice. Rats. Humans, if they were hungry.'

'And the last time you read about a human in Britain being eaten by a snake?'

'Yeah, okay, Mr Biology. Although we've all heard about the bloke going to the loo and finding a huge great python.'

He smirked.

She blushed.

'Does a snail really vomit to move, as someone once told me?' she asked quickly.

'Well, it's a gastropod, which literally means "stomach foot". And I suppose it does essentially secrete mucus, which it slides on. So, yes. Vomit. Slide. Vomit. Slide.'

'Existing on a liquid lunch. And dinner,' said Miranda, beginning to walk back along the towpath. She could feel her stomach on the verge of making another announcement. 'Quite nice, though, to bury your eggs in the garden and let them hatch on their own, rather than spending nine months incubating them and several years saving them from themselves,' she threw back, over her shoulder.

'How many have you got?' he asked.

'Two. But they've gone now. So I'm foot-loose and fancy-free.'

'No father of the children?' he enquired, kicking a stone into the grass.

'He's gone too.' She flashed him a smile. Really, she thought, this is going to have to stop.

CHAPTER THREE

It felt very politically incorrect to get into a Jaguar and drive to the shop for her lunch, particularly with the collection of vehicles surrounding it. Alex's camper van was, as she had expected, a faded orange with a scratchy cream top. How awful, she thought, to have to live in something so small when you were so tall. And where did he shower? Or maybe he didn't. She had read somewhere that after a while you didn't smell, that your body was self-regulating. Or maybe that was your hair. Whichever it was, she didn't believe it for a minute. Otherwise tramps would smell fragrant. Maybe you simply stopped smelling any worse.

She returned with a pie, a packet of crisps and a bottle of sparkling water. 'Woo-hoo. She went and bought *the* pie from the local shop,' Will exclaimed, as she joined them on the groundsheet where they were chatting.

There was a lull in the conversation and they watched with interest as she bit into it. She swallowed and they waited expectantly. 'Well,' she said eventually, 'if I had to describe it, I'd say it was worm, with a hint of parsley. Or loam. Beautifully minced. Anyone else want a bite?' She held it out.

'No, you're all right. Don't mind if I don't,' said Brian, a grizzled veteran of the volunteering sector, who had been getting rid of overhanging branches on the path.

'Is it supposed to be a meat pasty, or something else?' asked Alex, peeling a hard-boiled egg.

'Well, the woman in the shop said she thought it was cheese and onion. But since it appears to be brown and sludgy, I can only assume it's meat. Are you vegetarian?'

He shook his head. 'I'm all about sustainability. Eating food that's in season. Having organic and ethically treated animals. Eating fish that are plentiful and not caught in bloody great drift nets that denude the sea.' He looked around at the others. 'Yes, I know, I'm on the well-ridden hobby-horse again. I'll just dismount over here and take the spurs off.'

Miranda felt now as though she should be apologising for devouring a pie made of indeterminate animal, which had probably been treated very badly and didn't even taste nice. But bugger it. It had filled the hole in her stomach and it was dead anyway.

Will gestured to the blue sky. 'I love this country. Pissing down with rain this morning and now it's like the Caribbean.'

'Which is like the Caribbean, really,' said Miranda. 'Pissing down one minute and baking hot the next? Or, at least, it is at some times of the year ...' She tailed off.

'A favourite holiday destination?' asked Teresa, her mutton hair seeming to express rank disapproval.

'We have friends in Antigua. Very good friends.'

'Naturally,' said Teresa.

She really doesn't like me, thought Miranda. And then, because she could have gone either way, she decided to antagonise her. 'Um. I also have friends in Switzerland, who I visit on a regular basis. Oh, and friends who have an ocean-going yacht

– I join them when I can.' She noticed Alex shooting a glance at her and stopped. Then added, 'When I'm not camping in, er, Lancashire.'

Alex flashed her a massive smile. Clearly he didn't believe her for a minute.

Lunch packed away, they walked back to the towpath. She was gratified to see him manoeuvre a spot beside her.

'Lancashire, eh?'

'Yes,' she said firmly. 'A huge favourite.'

'Whereabouts?'

'Chilterns,' she threw back.

'My goodness! I can only assume they must have got up on their tiptoes and shuffled north, then.'

She chuckled. 'Never was much good at geography. Where are the Chilterns then?'

'Not far from here – the area near Henley to the south-east. You'd be in the Yorkshire Dales if you wanted hilly near Lancashire. Beautiful part of the country. And you don't have to camp to enjoy it.'

'Is that where you're from?' she enquired.

'No,' he responded. There was a beat before he continued, 'I'm from loads of places. We moved around a lot when I was growing up and I've continued the trend.'

'Where do your parents live now?' she asked.

'They're divorced. My mum lives on the Isle of Wight. My dad …' he hesitated '… my dad … Last time I spoke to him he was in Spain somewhere. And it was raining.' His voice held a note of finality, as though that was all he would be saying on the subject. 'Are you from London?'

'Yup. Grew up in Camden Town, before it got quite as skanky as it is now. It's all about ripped tights, piercings and …' she'd been about to say 'dreadlocks' '… it's a bit druggy. You see people coming towards you smacking their gums and looking wild and …'

'You realise it's your father checking up on you,' he finished promptly.

'Exactly.' She laughed. 'Then we moved to Primrose Hill and I spent all my time kissing boys in the park.' Now, why had she said that? Freud would have had a field day. It was absolutely, without a shadow of doubt, because she had been looking at his lips as he spoke. She went through the routine in her head: *I am a forty-three-year-old mother of two. Leave this poor child alone and stop being predatory. Yuk.* What was it they called women like her, these days? 'Cougar,' she exclaimed aloud.

'Where?' asked Alex, pretending to look about in consternation. 'That would be a very unusual sighting.'

She bit her bottom lip. 'I was trying to remember something,' she said. And left it there, since there was nothing else she could say that wouldn't land her in it.

She realised with a jolt that it had been ages since she'd had such a nice time. Flirting was very therapeutic, even if it did feel wrong with a boy who was barely out of short trousers.

She donned her gloves again and got stuck into the path clearing, finding it satisfying in a way that she had never found cleaning the house. Maybe it was because everyone was working together. If cleaning the house had been a team event instead of a lonely chore, which was only noticed when it hadn't been done … In fact, after careful consideration – she stretched, hands on her waist, leaning backwards and admiring the blue of the sky – she would have to say that the best time she had had recently was the evening of celebratory divorce drinks with Hannah. They had laughed so much she had almost thrown up a kidney. She had also cried quite a lot. But somehow she had still had a good time. That was a bloody sad indictment of the last few years of her life. She bent down and picked up a load of prickly brambles, which had been thoughtfully cut into manageable pieces. She had taken off her jacket as the day had warmed up, but she was beginning to feel like a cheese wrapped in plastic. The wicking shirt, which was supposed to allow her skin to breathe, was sticking to her back. If her skin *was* breathing, she imagined it would have its mouth wide open, gasping for air. A drop of sweat fell off her nose.

Right. That was it. She took off her shirt, revealing a decidedly skimpy vest top and a wretchedly ugly sports bra. It couldn't be helped. It was either that or suffocation. She did an impression of a cormorant drying its wings, then carried on picking up rubbish with renewed vigour.

An hour later, Will called another break and handed out bottles of water. Miranda drank hers thankfully.

'Hot work, eh?' Alex tried unsuccessfully not to look down her top.

'Any hotter and I'll be down to my pants,' she said unthinkingly. And blushed. She could feel the heat staining her chest. Even her ears felt hot.

'Come on, sun,' he said quietly.

Which didn't make her feel any cooler.

* * *

Driving home, with scratches up her arms and smelling like a navvy, as her mother would have said, she had to confess to feeling satisfied and rather virtuous. She couldn't wait to tell her friends about it. Her real friends – those who weren't tainted with a whiff of Nigel, so not Lydia or Estelle or anybody who had set her up with shit dates.

When she unlocked the front door, she wanted to embrace her house. There was nothing quite like a shower after an honest day's work. It seemed so long ago that she had been standing in this cubicle, trying to activate herself. Naked and still damp, she weighed herself. How depressing, she thought. All that exercise and I'm still fat.

Miranda was not fat. In previous centuries she would have been described variously as 'voluptuous', 'Rubenesque' or 'hourglass'. But it was hard to find clothes that fitted – they all appeared to have been designed for flat-bottomed and -chested girls. Or boys, even.

The one decent piece of advice she'd had from her mother was to buy proper bras. Rigby & Peller made excellent, comfortable upholstery for her top half, and after a fitting ('Madam has a fuller left breast'), she liked to nip into Harrods for tea and to use the luxury washrooms.

She checked her breasts for lumps and idly wondered if she could ever have worked in a strip joint, showing her wares, as it were. In her teens she'd been addicted to a magazine that was almost entirely about girls and women prostituting themselves because of their circumstances. If it wasn't actual prostitution, it was staying with a hideous husband, or drug-smuggling. It had been a sort of forerunner of *Heat* magazine, which was still about women marrying for money but now they were famous.

It was seven o'clock on a Saturday night. This was when she missed having someone to hang out with. Even Nigel. It seemed sad opening a bottle of wine with no one to share it. And she missed cooking for two. Or four, when the family had been together. 'Oh, listen to yourself,' she said aloud, remembering how she'd complained about being a skivvy, sometimes cooking separate meals for the children because she'd allowed them to become faddy eaters.

She opened the fridge door and ate a piece of celery while debating the options. Omelette. That was about it. She closed the door, grabbed a stash of flyers from beside the phone and ordered a takeaway sushi before flumping down on to the sofa and switching on the television, which felt wrong, considering the bright evening, but she hadn't got the energy to walk to the shops, let alone gather food there.

The enormous beige linen sofa gathered her in, and a faint breeze from the window stirred the curtains. She half watched *The Vicar of Dibley* – it was an episode she'd seen a number of times, with Geraldine, Dawn French's character, becoming a radio star. There was something strangely attractive about the owner of the manor, David Horton. Or was it his house? Or the fact that he was so capable?

The doorbell rang, and a man in a crash helmet handed her the sushi. She couldn't have worked as a food deliverer, she thought. Couldn't have coped with the semi-permanent helmet hair. And, luckily, I don't have to. Yet. Standing in the kitchen, she ate the rice and fish with her fingers, rinsed them under the tap and wiped them on the tea towel, which she then threw into the laundry basket with a Note to Self that she should put it in the wash the next day.

She sniffed her fingers and went back into the bathroom to wash her hands with soap, sniffed again, then slathered on almond hand cream. The mirror reflected a face with a hint of suntan. Miranda leant forward to peer closer at her crow's feet and the lines on her forehead. She was definitely going to get them done. Botox. That was the answer. All her friends looked so much younger than she did after their bi-annual visits to the doctor in Harley Street. Apart from Lydia, who was old school and didn't even moisturise, let alone Botox. Hands like a pumice stone and the toes of a tree climber.

She got out a mirror that magnified by thirty and stuck it on the wall tile. When she had wanted to be a vet, she had asked for a microscope for her birthday and, for about six months, had studiously examined everything under it, from ants to scabs. But it was never as good as the science programmes where you could see the chomping hairy mandibles of a beetle or the inside of a wobbly pink human intestine. She loved her magnifying mirror, though. You could see only a little bit of your face at a time, which was fascinatingly hideous. Her eyebrows looked like spindly thorn thickets, with outlying stragglers. She plucked them and checked her chin to make sure nothing was growing there. Age, her grandmother had once told her, may give you wisdom but it also gives you excess hair and fallen arches. Age is not for wimps. God, it would be so easy to get depressed about everything drooping and growing hair.

Meanwhile, there was a nose to be attacked. Its pores were the size of bubbles in a yeasty bread mix and needed to be dealt with. That took a few minutes, and while it was relaxing after its pummelling, she peered up her nose. Bodies. So complicated. Hair inside nostrils to sift out particles in the air. Skin, with its pores opening or closing. She imagined her entire body as a vast collection of pulsating sea anemones, expelling and swallowing minute motes.

She dabbed toner everywhere, then mixed up a face pack with organic powder she had been given as a birthday present. It smelt of damp nappies, but was exceptionally good at calming down punished skin.

Back on the sofa, under a thick layer of night cream, she flicked through the channels. Telly was so boring on Saturday night. She shifted to Sky and rolled down the things she'd recorded, settling on a drama series about Sherlock Holmes, which had been getting good reviews. The cushions were comfy, the temperature was perfect and Dr Watson had a very good bedside manner. He had barely got his feet under the valance before she was fast asleep. She woke up as the credits were rolling and decanted to bed without cleaning her teeth.

The next day, Miranda woke up with a spring in her step and took a moment to remember why. Oh, yes. Towpath clearing. She quickly checked the time, having forgotten to set her alarm. It took her a moment to work out that the digital clock actually *was* showing five thirty-seven a.m. – the earliest she had woken up naturally since she'd last had jetlag.

She bounced into the bathroom and smiled at herself in the mirror. Natural light made you look so much better. She brushed her teeth with fennel toothpaste – bought because it was the sort of thing Nigel sneered at – then mint, because it felt fresher, and virtually skipped into the shower. 'Oh, what a beautiful day,' she trilled, as she shaved her legs.

She had two pieces of toast and a boiled egg, which she had undercooked so seriously that it looked like a jellyfish in a shell. She squiggled it around with a spoon to make it less offensive, then wolfed it down. She was ravenous so she followed it with a bowl of cereal and leapt into the car.

She arrived at the towpath with a tub of salad, a vegetable wrap, an apple, a banana, a smoothie and a bag of organic carrots.

'Don't tell me, you're more hung-over than a quadruple bypass patient on an operating table,' Alex commented, as she reeled off the list to him while they waited for the others to arrive.

'Actually, no,' she said primly. 'I had an early night after dining on sushi.'

'You were knackered?' he sympathised.

'Yes, I was.' She smiled. 'I know it sounds pathetic, but I really was a bit wiped out. A combination of fresh air and a little exercise.'

'It's what happens if you're not used to it.'

'And you?'

'Well, I suppose I'm used to it.'

'I meant what did you get up to last night?'

He hesitated. 'I had to have a meeting with my father.'

'Have a meeting with him? You mean you went to see your dad?'

'No. It was a meeting – it's complicated. But I didn't get back till … erm, back until late, so I didn't have a huge amount of sleep.'

'And how was that?' she asked idly, to keep the conversation going.

'Fine,' he said. And bent down to do up a shoelace that didn't need tying. 'So, no aches and pains, then? No massage required anywhere?'

'You offering?' she asked, addressing his ear.

He stood up. 'I think I possibly am,' he said, his green eyes alight.

He's only saying that because he feels safe, she thought. Because I'm so much older. Because I'm no threat. Treating me like he would his mother. But she couldn't prevent a tingle of excitement. 'Shoulders could do with a rub, then, if you really don't mind.' She turned to present them.

His hands were strong and she winced a little as he worked on her.

'Hey, can we all have one of those?' asked Teresa, emerging from her scruffy Fiat with a cooler bag that contained her lunch.

Alex merely grinned and carried on massaging Miranda. 'How's that?' he asked.

'Me love you long time, meester,' she responded, in a higher voice than she'd meant to use, actually feeling rather hot and bothered and trying hard not to be turned on.

Will's Land Rover pulled up, drowning Alex's response, but it appeared to signal the end of his ministrations and they got to work soon after.

It was a beautiful day and Miranda stood up frequently to stretch and look about her. On the canal, a shimmering drake was bothering a drab duck in an area of dark, still water. She knew she should be appalled by the huge expanse of green duckweed and algae bloom, but it was the most brilliant colour. It made the bank on the other side look positively dull.

She had stuck her hair into a large clasp at the back of her head, but red-gold curls had escaped and had glued themselves to her face by the time the call for lunch went up. 'Phew,' she said, as they walked back to the meeting area. 'It's awfully hot and sticky.'

'Maybe you should wash it,' said Alex, as he went past.

She snorted.

'I'm so sorry,' he said apologetically. 'Something a friend of mine used to say every time I said it was hot and sticky. Reflex action. Really. Sorry.' He did look a little pink around the ears.

'It's fine. Honestly. Don't worry about it. I've heard worse. Much worse. And I definitely could do with a freshen-up.' She grinned. And now *she* was embarrassed. 'A freshen-up.' That was so bloody Surrey.

It was peculiar how, even at her age, she reverted to being a teenager, given half a chance and a following wind.

After lunch, they worked with fewer breaks to clear the last stretch of towpath they were dealing with that weekend. Miranda wondered whether she would do the volunteering thing again. It had been a nice idea, but apart from Alex, she didn't like the others much. They were all a bit holier-than-thou, with bad skin and terrible hair. She smiled at that. Hers had gone mad with the combination of heat and sweat. She took off her glove and wiped her brow with the back of her hand. Her nails were filthy, even though she hadn't done anything without gloves on. Yuk. That must be from the inside of the gloves. Someone else's body detritus.

By five o'clock, it was all done. The team gathered gratefully in the shade of a tree – now shorn of its lower branches – and drank bottles of water. Will thanked them all for their hard work and said that anyone who wanted to see the job through to the end was welcome to come again. Everyone except Miranda intimated that they'd be doing just that.

She couldn't decide. On the one hand, it would be a waste of the wicking shirt and the trousers if she didn't. On the other, she might just go and get a job.

She got into the Jaguar and was sitting with her eyes closed, anticipating the drive home, when she was startled by a knock on the window. 'Alex. You gave me a fright,' she said, her heart beating unnecessarily fast.

'Sorry.' He smiled. 'Again.' He leant his forearm on the car roof. 'I'm sorry for my very poor attempt at humour earlier. Can I take you for a drink to make up for it?' He hastened on before she had a chance to speak. 'There's a really pretty little pub about a mile away. It's on your way home. They do coffee. Or … erm … other things, if you don't want a drink of an alcoholic nature?' he ended, raising his eyebrows hopefully.

'How could I possibly say no?' she answered. 'A nice glass of something sounds just the job. Only the one, mind you, since I do have to drive home.'

Alex began to explain where the pub was, but saw that she had lost him beyond turning left on to the main road. 'Tell you what, why don't you follow me?'

'Much easier,' she agreed.

It was a relief to get the air-conditioning going in the car. She tuned in to Radio 2 and jigged along to 'Honky Tonk Woman', singing the few words she knew and humming the rest. She was going to a pub with a dreadlocked eco-warrior. Not that he was a warrior, but it was a very sexy word redolent of a bygone age when men were men and women wandered about in long skirts applying hartshorn and experimenting with plaits.

'Whoa, lady,' she said aloud, running her hand along the nape of her neck and lifting her hair to get a bit of ventilation.

The verges were verdant with flowers, trees and bushes, all bursting into life. It was like a scene from a 1950s film with euphemisms for sex. Peonies exploding. Pods popping. Stamens thrusting. Miranda felt an excitement she hadn't experienced since the very first blind date after her divorce, when she'd thought that she was going to be properly pillaged. How misplaced *that* had been.

The photograph of Marc – that was his name – had shown a stocky man with close-cut hair in the Russell Crowe mould, standing by a stallion with muscular nostrils and a look in its eye. She had spent about three hours getting ready – even bought new clothes and underwear to emphasise the new leaf she was turning over.

And then she had met him. She would literally have preferred to have had dinner with his horse.

His wallet had been bursting with platinum credit cards and fifty-pound notes – he had made sure she noticed them when he took out a picture of his new Labrador. But he had been an unreconstructed bore who could barely wait for her to finish a sentence before he was leaping in with long, tedious stories, all of which he started, 'I must tell you about this funny thing that happened to me …'

Under her breath, she replied, 'No, you don't have to tell me and it won't be funny.'

Her mobile phone startled her by ringing very loudly where it nestled in her crotch. She put the hands-free earphones in and answered.

'Hi, Mum.'

'Oh, hello, Lucy. Listen, I'm driving so I might lose you if I go into an iffy patch. How are you?'

'Fine. How are you?'

'Feeling pretty good, actually. Everything okay, or were you after something?' She might as well cut to the chase, since Lucy generally only phoned to lecture her about splitting up the family or how she should invest her cash.

'Hmm. I saw Dad yesterday and he said you still had some of his books, which you said you were going to give him back. I thought I'd save you a trip by picking them up from you this week.'

Miranda bristled. She consciously kept her voice light. 'I wonder which ones they are. He did take the couple he'd read, and the yard of books he bought at Sotheby's to put on his office bookshelves,' she said sweetly. 'Sorry. You're going to have to tell him to give me a ring and let me know what he's talking about.' He wouldn't because he was a coward and that was why he had drafted in Lucy to ask her.

'Leatherbound books, he said,' Lucy countered, obviously having been briefed by Nigel.

'Yes. The ones he bought by the yard, as I said. No doubt he's finished reading them all and is desperate for the sequels,' she said bitchily. Nigel read the *Financial Times*, the *Telegraph* and some magazine called *Square Mile*, which she'd once read in the bath in the absence of anything racier.

'He says you know which books he's talking about. Apparently you claimed they were yours, but Gran says they were definitely hers and she gave them to Dad.'

'Well, I've no idea what you, he and she are talking about,' she said waspishly.

'Do you think you could check when you get home, though?' asked Lucy, relentlessly.

'Not tonight. I'm on my way to a …' She paused, unwilling to get into a conversation about where she was going and with whom '… friend's house. For dinner. I'll be late.'

'Oh.' Lucy sounded put out. 'Well, I'll tell Dad you'll do it in the morning, then.'

'No, you won't,' countered Miranda. 'You'll tell him to give me a ring and explain what I'm looking for.'

'I've already told you what you're looking for. Don't be mean, Mum. Which friend are you having dinner with?'

'Eh?'

'Which friend are you having dinner with?'

'Lydia,' she said foolishly, no other name coming to hand quick enough. Damn. Trust her to pick the wife of one of Nigel's best friends.

'On a Sunday?'

'Well, it was supposed to be lunch, but I was busy. So I'm dropping round now.'

'It won't be a late one, though, knowing Lydia and Justin. He's like me, up at five every morning. I must ring him – I heard a rumour about Standard and Poors.'

Miranda's eyes widened. Drat and double drat. That would be the cat put firmly amid the pigeons.

'I'm sorry, I can't hear you very well, Lucy. If you can hear me, lots of love. Speak to you soon. 'Bye.' She clicked the off button and glanced down to switch the phone off altogether. Ridiculous. Lying to your daughter about going to a pub with a young man.

'Young man.' She couldn't help putting on an accent. Like that actor in the sketch show. Who was he? She couldn't remember his name. Someone dressed as an old woman, ogling the man who came round to fix the boiler. Fix the boiler – oh, that's a good euphemism, she thought.

Feeling a little discombobulated, she concentrated on the camper van ahead.

They pulled off at a crossroads and within ten minutes were in the car park of a pretty pub with a bright display of hanging baskets at the front and a little beer garden at the back. 'Why don't you grab a spot outside and I'll get you a drink?' Alex said, holding her door open as she got out of the car.

'All right. Could I have a half of whatever the local beer is, please?'

'Crisps?'

'Salt and vinegar, please.'

'An excellent choice, madam. They'll complement the ale beautifully.' He flashed her a big smile and walked into the saloon bar.

Miranda sat on one of the benches under a stripy umbrella. There was a slight breeze and her hair danced. She closed her eyes to enjoy the moment. It was delicious. There was a soft murmur of bees and the susurrant sound of plants drifting in the gentle wind. She could hear a couple chatting at another table, but not loudly enough to disturb the rustic peace.

Bit annoying about Nigel and the books, though. If she hadn't had children with him, she could quite happily never speak to him again. She hoped there wouldn't be any marriages just yet. The ex-wife of the father of the bride. Or the father of the groom – although it was unlikely that Jack would be tying the knot any time soon. And Lucy? Miranda loved her daughter, but she could be trying, and her boyfriends had almost always been annoying. Although, to be fair, not annoying to Nigel.

She opened her eyes and turned to the young couple she'd heard talking. They were holding hands over the wooden table with empty glasses in front of them. She thought wistfully of her lost youth. Had she ever looked like that? She supposed she must have done when she first met Nigel. Or had she? Her head had been full of other things, like not having to work unless she wanted to. And Nigel had been the human equivalent of the wardrobe full of fur coats in the Narnia books, a window on to a different world. A world of adults making adult decisions, like where to buy a house. Organising a mortgage. Choosing stuff that wasn't crockery and cutlery, saying things like, 'Oh, yes, a king-size bed is much more suitable,' and knowing that they were *married*, so it was a proper marital bed. Then, of course, the ultimate grown-up thing – even though you could get pregnant from the age of about twelve: having a baby. It had been odd telling Dad. Absolute proof that she was having sex. That a man was actually … she searched for the word that Nigel had used … 'banging'? Or was it 'slamming' her?

'What's making you smile?' asked Alex, ending her reverie with his arrival.

'Nothing. Rambling through memories. Can't even remember now. *Pff*!' She clicked her fingers. 'A moment that's gone in a flash of – What beer have I got?'

'That is one interesting flash,' he dropped a packet of crisps in front of her, 'and it's called Brakspear. A fine drop of ale, if I do say so myself.'

She downed half of it in one. 'Excuse me. A bit thirsty.'

'Can I interest you in a thinly sliced potato drenched in a delicious marinade of sea salt with a hint of balsamic?'

'Don't mind if I do.' She reached into the bag and took a few.

'England on a balmy evening like this is heaven, don't you think?' He necked a pint of very pale apricot liquid.

'Gorgeous. Why would anyone be anywhere else?'

'All we need now is the thwack of leather on willow.'

'That's the sort of dodgy thing they get up to in the shires,' she said.

'Not a cricket fan, I take it?' he asked.

'You are?'

'Love it. A game of strategy. The only thing my father taught me,' he said, and stopped.

'He must have taught you more than that.' Miranda tucked a stray curl behind her ear.

'Not much,' he said curtly. 'What will you be doing next week?'

Miranda raised her blue eyes to his leaf-green ones. 'Something rather akin to what your father taught you ... not much. I've got a few friends I'll be meeting up with, and a play at the Barbican that another friend has press-ganged me into seeing. It sounds like one of those experimental pieces where I'll spend the entire evening wondering whether I've missed the point, and concentrating desperately to see if I can grasp something to talk about intelligently afterwards. And no doubt coming up with the stock word ... "interesting". Apart from that, same old, same old.'

'You should get more involved with the eco side of things then,' he said, taking another long sup of his drink.

'Maybe. Is that lime and lemonade?' she queried.

'Lime and soda with a dash of Angostura bitters. Tastes almost alcoholic, but allows me to retain my driving licence. You have children, I think you said?'

'Two. One in banking, the other on a rather extended gap year.'

'As in?'

'As in over a year now, and not much to show for it,' she said, with a sigh.

'Except that he can probably hold his own with anyone, has a better view of the world than those who don't travel more than ten miles from their own door, and speaks a few languages?'

'Yes,' she said. 'I'm very proud of him. My ex-husband thinks he's wasting his life.'

'I've got a friend whose parents thought exactly the same. He now runs one of the biggest student travel agents in the world. Hugely successful. Rolling in dosh. Gives loads of it to charity.'

'And now has ecstatic parents?'

'And now has ecstatic parents,' he echoed.

'Not that Jack's doing much at the moment. If his emails are anything to go by, he's learning how to surf in Indonesia.'

'A necessary survival skill. Imagine how useful that could be if there was a sudden deluge and your house was washed away.'

'I'd be in the house, surely.'

'And he'd be coaxing you out of the window on to his surfboard as you were heading for the weir.' He nodded sagely.

She laughed. 'Is that how you ended up doing this canal-clearing thing?' She gestured airily.

'No. I did it to – erm – annoy someone,' he said.

'Your father?'

'Yes. He thinks it's all about capitalism. We don't always see eye to eye.' He grinned. 'It's a long story. And you have to get home, you said.'

'Did I? I meant I can't drink much because I have to drive home. I can certainly make time for what sounds like an interesting story.

There's nothing I like better than hearing about other people's complicated home lives.'

'Since you have one of your own?'

'Well, it doesn't sound as exciting as yours. But I'll show you mine if you show me yours.'

'Depending on where we start with the life history, it'll take a lot longer than one drink,' he said, his eyes crinkling attractively.

She put her head on one side, considering. 'Fine,' she said, after a few seconds. 'And what would you suggest in that case?'

'Have dinner with me,' he pronounced, his even white teeth showing between what she had thought were eminently kissable lips since the moment she'd met him.

CHAPTER FOUR

While he was at his minor public school, Nigel had been called before the headmaster to explain how he had come to be in possession of a packet of cigarettes and a hip-flask full of whisky. During the complicated explanation he had given, in which he had blamed dark forces and a boy who was swotty, spotty, blond and a bedwetter, he had discovered an aptitude for lying. It was standing him in good stead now, but what he needed were the books his mother had given him and which he had mixed up with two yards of leatherbound dictionaries bought in a drunken moment from Sotheby's.

When Miranda turned on her mobile phone on Monday, there were several texts and voicemail messages, at least half of which related to the books. 'Pesky blighter,' she said aloud, making an avocado, cottage cheese and tomato sandwich for breakfast – she'd had no dinner the night before. There was also a message from Alex, suggesting dinner on Wednesday at Zuma, a very smart restaurant in Knightsbridge. That struck her as odd because he didn't look the type who would know its name, even less frequent it.

Was he expecting her to pay? Or go halves? Well, if that was the price of hanging out with younger men, she supposed she'd have to bite the bullet.

The trouble was that she had recently put what was left of her cash into a copper-bottomed scheme that Lucy had organised. It had been paying such rich dividends that she had taken out a mortgage on the house and piled in more. She envisaged it growing year by year into a kind of enormous, bouncy pension that she could lie around on in her old age – but it left her very short for day-to-day expenses. That was one major disadvantage in not having Nigel to sort out the finances. And the reason she needed a job.

She composed a text, saying she would love to have dinner with him, then hesitated over whether to put an 'x' at the end of the message. She put it on, took it off and put it on. Then took it off just before she pressed send. A date. With a man who was only a bit older than her daughter. Or thereabouts, since she didn't know for certain how old he was. If he was thirty, he was thirteen years younger, therefore two-thirds her age. Or was that three-quarters? Her maths had always been a bit foggy, particularly round fractions.

She finished her breakfast, and put the items in the dishwasher. Oh dear. Is that one of those non-eco things I shouldn't be doing, like brushing my teeth without using water? Or was it okay as long as the dishwasher was full? But that meant there would be bits of dried food mouldering away in it, smelling like a teenager's bedroom.

After a quick shower (saves on water), Miranda threw on an orange and cream Diane von Furstenburg dress and carefully put on her makeup. She had a hair appointment at eleven thirty, which would leave her with just enough time to get to the Lanesborough, near Hyde Park Corner, which did a very fine pot of loose-leaf tea. There she would do battle with her mother. It was a ritual she felt sure neither enjoyed much, but it had become so entrenched in their lives that it would be difficult for them to back out now.

Her mother. Where to start? She had got to that age where every action was accompanied by an equal and inapposite reaction. Bending resulted in a little exhalation, a 'pah' of effort. Sitting down occasionally concluded with a full-blown 'aaaah'. Was it legitimate, she wondered, to say that she loved her mother but didn't like her very much? That seemed churlish when Miranda knew how much effort it took to raise a child.

A few hours later, in the unforgiving daylight of the glass-domed room, her hair newly highlighted and blow-dried (such a treat after two days of it being sweaty and itchy), she watched as her mother ever so slightly touched her tongue to the cup while sipping the Lady Grey. It was just one of the habits that irritated her. Mothers. Couldn't live with them, couldn't shoot them. Although there were those who did, obviously. Her parents had loved *Some Mothers Do 'Ave 'Em* – if Miranda ran the BBC (or was it ITV?), she would commission a show called *Some Children Do 'Ave 'Em*. It would feature a mother who was constantly at you about *everything* and a father who forgot your name but remembered the hamster's.

She had a forlorn hope that she would never look like her mother, but was very aware that at some stage she probably would. In which case, she was heading for a mouth like a sucked lemon and long earlobes.

Nigel had cloyingly called her mother a stunner, and it was true that photographs from her youth showed some similarity to Diana Dors. But for half a century she had been married to a philandering workaholic and the stress had left her features crabby and disappointed.

'What *are* you going to do with that boy of yours?' her mother asked, reaching for the pot of clotted cream.

'Jack is perfectly all right, Mum. He phoned me the other day from Indonesia. He's on his way to Borneo and I think he said he was volunteering to help at an orang-utan centre. It sounds like he's having a great time and getting work experience,' she lied.

Her mother spread a large dollop of strawberry jam on her creamed scone and then consumed half of it. At least I'll have inherited excellent teeth and digestion, thought Miranda.

'He needs a sense of direction,' said her mother. 'If you hadn't got divorced, he might have stayed on the straight and narrow. Been working in the City now and saving for a house.'

Miranda listened to the well-trodden rant and continued to sip her tea. Thank goodness for Jack. Weird how Lucy had become so like her father. She had been such a sweet child. Rather like a stuffed squid when she was going through the terrible twos, with dimpled arms and legs that didn't seem to bend in the middle, but she had turned into a pretty little girl.

'Did I ever have a comfort blanket, Mum?' she suddenly asked.

Her mother looked disgruntled at being interrupted just as she was getting into her stride about feckless youth, but finally said, 'No, not a blanket. There was that stuffed polecat you had from Uncle Ben. You used to suck its ears and scream like a banshee if we didn't have it with us. Why?'

'I was remembering how Jack used to take a funny little bear everywhere until he was about eleven. And Lucy had that pink satin blanket from a doll's cot. I found it the other day when I unpacked a box of odds and sods that'd been in the cupboard under the stairs.

She must have lobbed it in there years ago – terrible reek of moth-balls. I think I've finally found her sentimental streak.'

'She's a wonderful girl, Lucy ...'

Before her mother could begin a new strand involving her beloved granddaughter, Miranda cut her off by enquiring sweetly if she wanted a top-up because she was definitely having more Darjeeling, and waved over a waiter.

'Did you have a good weekend?' asked her mother, searching for a neutral topic.

'Er, yes, actually. I did some volunteer work at a canal in Oxfordshire,' she said, clasping her hands together and giving her mother a challenging look.

'Did you?' her mother asked, horrified.

'Uh-huh. It was really good fun. Thought I needed to get out more – do something constructive. It's a precursor to getting a job. Yes. After all these years. And before you ask, no, I don't think it will be in the acting world – I'm far too long in the tooth. I don't know what kind of job, except it won't be lap-dancing, circus work or anything else that will embarrass the children. Although I quite fancy burlesque ... Mum, you should see your face! Anyway, I went to Oxfordshire and met some very nice people.' Not a total lie. One of them was *very* nice.

'Really?' her mother asked in disbelief.

'Yes, Mum. They were. Perhaps not the sort of people you'd meet at the Rotary Club, but good sorts.' What on earth was she saying? She'd be using expressions like 'There's nowt so queer as folk' next.

She pressed on, 'I enjoyed it so much I'm going to go again.' So there.

'Well, it's very singular of you, Miranda,' her mother said. 'If you're going to do charity work, why not do proper charity work? Doesn't Lydia do something with disadvantaged children?'

'Yes. I think she knits them into socks for the army. But I wanted to do something energetic.'

'You never used to say that at school.'

'That was rather a long time ago. And I was utterly hopeless at hockey and netball. It's very dispiriting to be the last person to be picked for the team and it puts you off doing anything energetic. If you remember, I was only good at shot-put, and nobody wants to be good at shot-put unless they're lesbian.'

'Miranda!' Her mother's eyes darted to the next table.

'Oh, all right, not lesbian, then,' said Miranda, wanting to voice the L-word again. 'Fat.' What was it about being with her mother that always made her sound like she was seven? 'The point is, I'm going to go and volunteer again – and I met a rather scrumptious man, who I'm going to have dinner with on Wednesday.' There. It was out.

'From canal clearing?'

'Mum, you've done that face where you look like Lamb Chop eating a pretend carrot.' She laughed. 'I think he might be mixed race. He's got dreadlocks. Down to here.' She gestured to her waist. 'And now you're doing what Butter and Marg did when they wanted feeding,' she said, talking about the goldfish she had won at a fair. They had lived in a bowl that eventually went a livid green and killed its occupants.

'Does Nigel know?' she eventually asked.

'Mum, I'm not married to him any more. I'm a free agent, just like he is. He doesn't have to tell me about his latest floozy, and I don't have to tell him what I'm doing.'

'Have you told Lucy? Or Jack?'

'Nope. They've left home. It's nothing to do with them.' Yet. 'And it's a dinner date, not a wedding.'

'But mixed race.' Her mother shook her head.

'Mmm.' Miranda reached for the teapot. 'He might not be, though. I have no idea. Doesn't matter either way, though, does it? I think he lives in a camper van. Or that seems to be what he lives in. I don't know very much about him. I will by Thursday, if you want me to keep you posted?'

Her mother tightened her lips, realising she was being baited and refusing to capitulate.

Miranda left the Lanesborough feeling rather as she had on leaving school, a combination of exhilaration and trepidation. Her dad wouldn't approve of Alex either. He approved of Nigel and men like Nigel. He read the *Daily Telegraph* and believed there was too much immigration and that too much of what he paid in tax went to social-security scroungers. On the other hand, they had a cleaner from the Philippines and he kept quite a lot of his money in offshore accounts. 'If it wasn't for the stupidly generous state hand-outs encouraging people to sit at home watching television and producing more children, there would be people available to do the jobs,' he would declare, to anyone who would listen. 'As it is, we allow thousands of people to come here and most of them are instantly able to access stuff that we pay for. Why should they be able to go to our hospitals for treatment when they've contributed nothing, and send their children to our schools when they don't even speak English?'

Who was it who said you were only an adult when your parents were no longer around?

Maybe she was having a mid-life crisis. How do you know whether it's a mid-life crisis or something you'd have done anyway? A friend's husband had done a classic: he'd run off with a twenty-year-old Norwegian student, spent all his money on renting a smart flat and buying a Porsche, and started wearing low-slung jeans and tight-fitting shirts that looked ridiculous with his mini pot-belly. He'd come crawling back two years later, wanting to be part of the family again.

But Miranda had always had a nice car. And she tried to be on trend if not trendy – maybe she'd have a look for a funky top in one of the high-street shops for Wednesday. Aha, and that's how the mid-life crisis starts. She smiled. 'You can drop me here on the corner.' She handed the cabbie a twenty-pound note. 'Keep the change.' It was odd, she thought, how you tipped cabbies and hairdressers, waiters and waitresses, but not gas fitters, car mechanics, salespeople, hospital porters. All of them did you a service, but only some got a little extra cash. And, actually, the waiters and hairdressers she tipped were often bloody annoying.

She would have liked to be the sort of person who had the balls only to tip those who deserved it – the sort of person who took the service charge off the bill or demanded to see the manager. She had done it once and got so hot and sweaty that in the end she had meekly paid up.

Her mobile rang as she was searching for her house keys. Wedging the phone between shoulder and ear, she carried on rifling through her enormous handbag.

'Hi, Miranda. Wondered if you fancied going to a play tonight? I've been let down at the last minute so I've got a spare ticket.'

'What play?'

'I think it's called *Spurt of the Moment* or something like that. Written by some young person. You know me, I book them up so far in advance. Check on the Internet. It's at the Royal Court. Should be good.'

Amanda Drake was one of Miranda's closest friends. They had met at antenatal classes when having their first children and done instant bonding, having constantly answered to each other's names. Amanda's house was Miranda's second home, the place where she felt most comfortable. It was full of squashy sofas, huge televisions, palatial bathrooms and a light, airy kitchen where much gossiping was done over bottles of wine. It had been there that Miranda had done her sobbing before, during and after the divorce.

'I'm desperately trying to get into my house, and can't find my keys in this stupidly large bag. I'll call you in a moment,' Miranda mumbled, unaware that her chin had hit the mute button. She put her bag on the doorstep and took out its contents one by one. It was only when the objects were strewn around her that she remembered she had put the keys in the tiny front zipped compartment while she was in the taxi, so that she could reach them easily.

She piled everything back in and semi-shuffled into her house, turning the alarm off with concentration. She had set it off again the week before, and if there was one more accident, she would lose her police response. No one had told her that, had they, when she'd spent a fortune putting it in?

Miranda was on her way to the bin in the kitchen to throw away drooping roses from a vase on the dining-room table when Amanda rang back.

'Oh, sorry. I was going to phone you. Got sidetracked by a bunch of past-their-sell-by-date flowers. Is there anything sadder than a wilting rose?'

'Erm. A child with its leg blown off by a landmine?'

'Oh, make me sound callous, why don't you? I meant is there a *flower* sadder than a wilting rose?'

'A depressed daffodil? A weeping willow? A lethargic lily? A suicidal scarlet pimpernel?'

'Oh, enough of the aliteration!' laughed Miranda. 'And is there truly a scarlet pimpernel? I thought it was an eighteenth-century spy.'

'That too.'

'Let me look at my diary. I'm flicking through the pages as we speak. I'm almost sure I haven't got anything on … fnaw, fnaw …'

'Naked at four thirty of a Monday afternoon, eh? Who have you got round there, you saucy minx?' asked Amanda, in a raunchy voice.

'Ha. No one. But remind me to tell you of a rather naughty prospect which may be coming up. Literally. On Wednesday. Now. Diary. Here it is.'

'No. You can't do that. Tell me about the naughty prospect first.'

'Shan't. I'll check my diary, and if I'm seeing you tonight, I'll give you all the gory details later. And here we are. Nope. Totally free for – oh, look – the rest of my life. That is shabby. Really. Nothing in the diary apart from tea with Mother, and some dreary dinner party at Sally Thurston's next week.'

'Why do you say yes?'

'Habit. She means well. She's kind.'

'Kind of boring, you mean,' said Amanda.

'You're right. How do I get out of it, though, when I'm not doing anything else?'

'Start doing things.'

'Okay. You can give me this lecture later. What time tonight?'

'It starts at seven thirty or seven forty-five. How about we meet at six thirty in the restauranty bit of the bar downstairs?'

'Fine. Are we having dinner or just a vat of wine?'

'Maybe a light nibble. And you can tell me exactly what kind of light nibbling *you*'ve been up to.'

CHAPTER FIVE

The theatre was rammed with people drinking bottles of beer and eating olives. 'That's how you can tell we're in Kensington and Chelsea,' said Amanda. 'If we were in Streatham we'd be drinking full-fat Coke with a hot dog.'

'And in Camden, we'd be having a *line* of coke and an energy bar,' said Miranda. 'It's all healthy crack chic there now.'

'It's not like when we were young, is it?' Amanda put on an old-crone voice. 'When Camden was all fields and we had to walk three miles to school.'

'And you'd get seventeen gobstoppers for a penny and drink dandelion and burdock floats from a passing milkmaid,' finished Miranda.

'Oh, yes, I remember it well. Actually, I do remember when Notting Hill was a dodgy area. Now it's full of bankers and sleek women with fantastic teeth and shiny hair ... because they're worth it.' Amanda did the L'Oréal advert voice.

'That's why I moved there. I fit right in.'

'Well, you are a yummy mummy, so I actually think that, despite your protestations, you *do* fit in.'

'And you're a yummy mummy, too, so don't come the raw prawn with me, matey. How are the offspring?' asked Miranda, scoffing a pickled garlic clove and a piece of cheese.

'I've got serious empty-nest syndrome. It's okay when I'm at work, but when Peter's not around, I rattle about in that big house looking for something to do. No feeding of the five thousand. No unloading the dishwasher every night. No sewing on name tags or helping with homework. I miss them, don't you?'

'Well, I miss Jack a lot because I haven't seen him for so bloody long, but Lucy's still around. A mouthpiece for Nigel half the time, but that's fine.'

'Anyway. Enough of that,' said Amanda, draining her gin and tonic noisily. 'I'm going to get another of these and then you're going to fill me in about your date.'

Miranda always used to tell her children to stop wishing their life away when they said they wanted it to hurry up and be their birthday, but she had secretly wished away the days until Wednesday, and finally it had arrived. And even more secretly, as she stretched and wriggled in the cotton sheets and thought about getting up, she was wishing it was this evening. It was ridiculous – she had umpteen things to do, like finding a proper job (Amanda had suggested someone she could call about PR work), going to the bank to see exactly what amount of money she had to spend, and sorting out a man to fix the leak in the shower room.

It was strange how she had started to get calls on her mobile about advice on debt. How did they know? She cleansed her face and smothered on hydrating cream while phoning a plumber recommended by Lydia – she assumed Lucy had not phoned her the other night since there'd been no angry call.

Then she did what she had told her children *never* to do: she went shopping, knowing that there might not be enough money in the bank to cover it. But, she reasoned, the money would be there in about nine months when the scheme she had invested in came to fruition. And it was looking like 10 to 15 per cent interest at the moment, possibly even higher, according to Lucy. By two o'clock, she was practically dead on her feet, and some unkind mirrors with nasty overhead lighting had made her dread the evening ahead. She could only pray he had early-onset cataracts.

She wondered if Alex was running round his camper van right now, trying things on, polishing his natty dreads – if that was what you did with them – buffing up his feet.

Bugger this for a game of soldiers, she thought, as her breasts almost burst the seams on a red shirt, and went for a sit-down and a bowl of soup at a communal deli – she was definitely the fattest person there. A text pinged through. Lucy: still on the trail of the bloody books. She would have liked to tell Nigel to do his own dirty work, but that would involve a tetchy conversation with him. Not that it would start tetchy …

It was strange to reconcile the toady countenance he now had with the handsome young man he had been when she married him. On really bad days he looked like a bilberry, all swollen and purply. He would be easy to draw in a life class, just a series of massive circles. His attractiveness in every way had disappeared in direct proportion to his wealth. Peculiar how some women out there were prepared to allow such an abundance of flesh to land on them in the bedroom in return for a few baubles. At least she had had an excuse: youth, silliness and lack of ambition. Other men had been available, but she felt she had been unduly influenced by the approbation of her father. Yes, she'd blame it on him.

The leaves on the lime and plane trees lining the roads were barely moving in the sultry weather. Miranda felt hot and leaden as she walked back to the house empty-handed, debating what to eat so that she didn't look too bloated later. At least it was the sort of day when she didn't want to eat chocolate – it melted so quickly it reminded her of poo.

Earlier that day, a little orange Volkswagen camper van made its way towards Cirencester, Alex was feeling clammy. His father had insisted he go to see him that morning on a matter of some importance, and Alex assumed it was about his mother, who was periodically threatening to end it all.

He drove up to the gates and got out to tap in the day's code on the pad. It was his favourite time of year for the garden in front of the house. It was vast, but sectioned off into smaller areas, including a walled garden where hollyhocks and ornamental thistles poked above lamb's ears and lady's mantle. By summer, it would be a riot of colour, but now everything was quietly budding.

Belinda, the housekeeper, let him in and he made his way to his father's study where the wood-panelled walls gave the ticking of the eighteenth-century clock a pleasant *bok* sound. A tall, slim man with close-cropped silver hair and tanned skin was standing by the window pouring two glasses of sparkling water. One already rested on a filigree coaster on the walnut side table.

'Hi, Dad,' said Alex, sinking into the red leather chair and accepting a glass. 'What's up?'

'I've bought a small island off the coast of Spain,' his father said, 'to build a luxury hotel, a spa and a golf course – yes, I do know how you feel about golf courses, before you give me a lecture – and

I happen to know that a number of people are going to be very unhappy about that. No, not the golf course,' he added, as Alex opened his mouth to speak, 'about me owning the island. Right now, it's used as a very handy stopping-off point for drug-runners getting their stuff from Africa to Europe. I intend to stop that, obviously. I've been told they could make things nasty for us because we're talking about a lot of money. I myself am hiring a couple of personal bodyguards, possibly for the next couple of years, and putting in a little more security here at the house.'

'And you think I could be at risk too?' Alex asked bluntly.

'In a nutshell, yes. Let's face it, you're hardly difficult to track down in that orange van of yours. And not difficult to, say, kidnap. As my only son, you would be the perfect way for them to get at me and persuade me to allow them to continue. I don't want that to happen. In fact, I won't allow it to happen.'

'I can see that you might not like it, Dad, but why not let them carry on with it, and get the police involved?'

David Miller took a sip of his water. 'I have it on good authority that the police may be taking backhanders. As for letting them get on with it, you know I can't. Can you imagine the headlines if an island I own is used for drug-running?'

Alex grinned. 'Yes. Right. But won't they find somewhere else if you make it uncomfortable for them?'

'No. I think they'd try to make it uncomfortable for us by maybe shooting anybody who saw what they were doing. An innocent builder, for example.'

'What do you want me to do?'

'I need you to take a lot more care than you do now.'

'All right, I will,' Alex said.

'What will you do?'

'Take more care,' Alex said jauntily, raising his eyebrows.

'As in?'

'Why don't you just tell me what you want me to do, Dad, like you always do?'

'I'd like you to employ a bodyguard.' The clock ticked, and the leather chair creaked as he leant forward. 'I know you'd hate it. I know it's not your ...' he paused '... style. But it's not for ever. I've never asked you to change your way of life, have I?' Alex acknowledged that. 'Even though I do think it's about time you started thinking about laying down foundations for the future.'

Alex nodded. 'Yes, I know you do, Dad. And actually,' he said, 'I was going to wait and tell you this in a few months' time, but I may as well tell you now. Today I signed on the dotted line for my range of organic freeze-dried soups to go into Waitrose. For a not insubstantial amount of money.'

David let out a crack of laughter. 'Bloody well done, Alex. Congratulations. I know how much that means to you.' He got up from his chair and came round the desk to give his son a handshake and a clap on the back. 'Do you want a celebratory drink?'

'No, thanks. A little early for me. But now you come to mention it, I wouldn't mind a cup of tea.'

David picked up the phone. 'Belinda, a cup of tea for Alex, please, and a glass of champagne for me. Thanks.' The sun was shining between the slats in the blinds and he walked over to alter the angle. 'To get back to the security issue, what do you want to do? Obviously, since it's entirely my, er, fault, if you like, that the situation has arisen, I'm willing to put it through the company.' He raised a hand to Alex's instant objection. 'Maybe I shouldn't have used the word "willing". It *should* go through the company, since otherwise I could be facing all sorts of problems if you were to get kidnapped. Including raising the ten quid needed to free you.'

Alex smiled wryly. 'I don't know, Dad. It just seems a little over the top. You've done deals before where dodgy people have been involved.'

'That's the point. I'm not doing a deal with these "dodgy people", as you describe them. I want them off the island.'

'I still don't understand why they won't go and find another island. Yours can't be the only one, surely.'

'It's the most useful. Not many others are virtually uninhabited. Point is, I've taken advice, and the advice is, we need professional protection.'

'Is it worth the deal?' Alex wrinkled his nose.

'It most assuredly is. And before you ask, I'm doing as much as I can to make it ecologically aware. Solar panels on the roof, et cetera. However, it's going to be a five- or six-star hotel, and I refuse to have the sort of ecological bathrooms where you throw earth into the lavatory and occasionally lob in a hundredweight of worms. So don't even ask it of me.'

'How long would we have to have these bodyguards?' Alex asked, emphasising the final word.

'Until the hotel is finished and at least in its first working year.'

'Which would be about how long?'

'Three years, to be on the safe side.'

'Three years?' Alex was aghast. 'Three years of having someone—'

'Or two,' interjected David.

'Of having some*one*,' Alex reiterated, 'following me around everywhere. For God's sake, Dad. Talk about overkill.'

'Alex, you are my heir. And they know that. Please don't make me have to have you followed.'

Belinda knocked and came in with a pot of tea and a crystal glass of champagne. 'It's ethically sourced organic Assam tea,' she said to Alex, who was now pacing the room. 'Shall I pour?'

'No, thanks, let it mash. How are the kids?'

'Great,' said Belinda, her bosom almost visibly swelling with pride. 'One's taking GCSEs, the other's trying to decide whether to go in the army or do plumbing. I'd prefer him not to go into the army, what with Afghanistan and everything, but he's got friends who love it.'

'Yes, I can see that plumbing would be the marginally less dangerous option. Although I tell you what, there are some people whose pipes I would not like to riddle,' he said, with a grimace.

'Anything else I can get you?' asked the housekeeper, addressing David.

'A new van for my son, if you could. It's making the front of the house look scruffy.'

Belinda looked affectionately at Alex and left the room.

'I think she's got the hots for you, Dad,' Alex said, pouring the tea through the strainer into the bone china cup.

'Hardly surprising,' was David's riposte. He was well used to his son's ribbing. Belinda looked like a friendly dumpling. 'Anyway. What's it to be?' he asked.

'Let's compromise. I'll allow you to employ one minder. But can I have a right of veto? I don't want one who looks like a bloody great big gorilla with balloons under his arms. And if he's got to be around me all the time, I'd like him to have a reasonable personality.'

'Or her,' added David.

'Or her,' said Alex, perking up. 'You know, that would actually be quite cool. Halle Berry in *Die Another Day*. Angelina Jolie in that shit film *Lara Croft: Tomb Raider*. Nice. Hey, I'm coming round to this idea.'

'I think the likelihood of that is going to be about zero. But if you'd prefer a woman, I'll see what I can do. I'll send them round to the van, shall I?'

'Ha-ha. The house will be finished in a week or so. Send them there or the flat in London. Is there going to be a code? Three short knocks, followed by a long one, a finger of banana slid through the letterbox and a cough?'

'I can see this is going to be an endless source of amusement. I'll let you have a list and you can make your own arrangements.'

Alex drove back to his house in the pretty village of Shillingford and had a quick chat with the decorators before going to London and getting ready for his dinner date. He chose a pair of Alexander McQueen trousers and a Paul Smith shirt. He slipped on a pair of tan boots he'd had made for him, and tied his dreadlocks back. He had shaved that morning and was sporting a rakish five o'clock shadow. With a cursory glance in the mirror, he left with a confident air.

There was a distinct lack of confidence going on with Miranda. She was having a crisis. Every item of clothing she tried on looked atrocious. She had decided that her body looked like an old potato. Her hair was a mess. She could only see wrinkles and could have sworn her skin was starting to ruche in places.

She was almost tempted to phone Alex and tell him she'd got flu. Or the plague. Boils. Frogs. Anything. She looked at her watch. How could it be that she was running out of time? She'd been getting ready since three.

The mobile rang. Lucy again. She pressed reject call. A text pinged. Alex, saying he was on his way and was really looking forward to dinner. He'd also given her the postcode in case she didn't know where it was. As if. His text spurred her on. She decided to follow the tenets she had lived by since she was a teenager. One: if in doubt, get them out. Two: high heels good, higher heels better.

The woman who hailed the taxi on the main road in Notting Hill looked flushed but beautiful. She had tied her hair back loosely with a clip, and was wearing slim black trousers, towering stilettos, a stunning blue shimmering shirt unbuttoned dangerously low, and diamond drop earrings – a twentieth anniversary gift from Nigel when he was feeling guilty about the affair with his secretary.

Fashionably late, she arrived at Zuma and was directed to a table where Alex was perusing the wine list. He stood up and kissed her on one cheek, setting off a chain reaction through her sensory zones and making the hairs on the back of her neck tingle. It had been an age since anything this exciting had happened to her follicles.

She smiled flirtily. 'Sorry I'm late. Have you been waiting long?'

'Hmm,' he said. 'The temptation to say "all of my life" is quite strong.'

'But luckily you resisted it because it was far too corny,' she responded.

'Exactly. I arrived about ten minutes ago, to make sure our table was okay.'

'What would you have done if it wasn't?' she asked, opening the menu without looking at it.

'Asked to be shown another, of course.'

'Naturally,' she said, 'since you're obviously a frequent customer.'

His bright green eyes crinkled attractively. 'I can see I'm going to have to disabuse you of the notion that I live in a swamp, make my own clothes out of spinach and grow fungus under my fingernails.'

'A fungi to be with,' she quipped.

'Well, I do hope so. Before we get into the story of my life and you tell me how you came to be so gorgeous, shall we order some wine?'

'Thank you. Yes. White okay?' He had called her *gorgeous*! She felt like a teenager.

Alex addressed himself to the wine list, giving Miranda time to study him more fully. The sage green shirt with small cream stars had a couple of buttons undone and highlighted his smooth brown skin. He was wearing stone-coloured trousers, and she could see a booted foot coming out from under the table.

As if he could feel her scrutiny, he glanced up and caught her eye. 'All satisfactory, madam?' he asked.

She blushed to the roots of her hair.

He smiled. 'Hey, don't think I haven't been doing the same. You look beautiful. That blue shirt makes your eyes look the colour of cornflowers.'

Miranda was feeling too hot to make any intelligible response. He turned to the more innocuous subject of wine. 'How do you feel about a sauvignon? Or a pinot grigio? Or chardonnay?'

'Chardonnay, but not too oaky. If you fancy that?' She was all of a dither, and her voice had gone up a notch. Calm yourself, she said slowly, in her head. You're forty-three years old, for heaven's sake.

He waved at the waiter and ordered a bottle of chenin blanc before opening the menu.

'How do you square all this with your eco-credentials?' queried Miranda, gesturing to the selection.

'I do what I can where I can. And I ask before I decide. You don't have to wear a hair shirt to want to do the decent thing by the planet. I do think we should eat a lot less meat, but I also accept that we wouldn't have the meadows we do if there weren't sheep roaming the hillsides chomping up the grass and leaving handy droppings for the plants. Has that helped you make any decisions on what you want to eat?'

'A small pile of seaweed and an organic carrot?' she suggested.

He grinned at her. 'Honestly. I'm an eco-fan, not an eco-bore – I hope. And please, please, order what you want. My father is an out-and-out protein scoffer. He would eat a whole cow every day, hoofs cut off, arse wiped and on the plate – except that his doctor would have a go at him. My mother thinks food is only safe to eat if it's covered with plastic. As I said, I do my best, but I accept that the world changes slowly.'

Miranda was quiet as she ran through the menu. She wasn't going to risk it.

'You ready?'

'Yes, I think I am.'

His mouth twitched as she ordered a selection of vegetable dishes. He ordered some dishes that she hadn't seen, explaining afterwards that he was a friend of the chef and had phoned ahead.

The restaurant was packed, with a hubbub coming from the bar area to the right of the entrance. Their table was one of the more discreet ones, but it still felt buzzy.

'Where do your parents live, then?' Miranda asked, after the waiter had left. He raised his eyebrows. 'You said your dad eats cows and your mum eats plastic. Earlier,' she explained.

'Oh, yes, I did. Dad lives in Gloucestershire. Mum currently lives in Hampshire. The Isle of Wight. Just getting divorced for the second time and presumably working on a third husband.'

'Not very good at being on her own, then?'

'No. Although she does prefer the company of adults. She wasn't around that much when I was growing up.'

'Where was she?'

'Charity stuff, I suppose,' Alex said smoothly, not revealing that he had had a nanny for most of his childhood. 'And then she divorced my father when I was ten and married a man who was an idiot. Luckily, I get on well with Dad most of the time, and he got custody of me.'

'Only child?' empathised Miranda.

He nodded. 'You too?'

'I spent my childhood wishing I was creative enough to have an imaginary friend.'

He laughed. 'I spent my childhood roaming round the est– countryside,' he stumbled slightly, 'un-damming streams, saving chicks that had fallen out of the nest, foraging for mushrooms.'

'How idyllic. And did you always have hair like that?' she asked.

'It was an act of rebellion when I was about twenty-five. It's quite fun creating dreadlocks. You have to put special wax in your hair and eventually it does it itself. I'm considering chopping them off.'

'That would be a shame if you have to put so much effort into it. It must be like a big, comfy pillow when you sleep on it. And if you cut it off, you might end up on litter-picking duties instead of being given the big, butch equipment.'

He looked confused for a second, then his brow cleared. 'Oh, right. Samson and the hair. I get it. I do think it gives me an air of latent strength that would be sadly lacking if I had a short back and sides.'

'You could have a long back and sides,' she suggested.

'Which would be what it is now.'

'No,' she corrected. 'You'd have long back and sides and a short top. Which is an unusual look, but one you could possibly pull off.'

'Hmm. Like a mad monk.'

'And with the dreadlocks, do you have to avoid getting water on them?'

'Only if you want to have scurf up to your ears and get a great itch going on. You wash your hair as often as most people. But unlike your lustrous locks, I merely let them dry naturally. And occasionally shape them into dogs, squirrels or swans.'

'Nice,' she said. 'Like balloon animals. You could wake up of a morning and decide to go on safari.'

'Is that how you'd like to wake up, an animal on your head?'

'I could say I'm just "lion" here! I do look like a lion's sat on my head sometimes. I have to get the water buffalo in to lick me into shape. It's a jungle out there in Notting Hill.'

He laughed. 'So, you're divorced with two children and you live in Notting Hill?'

'Correct.'

'You do good deeds at weekends?'

'Erm … correct?' she essayed, with a slightly guilty expression.

'You did a good deed last weekend?'

'Correct.'

'And your favourite colour is green?'

'No, I don't really have a favourite colour. Do people really have favourite colours?'

'I have absolutely no idea. Particularly not when you've got to our age. I was sort of being ironic. I was saying you loved green as in ecologically.'

'Oh,' she said briefly. She had been startled by 'our age'. Strictly speaking, they were the same generation, she supposed. And they were technically on a date, she supposed. So she should stop worrying about the age difference … she supposed.

'What do you get up to, then, when you're not tidying canals?'

'I have endless lunches and go shopping. I have manicures, pedicures, massages and hair-dos. I do charity work with children and animals and, in my spare time, I dabble with world peace and global warming and make small soft moccasins for millipedes,' she said gaily.

'Phew,' he said, taking a sip of the wine that had been poured. 'I'm surprised you managed to find a hole in your busy schedule to have dinner with me.'

'There's a half-finished pile of slippers at home,' she pronounced.

'Is it a rush order?'

'It's imperative they're finished by the weekend. There's a hoe-down.'

'Is that generally what you say when people ask you what you do?'

Miranda thought back through the evenings with the Nigel-clones. 'If I do, they usually say' – she put on a Queen Mother accent – '"No, but, really, what do you do?"'

'All right,' he said, 'but, really, what do you do?' he asked her, in an even higher voice.

'Oh, you have disappointed me. I was hoping you were going to come up with something more interesting than that,' she said, with a properly disappointed expression.

'I'm genuinely interested in what Ms Miranda Blake gets up to,' he said. 'Like, what did you do today?'

'*Weeell*,' she said slowly, trying to decide whether to lie or not. 'Actually I did go shopping, but couldn't find what I was looking for. I organised a plumber because I've got a leak – that's L-E-A-K, not L-E-E-K. Cleaned a bit at home. A rather boring day, all in all. You?'

'Essentially spent the day talking to my dad and dealing with a few bits and pieces here and there.' He was always a little cagey, having been targeted by gold-diggers for most of his life.

'What a dull pair we are.' She sighed, picking up some fried seaweed with her chopsticks. She wished it was the meat sizzling at the next table, which smelt heavenly.

'Yes. It's amazing we find anything to talk about, isn't it?' His smile belied the statement.

'In reality, I do what many women in my position do when they suddenly find that, after years of being everyone's skivvy, they're beholden to no one. They run around trying to find something to do. Hence the canal. And I'm trying to sort out a job, or it'll be out to the scullery after dinner for a spot of washing-up.'

'Hopefully it won't come to that,' said Alex. 'I'm sure I could sell some of your caterpillar carpet slippers. This area's ripe for them.'

'Moccasins for millipedes. They wouldn't fit caterpillars,' she corrected.

As successive dishes came, the conversation flitted from one topic to another until eventually Alex asked for the bill.

Miranda reached for her purse and took out her credit card.

'Thanks, but I'll do this,' said Alex, handing his card to the waiter, without even checking the amount.

'Tsk tsk. You should *never* do that,' said Miranda. 'They might have put somebody else's food or drink on our bill. Or whatever.'

The waiter handed the console back to Alex for his PIN. 'Well, that seems very reasonable,' he said, looking at the amount.

Miranda had not managed to extract the information required to know whether it was all bravado on his side, and whether he would now have to live on scrumped vegetables for a month, but she accepted the comment at face value.

'Would you like to have a drink at the bar?' he asked.

She looked doubtfully at the packed area full of skinny women, with over-inflated beaks instead of mouths, and predatory men in sharp suits. 'No, I don't think so. But there must be somewhere else we can have a quiet drink,' she said.

'Hmm. A friend of mine has lent me his flat just around the corner. We could go there – if that doesn't sound too whatever-the-word-is – forward for a first date?'

She flicked him a saucy look. 'Oh, go on, then. And it's certainly a better idea than the shark-infested pool over there.'

* * *

Her high shoes tapped as she walked alongside him. Morse code for 'Ooo-er'.

Ten minutes later, he was letting her into an imposing building with a porter on the door, who nodded as they went past.

'My God,' she said, as they went into the first-floor flat. 'Who is this friend? Can I have him as a friend too? This is incredible. What beautiful artwork.'

The flat was on one level with blond-wood floorboards, white walls and big sofas in thick beige cotton. A giant painting of two swimmers hung over one, while a turquoise and green statue loomed over the other.

'He likes to support up-and-coming young artists,' said Alex, standing behind her as she admired the painting. 'What can I get you to drink?'

'Vodka tonic, please, if you have it.'

'Coming right up,' he said, and went through to the kitchen. 'Ice and lemon or olives?'

'He keeps a very well-appointed kitchen. Olives, please.'

She could hear cupboards being opened, and continued to admire the art on show.

'There you go,' Alex said, handing her a heavy tumbler.

She sat down on one of the enormous sofas and kicked off her shoes, then tucked her feet underneath her. 'Lovely,' she exclaimed, taking a bigger gulp than she'd meant to, and coughing. 'Sorry,' she spluttered, eyes watering.

He waited until she had subsided, and said, 'I once snorted with laughter and virtually shot beer out of my ears. I swear some of it actually leaked out of my eyes. The barman had to mop up with a tea towel.'

'Would you mind if I staggered inelegantly to the bathroom to have a final jolly good cough in semi-privacy?' she gasped.

He pointed down a corridor off the sitting room, and Miranda sped off, making small choking sounds as she went.

The bathroom was sparkling clean. The products on show were all organic and proclaimed their ethical values. She opened one of the glass-fronted cabinets. Various bottles of herbal tablets faced her, along with a number of products relating to dreadlocks. Odd, she thought. Or maybe that's how they got to be friends.

'Feeling better?' he asked, when she returned a little more *compos mentis*.

'Mm. Yes. This flat – I assume – belongs to a friend you've known for some time.'

He hesitated. 'A very long time. It's great, isn't it?'

'Too right. You know, I have to be honest here and say that – you're probably going to laugh at me – I thought you actually lived in that camper van full time.'

'Bloody uncomfortable for a man of my stature. I'm not sure I wouldn't have ended up in traction if I had to do that. Although there have been occasions when I *have* slept in it and it ain't good. I had a crick in the neck and a kink in the back.'

'Funny how they've become so fashionable again,' Miranda mused.

'What – a kink in the back?'

'No. Camper vans. I was in South Africa a year or so ago, and there were these Airstreams on the roof of a hotel that were actually being used as rooms. Give me air-conditioned luxury any day. Were kinks ever fashionable?'

'Well, the Kinks were. "You Really Got Me".'

She looked confused.

'As in the song, "You Really Got Me".'

'How do boys *know* that stuff?' she asked. 'I bet you know the words, too.'

'You're right. We aren't too good on the emotional front, but we can say whatever we want by putting on the right song.'

Miranda managed to hold her tongue and didn't ask what he wanted to say now – with or without music. She certainly remembered that from the dim and distant past when there were rules for boyfriends. They'd been updated, but last time she'd looked, you definitely didn't ask them anything too personal on the first date.

Her eye was taken by a beautiful leatherbound book on the coffee-table, a copy of *Peter Pan*, which reminded her that she had to deal with Nigel's books. And thinking of Nigel suddenly made her feel self-conscious – and old.

She stood up abruptly. 'Thanks very much for the drink. I really ought to be going,' she said. Could she have sounded any more prim? Any minute now I'll turn into Miss Jean Brodie, she thought.

'Oh. Yes, of course.' Alex stood too, looking surprised.

She slipped on her shoes and walked to the door, where there was a slightly uncomfortable moment as she tried to shake his hand and kiss his cheek. She flushed as he moved his head to the wrong side, and they kissed full on the lips.

Alex contemplated pressing his advantage, but pulled back at the last moment. He didn't like to rush.

CHAPTER SIX

The newspapers were full of the freak heatwave that the south of Britain had been experiencing for a week. Nobody had written the clichéd headline 'Phew What a Scorcher' yet, but it was only a matter of time. Commuters on their way to work were heavy-eyed and lethargic after a night of thrashing around in bed trying to get cool. Even the pigeons seemed uncomfortable, jumping from chip to pavement on their sweaty pink legs.

By ten a.m., the cloudless sky had deepened to royal blue and the air shimmered. Alex had a cool shower and dressed in thin cotton combat shorts and a fine grey T-shirt with the indistinct logo of a motorbike on it, ready to interview the selection of bodyguards chosen for him by his father. The flat was baking and he opened all the windows to catch a whisper of fresh air.

He checked his phone to see what time it was. It was, rather annoyingly, half an hour until the first appointment. That was no time for him to get his teeth into anything constructive and too much to just fiddle about.

He opened his laptop and tapped in Miranda's name on the search bar. He was surprised to find absolutely nothing. She didn't appear to have a Facebook account, even though her son was back-packing. She must be a strictly email type. Her husband's name yielded a small item in a financial newspaper about some dinner he'd hosted, which had been full of totty masquerading as bankers.

What was the name of her daughter again? Lucy. That sparked results on his Google search. Well, well, well. So she was hanging out with the ever so slightly unsavoury Tory MP, Andrew Flight. He'd been making waves with his right-wing comments about gay marriages and the role of women in the Church. There was some suggestion he'd done it to get his name in the paper. Was Miranda happy about that relationship? Was that why she hadn't mentioned it?

Leaving the computer open, he padded through to the kitchen to make himself a pot of green tea.

Alex passionately believed in doing what he could to help the planet, which he envisaged as a rather wheezy whale. But he also wanted to live in a nice flat and occasionally go for holidays in other places, which was both a good and a bad thing. Tourism had helped a number of countries where animals were being poached to extinction. Safaris had brought them back from the brink.

He was reminded of something his nanny used to say when he claimed he couldn't do some homework: 'Well, do your best,' she'd offer helpfully, before going back to her Barbara Cartland novel while sucking on a Murray Mint.

Living in a cave and bathing once a month – which he suspected was what Miranda thought he did! – would be best. Not having children to put discarded nappies on the flanks of the wheezy whale would be best. Not going out for dinner, drinking wine, having nice clothes would be best. Actually, just having no humans on Earth would probably be the very best …

The doorbell rang.

He answered the intercom, and could see a woman looking directly at the camera. He smiled. The first applicant.

'Good morning. My name is Samantha, and I've been sent by David Miller,' said a husky voice.

'Come on up,' he said, buzzing her in through the door.

As soon as he heard it click behind her, he opened his own door so that she could come in and went back to the kitchen to pour out a mug of tea. He almost dropped it when he saw her. Samantha was stunning. No two ways about it. She looked like Angelina Jolie but with lips that didn't resemble two fat slugs mating.

'Hellooo,' he said, stretching out his hand and hoping he hadn't sounded too much like Leslie Phillips.

'Hi. I assume your father told you I was coming?'

'Yes, he did. Would you like a cup of something? There's green tea on the go.' He gestured to the kitchen.

'Maybe a glass of water.' She raised her finely arched brows.

'Yes. It is a trifle warm,' he agreed, as he went to the kitchen. He came back carrying a glass that chinked with ice. 'Is that accent South African?'

'No.' She took a long draught of the water. 'Zimbabwean. Left about five years ago.'

'Please, pull up a pew.' Alex moved towards the sofa. 'Am I supposed to be interviewing you about your skills as a bodyguard, or did Dad go through all that?'

'Your father has comprehensively grilled me on my competence. But you're welcome to ask me any questions.'

'Just between you and me,' he said, getting comfy, 'what do you think is the likelihood of you having to rescue me or beat off would-be attackers with a knobbly stick?'

Samantha considered the question. 'From what your father has told me, this is a precaution similar to putting locks on both the front and back tyres of your bicycle when you chain it to the railings. Part of the exercise is to warn off thieves.'

'Or make them think it's much more expensive kit than it really is,' he suggested.

'Do you have an option?' she asked.

He laughed. 'Good point. No, I don't. Out of interest, what can you do?'

'I am SIA level three – Security Industry Authority,' she answered, in reply to his mute question. 'Capable of most things you'd expect from a bodyguard. Disarming assailants. Surveillance. Armed combat. Licensed to carry a gun, obviously. Can outrun most humans who don't do it for a living. And I can light a fire using sticks and mix a mean martini.'

Alex made a noise of appreciation. 'Sounds great. Particularly the martini part. Where do I sign up?'

She smiled, revealing beautiful teeth. He wondered if they were hers, or whether she had ever had to go into the sort of combat where they got knocked out.

'Your father told me there were a few of us he wanted you to consider. I know I'm the first. So, is there anything you'd like to know that might swing it my way, since I could do with a job that doesn't involve musicians?'

'The noise?' he asked sympathetically.

'The narcotics,' she said.

He nodded. 'Out of interest, if I did something illegal, would you shop me?' he asked.

'No.'

'Would you be with me at all times?' He sipped his tea.

'I'd be within shouting distance. I hope I can be discreet. You could describe me as your PA – that's what many people do.'

'Would you have to live here in the flat?'

She hesitated. 'If it was felt that it was imperative. But it's unlikely. Your father was talking about renting somewhere in the same building. Preferably alongside or one floor above or below. You know, he was even talking about a bug you would keep on you at all times.'

He grimaced. 'It does make you wonder whether this venture is worth it.'

'I would also say that nine times out of ten, nothing *does* happen,' she said optimistically.

The sound of traffic drifted through the windows. 'Would I be able to keep the windows open?' he suddenly asked.

'I think it would be unwise. This is the obvious place to target – and I understand you also have somewhere in the country.'

'Yes. I'm moving in soon.'

'I'd need to check that out too. Or whoever you employ would need to check it out,' she added smoothly.

'And you'd be in my camper van with me?'

'You could specify. I'd have to follow you otherwise. But up to you.'

He was silent. 'What does your boyfriend or husband, or whatever' – he hadn't noticed a ring, but maybe she didn't wear one when she was working – 'think of your job?'

'There isn't one,' she said briefly.

'Gets in the way?'

She didn't answer.

'Is that off limits?' he asked, at the point where the silence was verging on embarrassing.

'Not exactly. I'm a little uncomfortable talking about my private life since this is a business relationship. However, I can see that it is of interest,' she said slowly, 'so I will only say that my last, erm, connection was with a police officer and it ended amicably about six months ago.'

'Oh. Right. Is there anything you need to know about *me*?' he countered.

'Your father was under the impression that you were very much single. Is that correct? Because if there is someone else, they need to be brought into the fold, as it were.'

He was horrified. 'What? So anyone who's a possible date has to be "brought into the fold"?' he asked, emphasising the final phrase. 'That's going to put a bit of a dampener on the proceedings, isn't it?'

'Is there anyone?'

'Well … I mean … you know … there is someone who may be becoming … er …'

'I understand,' Samantha said. 'So we tell her what's going on and we keep an eye on things.'

'But she won't need a, um …'

'Bodyguard,' Samantha prompted.

'Yes. That. Unless we actually become better acquainted?'

'Exactly.'

'Bloody hell. Sorry. Excuse the language.' Alex shook his head, seeing nothing but problems ahead.

'Don't worry. I've heard far worse.'

'You're not going to be listening in to us, though, are you?' he asked, making sure he had it all clear.

'No.' She laughed. 'I don't think so. Why? Is she a Russian spy?'

He smiled. 'Nothing like that. We met during some canal clearing. It's early days. Well, I'll describe you as my PA, as you suggest, and then let's see how things progress,' he said, hoping that Miranda was not the jealous type.

Lucy Blake was having a trying day. She and Andrew were supposed to be having dinner with friends, but he wasn't answering calls, and when she'd texted him the details he had responded with **?** What was that supposed to mean? She replied, **Dinner. Rob and Laura. 8pm. AS ARRANGED. X** And nothing. No response. It was now seven o'clock and she couldn't decide what to do. She'd left a message on his mobile voicemail. She'd tried to make it pleasant, but it had gone rather pointed towards the end and she could never remember which option she had to press to re-record it.

She could see Canary Wharf glittering in the heat haze. The underground was going to be a nightmare. But taking a cab would add God knew how much time to the journey.

She hated uncertainty. If he didn't want to go, why didn't he say so instead of prevaricating with **?**

Her phone rang and she snatched it up.

'Oh, hi, Dad,' she said, disappointed.

'Hello, pumpkin. How are you?'

'Waiting for Andrew to call.'

'Hmm. What are you up to, then?'

She sensed her father knew something about Andrew that she didn't. Andrew and Nigel had met through the Conservative Club, and in a roundabout way it was how she had ended up in a relationship with him. She had been her father's guest at a fundraising dinner for the Tories, and had immediately found a kindred spirit in the MP – she felt he had an aura of greatness about him, and her father had seemed to feel the same.

'We're going out to dinner tonight, if he ever phones and confirms it,' she said tetchily.

'Anyone I know?' Nigel asked jovially.

'I don't think so. Rob and Laura?'

'College friends?'

'No. Friend friends. Why?'

'Oh, nothing,' he said airily.

There was a pause.

'Anything I can help you with, Daddy?'

'Any news on those books from your mother?'

'No,' she said, in an exasperated tone. 'Why don't you ask her yourself?'

'I have,' he said, with a huff. 'Thing is, as you know, she isn't my greatest fan, and I get short shrift. That's why I thought it might be better if you did it.'

'Why is it so important to have them back, anyway?'

'As I said before, I'm going to take a whole load of things for auction at Christie's. And, strictly *entre nous*, they're worth quite a bit of cash.' He hastened on: 'It's not as though they were hers in the settlement.'

She laughed. 'You know I wouldn't care if they *were* hers,' she said. 'You're the one who made all the money.'

Lucy held no truck with women getting the lion's share of divorce settlements. If they were clever enough to get a job and earn money, they could pay a nanny to look after the children. She would have loved to have had a nanny. She imagined it was like having a constantly indulgent parent. And it sounded good saying you had one. It implied so many things, foremost among them that your parents were stinking rich.

'I could do with having those books as soon as poss so that I can do them in a job lot.'

'It is a bit boring having to keep asking her, though.'

'I know, Lucy-loo. You do this for me and I promise to take you for a slap-up meal at Cipriani.'

'I'll see what I can do. I don't know what to do about Andrew, though. Should I wait or not? It's *so* annoying.'

'I'd get yourself to wherever you're supposed to be. He'll turn up.'

Seven o'clock in Britain was eight o'clock in Spain. In the port of Alicante, tourists were flooding into the bars and restaurants. Girls were falling out of tiny scraps of acrylic clothing like squeezed pork sausages. They were hanging out in gangs – hyenas scenting prey – ordering sangria, cocktails and alcopops, their heavily made-up eyes swivelling to track a target. There was a strong smell of deodorant, cheap perfume and hot nylon. Happy Hour meant that some of them were already the worse for wear.

Captain Jon Wallis swerved to avoid two of them as he manoeuvred his silver Audi through the city. Ten years ago, he would have been one of those propping up the bar and looking for an easy lay. Now he had bigger fish to fry. He checked his Rolex. Fifteen years in the army had made him an inveterate timekeeper and he had never once been late for a meeting. One afternoon he had been the only person to turn up at the appointed hour because of a multiple pile-up on the motorway and a collapsed building in town.

He had left his car in a side-street, neatly packed his jacket, tie and shoes into the small rucksack he always carried in the boot, and run to the meeting in the trainers that he also invariably had with him.

At the age of forty-six, he could pass for a decade younger. He had gone into the army straight from university and had left after the war in Bosnia where he had distinguished himself by his calmness under pressure. His pulse rate was still fifty beats a minute, and more than one woman had been transfixed by his enviable six-pack. He also had a swoon-inducing scar on his torso, which he would tell them was from shrapnel, but was in fact from an accident when he was eighteen and had drunk far too much. He had decided to sleep in a skip and almost bled to death after impaling himself on a broken glass table.

The army had been good to him. He had been born into a family on the verge of an arduous breakdown. His parents were scrappers. He couldn't remember a time when there hadn't been shouting and screaming. Even breakfast was conducted under a hail of abuse and occasionally of thrown objects. When he was old enough to understand, he realised that it was a relationship held together by financial necessity. His mother would have left, but with four children to feed she needed a provider. His father would have left, but he couldn't deal with the idea of handing over the house and having to downsize. Instead he had got his kicks from having sex with other women and not caring whether his wife found out. Jon's three siblings had followed their leaders and gone into similar relationships, resulting in a collection of people who the *Daily Mail* would have held up as social-security scroungers. Not one worker among them, but endless nephews and nieces with whom Jon had sporadic contact. He quite liked his sister Annie, who had provided him with his first niece, but he had absolutely nothing in common with his brother Mark – or Spud – and openly detested his other brother, Owen. Owen had left home at sixteen and moved into a flat with a girl who was having his child. He had deserted her when the child was a toddler.

Jon had not spoken to Owen or Spud for about twenty-five years. He had surprised everyone by getting good grades at school and going to university, where he had studied business management. The army had come recruiting and he had signed up because he needed the money. He had loved the camaraderie, the brain-cleansing nature of fierce exercise. Within a year, he would have died for his colleagues, his mother and possibly Annie. His father had died of a heart attack at fifty-four, leaving him with an obsession about blood pressure and a date he had to exceed. Every birthday, he thought about getting closer to the point at which his father's heart had stopped beating.

When he was in the army, he discovered that death was sometimes a blessed relief. One soldier in his unit had had the lower half of his body blown off. He had survived with emergency surgery, but died later. Jon reckoned he had lost the will to live along with his genitals. How could anyone want to live like that?

Jon had made a number of vows in his life. He would not be poor. He would do his damnedest to stay healthy. And he would not marry until he was sure – although that word was something of a movable feast. As one ex-girlfriend had put it, it was essentially a bastard's charter. He sometimes wondered whether his mother had been as unfaithful as his dad. When the four of them had posed for pictures as children, the resemblance was not striking – completely absent, even: Owen, the eldest, was swarthy with dark hair, Annie pale with red hair, Spud with mousy spikes and Jon the blond, blue-eyed cherub, whose looks belied the troubled soul beneath.

He had done well at school to spite Spud, who had not shown any brotherly love by egging on the bullies. Jon had never been short of a fight – or, conversely, a girlfriend. In his thirties he had narrowly avoided marrying a jazz singer and had even put down a deposit on a small house in Basingstoke. Now here he was, zipping along the N332 to Santa Pola from Alicante in a top-of-the-range Audi, having just authorised an extension to his large but comfortable house in the hills with a view to the sea and, on a clear day, to North Africa.

It could all have been so different, he thought. He could have been up to his ears in children and heading for divorce, like so many of his mates.

His business dealings since leaving the army had been lucrative, and had taken an interesting twist a few years earlier. If women had thought him a difficult man to know before, they would have found him near impossible now – even though, on the face of it, ex-Captain Jon Wallis was a charming, articulate, funny escort.

The evening sun was at an oblique angle, shooting light green flashes across his windscreen as he turned down a small road and parked. He checked before getting out of the car, then pressed the locking logo on the key fob as he walked to the door of the discreet beach-side restaurant. He gave a small smile as he approached the table where two men were already sitting, one of whom was a local dignitary.

'*Hola*, Jorge,' he said, clasping the man's hand. He nodded at the other. 'How are things, Andre?'

Andre, a thick-set man in his thirties, pushed out his bottom lip and jerked his head – the time-honoured signal for 'Perfectly okay, thanks.'

'I assume Miguel is on his way?'

'Some traffic on the main road, apparently,' said Jorge.

'Hmm. Didn't notice any myself. Must be using a different main road,' said Jon, knowing full well that it wasn't true. He took the wine bottle from the table and poured himself a glass of Faustino V. One of the benefits of living in Spain was that you could always get a nice chewy bottle of Rioja.

Miguel arrived twenty minutes later, complaining that he had been stuck nose to tail on the coast road.

Jon cut him off with a laugh. 'Now, you know that's bollocks, Miguel. I drove along the same road about half an hour ago. You never leave yourself enough time. There's always one who likes to make us all wait. Acquaint yourself with the menu and let's get on. I have to get back to the house by ten.'

'*Una chica*?' asked Andre, with a smirk.

'*Sí, claro,*' he responded.

The food was ordered and delivered to the corner table, which to the casual eye looked no different from any other. But it was positioned so that all four men had a view of the door, albeit obliquely.

'To business,' said Jorge, cutting into a piece of fish. 'I have discovered that Miller has hired a bodyguard for his son. So our plan no longer works. Any suggestions?'

'I still think we're better off targeting the locals,' said Andre.

'We've been through this before,' said Jon. 'We need them on our side. The important ones are all getting a cut, as you know. And the others are suitably scared. We need Miller to be compliant, not bloody-minded. We only ask for what he's prepared to give. I don't doubt he's got access to, er … people similar to those, er … people we have, and we don't want this getting to a stage where the police who are not in our pockets decide to get involved.'

'What, then?' asked Miguel, taking a long drink from his wine glass.

'I still think that "holding" key people is a worthwhile strategy. And it doesn't have to be traumatic for those involved, as discussed.'

'Why do we have to have our meetings in these places where we can't talk about things openly?' grumbled Andre.

Jon replied smoothly, 'If you think tabs aren't being kept on our homes, you're a fool.'

'They could follow us here.'

'We'd see them. Unless we were being idiots and not checking our rear-view mirrors. Or checking ahead of us for that matter.'

Miguel looked uncomfortable.

'In the absence of any other ideas,' Jon put up his hand to still a protest from Andre, 'any ideas that don't involve eliminating the locals and bringing down the national police, I suggest we continue to liaise with Oxfordshire.'

CHAPTER SEVEN

It was the weekend, and Miranda decided it was time she got to grips with the follicle foliage. She was in the shower, wondering whether she would get to see Alex naked at some stage. While she had her eyes shut, she could imagine them entwined, like characters in a Pre-Raphaelite painting. Then she stepped out and caught sight of herself. Ruddy hell. She appeared to have a small stoat clamped to her crotch. It was non-stop, this topiary stuff. You coiffed one day and it all crept back again when you weren't watching. She should get it lasered off. Except didn't they say it only worked if you had hair like a badger's, all thick and black? And you had to have it done umpteen times, anyway.

One of her friends was a massive fan of the Hollywood, where there was nothing left in the entire area – total deforestation – but she was buggered if she was going to go around looking like a pre-pubescent girl. Or would it be expected? Would Alex take one look at her lady garden and hoof it? She had always kept it neat and tidy, trimming it into a nice triangle. But should she go and get it waxed – lie there with her legs akimbo, everything on display for some stranger to whip it off? And what about re-growth? She could imagine it being as itchy as hell with bumps under the skin as the hairs tried to poke their way through the traumatised area. It didn't bear thinking about.

She suddenly remembered that she had some waxing strips in the cupboard from an unsuccessful attempt at doing her legs, way back when. She had come to the conclusion that it was a lot easier just to get the razor out and shave everything – and you could guarantee smooth skin when you wanted it. The waxing lark was all about letting the hair grow long enough to get a good finish, which meant you spent most of your time with hirsute legs.

She read the instructions on the packet. She warmed the sheets between her hands and carefully pulled them apart, revealing the sticky pink goo between. She laid one half on the rim of the bath, looked in the mirror to check she had it in the right position, laid the strip on the requisite area and pressed down firmly, then ripped it off. Well, that wasn't so bad, she thought, folding it in half and putting it in the bin. She grabbed the other half and applied it to the same area to get rid of the stragglers. With a flourish, she ripped it off and watched fascinated as it stuck to the side of the bathroom sink. Whoops. She tried pulling it off fast, but that resulted in it adhering itself and its furry contents to the underside as well. She opened the cupboard to get out her nail-varnish remover. That should do it. But it didn't. The wax retreated into lumpy clumps. It was at times like these that she wondered what would happen if she had a heart attack and died right there on the spot. Would people look at the evidence and correctly surmise what had been going on?

Meanwhile, what to do? One half of her bikini line was red and lumpy while the other half looked like virgin rainforest. Was it better to finish the job and then deal with the hairy bathroom sink or vice versa?

She grabbed her mobile and phoned Amanda. 'Thank God you're around,' she said. 'How do I get a wax strip off the side of a stone-finish bathroom sink?'

'I don't know. Have you tried Googling?'

'No. You couldn't do me a huge favour and do it for me? I'm nowhere near my computer and by the time I've booted it up I'll be even more stressed.'

'Hold on while I go and check.' Miranda heard the sound of a door opening. 'I didn't have you down as a home depilator,' said Amanda, conversationally.

Miranda pictured her walking along the corridor to her office at the other end of her house. 'Did it on a whim.'

'A quim, you say? How very old-fashioned.'

'You know I said whim.'

'Here we are. Dum, dum. Hmm. Well, quite a few mention ironing it with a cloth on the top to melt it and get it absorbed. Sounds reasonable. Rubbing alcohol. Surgical spirit. Do you have any surgical spirit?'

'I might have some turps. Is that the same?'

'Don't think so. Hold on a tick. Turpentine. Says here it's used by artists to thin paint. Oh, and it comes from pine trees. And was used for cuts, abrasions, as a treatment for lice, a chest rub, and taken internally for intestinal parasites, apparently. Although not these days. Have you got intestinal parasites?'

'Not any more. Should I try the turps?'

'No, I'd try the nail-varnish remover. And if all else fails, get a little man in.'

'Oh. Midgets are good at getting rid of bikini wax stuck to the bathroom sink, are they?'

'Ha-ha,' said Amanda, sarcastically. 'Now, unlike some people, I have things to do. Speak later.'

Miranda found it worked surprisingly well, the iron and cloth trick. She scrubbed at what was left with the nail-varnish remover and stood back to examine it. 'A blind man would be happy to see that,' she pronounced.

She readdressed herself to the lopsided bikini line, setting to with other bits of pink wax and eventually, light-headed from hanging over her nether regions, was moderately happy with the thin triangle.

She almost hoped that she wasn't going to have sex with Alex, or anyone else, ever again. All that worry. Would she be good? Would he be good? Would he want to do things that she absolutely would not countenance? She was getting stage fright and she wasn't anywhere near the stage. Ridiculous. I am forty-three years old and I am perfectly capable of handling whatever life throws at me. See how I dealt with the wax spill, she said to herself. No sea-birds or seals were hurt in the clean-up.

She logged on to her computer and checked her emails. Nothing from Jack. He was probably having a wonderful time. A couple of phishing emails asking her to give her bank details. Always tempting to involve them in a conversation and find out where they were from. And another from a favourite correspondent, Victoria's Secret, with the latest offers on sexy lingerie and T-shirts. She browsed the site, roaming through the brightly coloured underwear and getting more and more depressed. All those young, firm-breasted girls, with slim arms and hips. Their bottoms were so small and perfectly formed, like apricots. With a decisive click, she closed the computer and went to make a coffee.

Outside the window the lime-coloured leaves gently frittered in the breeze. A slightly scraggy squirrel scampered up the tree and along a branch, jerkily putting its head on one side as though someone had knocked.

Should she phone Alex and check if they were going to meet tonight?

After prevaricating and checking for biscuits (none), she rang and it went to voicemail. To leave a message. Or not leave a message. Leave a message … The beep went. He would know she'd called anyway … 'Hi, Miranda here. Erm, I seem to have forgotten whether we are or aren't seeing each other tonight. I've put it in my diary, but I've been a bit busy and I can't remember. Was it next week? Um. 'Bye. Did I say it was Miranda?' She pressed the end-conversation button. What a bloody lame message. How old was she? Ridiculous.

And now what?

The phone rang. Alex, she thought hopefully … but no, it was Amanda. Amazing how you could feel so dashed. 'Thanks for the info on the wax,' she said, rinsing out her mug. 'It worked like a dream.'

'You busy Monday night? 'S just that I've got a spare ticket to Cirque du Soleil at the Albert Hall.'

'Do you need to know now this minute? I'm not sure what's occurring. I'm trying to keep my options open.'

'What's occurring? Listen to who's getting down with the kids! And options open as regards the dread-locked one, I presume?'

'Exactly. I've left the worst message on his phone – like some cretinous teenager. I'm supposed to be seeing him tonight, and then who knows?'

'Woo-hoo,' sang Amanda. 'Well, I may try to find someone else and have you as a standby, then. Don't want to be left sitting next to some bloke smelling of BO and shaking dandruff over my crisps.'

'Why on earth would that happen?'

'If I had to sell my ticket outside. You can't get close enough to tell whether they're bath-shirkers before you're committed.'

'Amanda, it is not as though you're short of cash. Have a handbag seat.'

'Can't. It's against my religion. Like leaving food on the plate. All has to be eaten. Tickets – someone has to use them. If you come back to me and I haven't found anyone else, then it was meant to be. 'Byeee.'

'Oh, listen, before you go. You know you mentioned that friend of yours with a PR company? Can you put me in touch with her and I'll give her a ring? Things are getting rather crucial on the ready-money front.'

'I'll ping you her number. Lovin' you loads.'

'W'ever,' Miranda said, in her best yoof voice, and ended the call.

And because it was in her head that she should be reining in her spending, she thought she might have a little meander round Knightsbridge. She hadn't been to Harrods for ages. And she needed some more underwear, so she could nip into the posh shop opposite.

The ugly red lumps had gone down somewhat and she chose her loosest-fitting pants to avoid any chafing. Just in case she bumped into 'anyone', or agreed to have lunch with 'anyone', she put on a red shift dress, which showed off her legs, and fastened a suede belt round her waist to cinch it in. She discounted some of her shoes on the grounds of her inability to walk more than a hundred yards in them, and chose a pair of tan suede sandals. She rubbed a little oil into the ends of her hair to make it shine (and to smell nice too, if she was being honest), then applied some tinted moisturiser and a slick of lip gloss.

Studying herself in the mirror, she was surprisingly happy. She could have done without the crow's feet, but to compensate, her cheekbones were becoming more prominent. Yes, it was all about the loss of collagen, but she was determined to celebrate the positive.

She left the house, and as she made her way to her car, she noticed a woman across the road. She looked away quickly as Miranda caught her eye. For a moment, she worried about being burgled, but remembered that she had put the alarm on. She shook her head. She was just being paranoid. In fact, the woman seemed vaguely familiar. Maybe it was someone she'd met at a party. Miranda put the incident out of her mind and drove to Knightsbridge.

It was a nightmare. The traffic was diabolical and people were coming to fisticuffs over parking spaces. There are too many people in the world, she thought, and they all seem to have been piled up into this corner while the great cleaner in the sky has gone off for a nice cup of tea and a sit-down.

Could she really be bothered to go and fight for air over mountains of leisurewear? Consumption. It was all about consumption. Oh, God. Now she was sounding like the sort of people who tied themselves to trees and lived in burrows to stop a bypass. Maybe she should get a bike. Except you arrived everywhere sweaty and had to wear sensible shoes. And carry about a hundred chains and padlocks.

The car behind beeped at her to move forward, but she had suddenly noticed that a red Fiat was leaving right beside her. Excellent. Of course she wanted to go shopping. She put her hazard lights on and made sure no one could possibly steal the spot by allowing it only a whisper of space to exit. The car behind honked again. She ignored it.

By the time she had manoeuvred her Jaguar into an unassailable position for the parking spot, the driver behind was virtually purple with rage. He shouted obscenities at her as he drove past, and she arranged her features into those of a slack-jawed idiot while mouthing, 'But why?' It always cheered her up to see their faces when she did it.

She leant over to get her handbag, and while she was in the passenger foot well, she picked up a few bits of litter and rearranged the mat. She sat up quickly in time to lock eyes with the woman who had been watching her from across the road at home, who then pretended to wave to someone. Miranda knew it was a pretence because she followed the direction and no one was there. By the time she looked back, the woman had disappeared.

Coincidence? She thought not. Why would anyone be watching her, though, and how worried should she be? Surely there would be a perfectly innocent explanation. If she saw the woman again, she would challenge her.

Her phone beeped with a message from her daughter. Bloody hell. That frigging book scenario of Nigel's. She was almost tempted to give the damned things to charity. She rang her from the car. 'Hello, number-one daughter,' she said.

'Ha. *Only* daughter,' said Lucy. 'So can you do it? Honestly, Mum, Dad's just hassling me so much and he says you always have a go at him when he phones. Please. I'll come round and help you look through the boxes if you want.'

'No, it's fine. Tell him I'll get on to it this week. Honestly. And then tell him not to be so much of a – no, it's okay, I'll tell him myself. In fact, I'll send him a text right now and you won't need to get involved again. Really.'

'All right.'

'You okay, honey pie? You sound a bit miserable.'

'Oh, nothing. Good news about your investment, though, isn't it? I looked at it yesterday. We're doing well. I must say, it seems to be going brilliantly.'

'Yes, you can give your halo a little polish for that. It's a shame I can't take some of it out right now – I could do with the cash.'

'But it only works because of the sum involved.'

'I know. You've explained. Every time I hand over my credit card, though, I can hear the voice that says it's idiotic because I'm paying so much interest.'

'In a year, you'll have more cash than you can shake a stick at. It will all pale into insignificance.'

'So you say. All fine with Andrew?' she asked, a mother's intuition.

Lucy hesitated. 'I don't know, Mum. I think so. He's a bit distracted at the moment – he's probably got loads of things on at work. I'd better go – I've got tons of work to do myself. Don't forget to send that text to Dad, like you promised.'

Miranda sent a very curt one, which said she would deal with it when she could and that he was *never* to involve Lucy again. She debated softening the message with a kiss at the end, but settled for 'Speak soon.'

She pressed the key lock on the fob as she walked away from the car, enjoying the feeling. It was one of the things about modern life that she got a small kick out of. The fact that you didn't have to go round the car pushing knobs down and trying the handles to make sure everything was secure. And she loved her mobile phone with a passion. The way it freed you up from making arrangements involving second and third contingency plans. And having it ring with different tones so that if ever Nigel phoned it sounded like a duck. There were screw-top wine bottles, which meant that you didn't have to footle through drawers to find a corkscrew. Google – the double click revealing the answers to all your questions, no matter how idiotic. Toaster bags. Plus, she had a sneaking fondness for scanning her own purchases at her local Tesco.

She should compile a list of reasons to be cheerful for when she was feeling gloomy and getting swamped by all the bad things about modern life. Parking attendants waiting to leap out and put a ticket on your car even though you'd only gone two minutes over time. Companies that insisted on giving you endless options to press when you phoned them, then cutting you off. Junk mail in the computer inbox with endless scams about security details for your bank. The inability of most sales assistants to do the simplest mental arithmetic.

One evening, during a date with a man so tedious that she knew she would never see him again, she had introduced the likes and dislikes list as a talking point. Martin – was that his name, or was it Matthew? – had said the thing he loathed most was ordering his shopping online and it not being the right stuff when it arrived. 'I ordered salmon, puff pastry and tomatoes – along with loads of other things, obviously,' he had said, in his annoying, toffee-nosed accent. 'They thought cherries were a suitable substitute for salmon. I mean, *really*. Can't bloody produce cherries *en croûte* as a main course, can you? Friend of mine got the wrong bag altogether. Can't recall what she'd ordered, but she got three packets of cheese and a Caesar salad. Not what you want, is it?' Miranda still thought – as she had said at the time – that it sounded a fun way to cook, like *Ready, Steady, Cook* on television.

It was as she was pottering along, debating what else she liked or loathed about life, that she suddenly spotted Alex deep in conversation with a stunning woman. She stopped dead, which resulted in a massive tut from someone close behind her who almost cannoned into her. Feeling ridiculous, she quickly nipped into a shop doorway, flattening herself against the wall and poking her nose out to check what was going on.

Every woman's nightmare. Slim with big boobs. She couldn't see much more from this distance. And Alex was giving her that special smile. Actually, she couldn't see that. But she imagined it. So that was why he hadn't phoned her about this evening, the two-timing testicle.

She bit a small piece of hard skin on the side of her thumb and chewed it off while she thought. 'Ow,' she exclaimed, and looked down to see what damage she had done. She had drawn blood. That was going to sting. She tentatively peered out again. They'd gone. Now what?

Stepping down from the ledge she'd been on, she tried to walk normally while hugging the wall and expecting at any minute to have to dive into another doorway.

The couple were nowhere to be seen.

And now the last thing Miranda felt like doing was shopping.

Oh, come on, buck up, she told herself sternly. It'll be one of those things you read about in books. She'll be his long-lost sister. Or a friend of a friend, perhaps, who wants help. I'm being unduly over-dramatic. I'll go and buy a pair of shoes. That always helps. Or maybe I should ring him again … She got her phone out of her pocket and spooled to his name. Her finger hovered over the button. Oh, what the hell? she thought, and pressed.

It rang and rang, then went to voicemail again. She bowed her head as the message rambled on, and the beep arrived. 'Oh, hi, Alex. Not to hassle you or anything,' she said, 'but I was hoping to see you this evening. I've been asked by a friend to go to dinner, so I'll probably do that if you don't phone back in the next, erm … half an hour, say? It's Amanda by the way. I mean Miranda. Sorry. Don't know what I'm talking about. Although actually it's Amanda who's asked me. Tonight, that is. God, I wish I'd never started this message. Sorry. Maybe see you later. Or not. 'Bye.'

Shit. Talk about a messy message. And she wouldn't have cared so much apart from the vignette she had stored in her mind's eye.

Shaking her head as though to clear the image, she walked briskly up Sloane Street to Harvey Nichols, one of her favourite department stores. It was small enough to be manageable, although you could still lose half a day in there if you weren't careful. While Amanda said she constantly went into TKMaxx to bag a bargain but always came out with a candle and some underpants, Miranda would go into Harvey Nichols and always come out with a pair of Wolford tights and some body butter.

It was lovely and cool as she went through the heavy doors from the street. She browsed around the jewellery counter and inadvertently got sprayed with a hideously sweet scent reminiscent of dolly mixtures as she mooched round the makeup section. Urgh, that really is possibly the worst perfume in the world. She sniffed her wrist mournfully. I bet it won't come off and I'll smell like a cheap tart until I have a shower and scrub it.

She reached out to another spray tester and, having checked that it was quite spicy, sprayed it over the top of the first. Bah. Now I smell like one of those hideous things you put in the loo, she wailed internally. She tried to wipe it off with a tissue from a box by a pile of cream blushers and powdery puffs full of glitter. 'Is this for grown-ups?' she asked, pointing to the latter.

'Yes, madam, it's for anyone who wants a shimmer on the skin,' the sales assistant said. 'It looks really nice with a tan, if you want to go bare-shouldered to a party, for example.'

'Thank you.' She smiled. But no thank you. Glittery arms. When are you too old for glitter? When do short skirts become muttony? When are tank tops trashy? She had seen a very slim woman with long blonde hair in the checkout queue at Topshop wearing a tiny pair of denim shorts, a pale pink vest with '06' on the back, and sky-high platform sandals. And she must have been about sixty. Close up, you could see that her legs were muscly but wrinkled, and her feet were practically rhino-like, with toenails like a griffin's claws. Her face had been one of those scary wind-tunnel affairs with a pair of long, pale, swollen lips. Please never let me be so deluded that I think it's okay to wear young people's things when I ought to be wearing stout tweed to soak up the stains from balancing cups of tea on my bosom, she had said to herself.

It was unfair that old men could carry on wearing young men's clothes. Mick Jagger, 103 if he was a day, still looked reasonable in jeans and T-shirts. Maybe that was the point: it wasn't a pair of shorts. And he was a rock god, too.

She caressed a top that felt as light as a feather, then discovered it cost two thousand pounds.

By this time, Miranda had wandered over to the escalator, and although she had lost the impetus, she went up a level and whiled away twenty minutes feeling the fabrics on some very expensive clothing.

She checked her phone. No calls. Oho. No signal. She walked one way and then the other, checking to see if the little bars indicating a connection would pop up.

'Sorry,' she said, almost bumping into a woman carrying a collection of pale chiffon dresses. 'Oops.' She smiled as she stood on someone perusing a rail of pewter-coloured skirts. Bingo. A message.

It was the first time in history that Miranda had exited Harvey Nichols without buying some tights and a pot of body butter.

CHAPTER EIGHT

The text said eight o'clock for dinner, **Somewhere small – that's small as in casual, not small as in dwarfish.** Casual was almost her favourite word. It meant you could wear something you could eat in without holding your breath. Smart-casual was a nightmare because you never knew what the hell it meant. You could go to smart-casual and everyone was in jeans and T-shirts with a jacket … or wall-to-wall lycra and totter-me-home heels.

Weirdly, she had got back to her car to find it unlocked, which had freaked her out. She checked inside, but nothing was missing. She felt sure she had heard the thunk when the buttons had gone down.

On the way home, she rang Amanda. 'Wotcha,' she said.

'Howdeedoodee.'

'Hmm. I like that as a concept. Do I now have to say yee-haa?' asked Miranda.

'Only if you want to. What's up?'

'I appear to be going out with a man this evening,' she sang.

'Thank the Lord. She is out with a man … out with a man … out with a man this evening,' sang Amanda, in the manner of a sea shanty.

'And now I wish I'd bought one of the T-shirts I saw in Harvey Nicks for two hundred quid. Nothing on it. Plain T-shirt. But I

103

know it would have made me slimmer and younger. *And* given me pert breasts. Why is it that children eat your assets for breakfast?' she wailed.

'And for lunch, supper and snacks,' responded Amanda. 'Remember how we both enjoyed it – and them. And you would have to be insane to buy a T-shirt for two monkeys or whatever is slang for a hundred quid.'

'Two donkeys.'

'No, thanks, I've already had my tea. What *are* you going to wear?'

'Casual. I was thinking long floaty skirt and tight T-shirt.'

'Hmm. Bit hippie. Bit school run. Bit Sienna Miller boho but without the Sienna Miller body,' suggested Amanda.

'Oi. You're supposed to be my friend. What do boys like these days? Remembering that he's about ten years younger.'

'They like you naked and carrying beer, according to every article I read. But he's eco, isn't he, so probably unbleached cotton knickers and a scratchy pinafore dress in hemp.'

Miranda laughed. 'He's not like that at all, I'll have you know.'

'Do you think you'll be sleeping with him?' asked Amanda.

'Eeek. I dunno.'

'I know. It must feel a bit odd. I don't know whether I could have sex with anyone but Peter. It doesn't help that I'm a mess down there. Nobody should give birth to anything bigger than a ping-pong ball. Ten-pound babies do nobody any good. Smug singles and their smug snatches. Mine looks like a dead snake's mouth.'

Miranda chortled, and flicked on the indicator to turn into her road. 'Thanks for keeping me company on the way home. I may need you later to run through what I'm wearing. You going to be in?'

'I'm out at about seven. And whatever you do, you *have* to ring me tomorrow. I want to know *everything*. Speak later.'

Miranda slowed as she got to her garage and gestured to a young couple walking along to pass in front of her. Aah, she thought, they look sweet together. Young flesh always looks great. If only she had enjoyed hers more. She'd been too busy with children to notice its youthful tautness. She sighed.

Alex was wishing he hadn't told his father to employ a female body-guard. It was causing all sorts of complications in his head. While the idea of having one stunning woman on his arm and another hanging about in the vicinity should have been a wet dream, he could only foresee hideous unpleasantness.

Samantha would see him copping off with Miranda. Well, strictly speaking, not the copping-off part. But she would see him make his moves. Check out his *modus operandi*, as it were. She had shown no sign of fancying him whatsoever, so at least that wasn't an issue. But, worst of all, he was going to have to talk about his dad, and then he'd have to talk about the money, and – oh, bugger shit twat. He'd have to own up about the flat and explain that he had not been honest because of his experiences with fortune-hunters. On the other hand, she was a divorcee with children who had her own house and, from what he could gather, she was in no hurry to get married again.

It was odd having a bodyguard. Was she watching him right now? It was vaguely thrilling that he could call out and a gorgeous girl with a gun (he assumed) would come and protect him, even throwing herself between him and a bullet (he assumed). She was on speed dial 1 on his mobile phone. And she answered so quickly, he couldn't help but think she *was* watching him. Spooky.

'Problem?' she asked briskly.

'No. Nothing untoward happening this end. But I'm going out for dinner with Miranda tonight. And then ...'

'And then back to your flat?' she helpfully finished his sentence.

'Exactly. Erm ...'

'No. As I think I told you before, I won't need any other details. But if you're going to continue seeing her, she needs to start taking precautions.'

'This isn't going to be easy,' he said. 'Are we going to have to get his and hers bodyguards?'

She gave a short laugh. 'It's a possibility. But not one we need to discuss now. Or this weekend.'

'Tell you what, do you fancy a quick drink before I go off for my dinner? I'm not meeting her until eight and I could do with a sharpener. We could go to a pub nearby, and then you can, er, tail me to the restaurant.'

'Whatever you want to do, that's fine by me,' she said.

That took the joy out of it, being reminded that she was an employee. He ended the call. 'Take a letter, Miss Jolie,' he said aloud, as he trod lightly towards his wardrobe to choose a shirt for the assignation. A white shirt that was going through at the cuffs, and a pair of roughed-up jeans. Sorted. The album he'd keyed into his music system came to an end and he sauntered back to the sitting room to find the control pad. He was in time to see a woman looking up at his window. Odd. Was he becoming paranoid? It wasn't being paranoid if they really were out to get you. He'd mention it to Samantha.

He opted for a Kings of Leon album. He did a drum roll on his leg, finished with a flourish and headed off to the bathroom to enjoy a leisurely shave and a shower.

Miranda called Amanda at half past six.

'Don't tell me, you're going as an emperor penguin,' said Amanda, before she could say anything.

'No. Damn sight easier if I was. The bedroom looks like I've shouted, "*Expeliamus*," at the cupboards. Clothes every-bloody-where. I've got five outfits. You ready? Number one. Jeans and white shirt.'

'A classic. You can't go wrong with that.'

'Except that jeans leave marks all over your body when you've been sitting in them for too long, and if I do – oh, even thinking about taking my clothes off makes me feel weepy.'

'And excited,' Amanda reminded her.

'Yup. Granted. So jeans and shirt, good, but creased body, bad. Second outfit, that long, navy, halter-neck dress with the silver clasp thing under the bust. Bad thing is that my bleeding boobs are so heavy I get neck strain, and the only bra that goes with it is a sturdy thing I bought from M and S.'

'Hmm. Third outfit?'

'My Rigby & Peller turquoise and brown bra and matching briefs with a brown, lacy wrapover top and brown skirt.'

'The underwear sounds right. But does everything have to be brown?'

'Yes, otherwise the underwear shows through. What's wrong with brown?'

'And the fourth outfit? Come on. I'm going out too.'

'Pink Gucci dress.'

'I love that dress on you. Why didn't you mention it first?'

'Because I have to wear boring nude-coloured underwear with it,' she said, through gritted teeth. 'And now you know why this is a frigging nightmare.'

'Fifth outfit?' Amanda demanded implacably.

'Flowery sundress with built-in support, so I can wear a pretty pair of frilly pants underneath.'

'Well, that sounds perfect. Why wouldn't you wear that?'

'It's a bit daywear.'

'Dress it down by throwing on a moth-eaten old cardi and wearing flat shoes. Sorted. Does it do up down the back or the front?'

'Back. Fiddly to put on, because I have to do it up round the front and squiggle it round to the back. There are three hooks and eyes, which are a bugger – like trying to get a ball through the netball hoop with humming-birds dive-bombing you.'

'What an exciting life you lead,' said Amanda. 'Wish we had humming-birds instead of pigeons. And instead of going on a date, which could end with a jolly good seeing-to, I'm wolfing down a seriously crap Scotch egg and then going to see some shit football match.'

'It's a fact that gobstoppers, aniseed balls and Scotch eggs in particular are never as good as when you were young.'

'And apples. They used to have umpteen varieties when we were young. Now you've got your Granny Smith, your Golden Delicious and those pink Gala apples that taste of sweet saliva,' said Amanda.

Miranda suddenly felt the clutch of fear. 'Am I just too old for this?' she asked.

'Stop it with your nonsense. You're only as young as the man you feel, they say. If he doesn't care, neither should you. Okay, so strictly speaking, you are middle-aged,' said Amanda, 'and, by the way, this lecture is only short because I have to get ready myself even if I don't care whether I'm wearing a ratty pair of knickers with no elastic or a bra stained with soup. You're not frumpy middle-aged. Middle-aged is knee-length tweed skirts and a perm. A paunch that sits either side of your waistband. Cankles. Comfy shoes. Batwing underarms. Chin hairs. A beard. Rheumy eyeballs.' Amanda paused to take a breath.

'Roomy eyeballs? How roomy?'

'R-H-E-U-M-Y,' Amanda spelt out. 'As in watery.'

'Yes. I do know what it means, thank you. Rant over? Feeling better?' Miranda asked.

'And it definitely is when you get the menopause. Although I cannot wait for the moment when I don't have to take precautions. I'm back on the bloody cap, and if the sodding thing pings off round the bedroom one more time …'

'Take the pill, then.'

'Can't. Makes me bloated and weepy.'

'IUD?'

'Last one made me have periods of biblical proportions. I bled like a stuck pig. Nope. The menopause sounds like bliss. Bring it on,' said Amanda, militantly.

'You wait until you're sweating like a turkey in Tupperware and you have vaginal atrophy.'

'Urk. What the hell is that?'

'I think it's when it dries up like a piece of parchment. I was listening to stuff about it on *Woman's Hour*.'

'Shit. Must be a nightmare walking. No wonder menopausal women get so warm. They probably have to wear fire-retardant clothes or they go up like tinder boxes,' Amanda proclaimed.

Miranda laughed.

'I don't know why we're taking the mickey when it'll be us one day not too far from now. How very depressing. The end of life as we know it. I'll be straight round the doctor's if I start smelling of lavender and eating Parma violets. I'm not buggering about with the black cohosh and red clover whatnot. I'll be demanding a pint of the best hormone replacement known to horse, which, if I'm not much mistaken, is where it's from. Horse urine. Or something like that. Now go away, I've got the no-makeup makeup to put on and it takes me hours.'

'And thank you very much, Amanda, for helping me, Amanda,' Amanda said, in a high voice.

'And fank you *vewy* much for being my vewy, vewy scwumptious fwiend. My best fwiend in the whole wide world,' said Miranda, in a teeny tiny voice, smiling as she put the phone down.

Alex was discovering that people can tick all the right boxes but not make your motor rev.

Walking into the pub, Samantha had said, 'I never drink on duty, so don't bother asking. It'll always be water. On special occasions, I might have carbonated.'

'Carbonated today, then,' he said, with a wink, then felt a total fool for having acted like some third-rate television host.

'Still, please.'

'Of course,' he said, feeling himself blush even as he ordered the drinks.

The problem was that either Samantha didn't have a sense of humour or it didn't march with his own.

Miranda was only too willing to go off on a flight of fancy. She would have mentioned the wink at the beginning, and he could then have said what a tosser he'd been and they could have pressed on.

But Samantha was a goddess – a rather boring goddess. Right now she was telling him about the care he should take even when she was no longer needed, because of his father's wealth. Risk of kidnap at all times. Blah, blah, blah. He could understand why she was constantly in demand to protect those in the film and music industries. She looked like she should be in films herself. He brightened. There was a rich seam worth mining.

'What?' she enquired.

'I was wondering whether you'd been approached to work on a film as an actress?'

'A stunt double. But it's not my bag. Hanging about for ages and risking broken bones for the dubious pleasure of saying to your mates, "That's me on screen there with the face you can't quite see." And also, you do have to train for it. I'm not willing to put in the work for something that doesn't seem to have much going for it.'

'Being on a film set? Showing it to your grandchildren when you're sitting in your rocking chair as wrinkly as a natterjack's nadgers?' Oh dear. Did he notice a disapproving tilt to the lips there?

She paused, then said steadily, 'I wasn't planning on having children – or grandchildren, for that matter. I like the job I do. I find it challenging and exciting without having to go into the imaginary world of films.' Suddenly she smiled. 'It's a strange world, full of instant and deep relationships that seem to shatter just as quickly. It alters your perception of reality and it's not my cup of tea.'

'By the way, I think someone was watching the flat today,' said Alex, changing the subject and taking a swig of his pint.

'Yes,' she said. 'I've noted down some information, and taken a quick snap just in case.'

He was impressed. 'Where were you?'

'Your father managed to get me a room near your flat. A bedsit.'

'A bedsit? I didn't know there was such a thing as a bedsit in that block,' he said, astounded.

'I'm not sure many people would know it was there. It does resemble a broom cupboard from certain angles.' She smiled again.

Was that a tickle of humour, he wondered. 'What do you do with the information?'

'Send it to your father on a secure link. I wouldn't worry. She might be on the lookout for property in the area. An architectural student. A strange tourist. Whatever.'

'Funnily enough, under normal circumstances I'm sure I wouldn't have noticed her. It's only because of you, really. Having a bodyguard.' He raised his eyebrows to signal his acknowledgement of how weird it sounded. 'I'm more aware of how so many people loiter about with no obvious intent. It's like when you injure yourself – like, you break an ankle – and suddenly you realise how difficult it must be to get around a city if you're disabled. You see a flight of stairs and your heart must sink.'

'To go back to this woman you've seen, your father obviously thinks there's a possibility of something untoward or I wouldn't be here. It pays for all of us to be vigilant. Now … shouldn't you be going?' Her eyes flicked to the clock over the bar. 'And, if you don't mind, I'd like to leave the pub first.'

'Of course. Cheers. See you later,' he said gaily.

Thank goodness for Miranda, he thought. A little verbal sparring, and then if he was lucky … He'd changed the sheets just in case. He hadn't felt fired up like this for months. He walked jauntily from the Devonshire Arms to the Abingdon, one of his favourite neighbourhood pubs with consistently good food and a nice, relaxed atmosphere. He had booked one of the leather booths and was sitting perusing the menu when Miranda arrived, looking like an English garden. All he needed was a haystack to roll her in …

'Hi.' She beamed. 'Sorry I'm a bit late. I was faffing around trying to make sure I wasn't early and overshot the mark.'

'I've only just got here myself. What shall we have to drink?'

'I've got a delicious riesling in my mind,' she said.

'Has it got glasses by the side of it and a plate of ham, as all good riesling should?' he asked interestedly.

'Yes. And a fish dish, but I can't quite see which fish on account of the fog,' she explained, and grinned.

Oh, yes, he thought. This is more like it. Utter silliness with a gorgeous woman who knows what she wants – and I want her.

There was no shortage of conversation or silliness as they ordered and ate their starters and main courses. Miranda had been careful not to order too much food in case her stomach needed to be on its best behaviour later, while Alex had ordered exactly what he wanted.

As they were desultorily picking at what was left of the food, she started talking about a book she was reading in which people could see each other's thoughts. She was trying to work out whether it would be an advantage or not. 'Obviously it would mean that having affairs would be a thing of the past – and that's got to be good. But then there are things you say in your head that are unkind, and the person would be able to hear them, which *isn't* good. I was paying for a pair of earrings the other day, for example, and this woman was behind me. I couldn't find my wallet, so to keep the wheels in motion, I asked her if she was waiting to pay and she said, "Yes," really angrily. And in my head I said, "No need to be so short. Or so fat. And anyway, nothing in this shop is going to make you look pretty." But obviously I didn't say it aloud. Who knows what would have happened if I had?'

Alex gave a bark of laughter, which had people in the other booths turning round to see if something was happening. He raised his glass to Miranda. 'You absolutely should have said that. But you're right. It could get very uncomfortable. The white lies we tell people to make them feel better – "No, I can't see that spot." And "Yes, of course I think you're intelligent" et cetera.'

'Rats. Thought I'd covered my spot. And I've always been thick. Don't hold back.'

'As I was saying, if everyone was honest maybe we'd all stop getting touchy about it. Shall we have another bottle of wine?' he asked, waving at the empty bottle.

'Are you trying to get me squiffy, sir?' she asked coquettishly.

'Might be,' he flirted back.

'In that case, get another one, damnit,' she said, pointing imperiously at him.

The waitress took the order and gave them the pudding menu, which they studied silently for a moment.

'You know, talking of being honest and open, I have something to tell you,' he said seriously.

Her heart sank. She'd raced through wife, terminal illness, sexually transmitted disease and jailbird before he said his next sentence.

'Where to start? I have a bodyguard. A female bodyguard. Because my father is convinced that I'm in danger from some dodgy types he's dealing with on a business venture or, rather, *not* dealing with, and they're a rum bunch. So, if you see a woman who keeps staring at me, it's probably her.'

Miranda let out a sigh of relief. 'Right. So that bird two tables back who looks like Angelina Jolie, and with whom I presumably saw you earlier, is your bodyguard?'

He nodded. 'Knightsbridge?'

'Friggin' Norah, she's beautiful,' she said grudgingly.

'But not as beautiful as you are,' he said, the American accent somehow taking the edge off the corniness.

'And this is exactly where I don't need to hear what your thoughts *really* are!'

'You'd hear them saying the same thing.'

'Hmm.' She looked disbelieving.

'You would,' he asserted.

'How long do you have to have a bodyguard for?'

'Bloody years, apparently. That's the worst-case scenario, anyway. It does seem preposterous.'

'What does your dad do?' she asked, her eyes aglow. 'Is he an arms-dealer? Drug-runner? Assassin? Oh, do say he's an assassin – there's something ineffably sexy about that word. MI5? Mr Miller, 003,' she said huskily, while pointing an invisible gun.

What a relief it was that she had obviously not checked up on him on the web – as he had checked on her. Unless, of course, she was being a good actress. Hadn't she said that was what she'd done before she'd got married? He lost his smile.

'What?' she asked, worried she'd gone too far.

'Have you not done a Google search on me?' he asked.

'No,' she responded, confused. 'Why should I? I don't normally even when they're a blind date. And you aren't a blind date. What would I have found if I had?'

His momentary ill-humour dissipated and he grinned. 'Sorry. Rush of blood to the head. Nothing. You would have found nothing to cause you alarm. Honestly. You wouldn't.' His hand covered hers on the tablecloth, and somehow there was electricity, a spark … a connection. Her lips parted on a small intake of breath.

'Did you want a pudding?' he asked.

'No. Not really,' she said, while her stomach tightened in knots of excitement.

'Would you like to come back to my place?'

'Yes, I would,' she answered, her heart beating a tattoo.

The bill was paid with no more words spoken, and in the taxi, they were suddenly together, thrilling with deep kisses and murmured noises of abandonment.

Alex gave no thought to Samantha, circumspectly following behind.

CHAPTER NINE

There were days when Miranda felt that nowhere could be as beautiful as Britain, and Sunday was one of them. The sky was almost aqua and as clear as the sea in the Grenadines. If a brightly coloured parrot fish had floated across her vision, she would have embraced it as an integral part of her vista. As it was, a coterie of parakeets was arguing in the tree opposite the bedroom window. She'd read somewhere that they were now considered to be native to this area of London, along with American bankers, fake breasts and tourists trying to find the Notting Hill blue door.

She lay in bed grinning to herself. The night had been fantastic with a capital F. She was a born-again slut – insatiable in every way. And she was glad she had decided to come home when she woke up at five o'clock in Alex's bed. A combination of too much alcohol and an unaccustomed body next to her – looking so young in repose and so appealing with his lithe limbs spread out, one hand under his pillow – had startled her awake.

The depilation had been worth it, but she wasn't prepared yet to perform her morning ablutions anywhere near her new boyfriend … if new boyfriend he was. So she had gone home and crept happily beneath the cold sheets for another few hours.

She stretched, and groaned slightly as her bones got stuck for a moment in the splayed-out recovery pose she'd assumed. Getting older was a pain, she thought, literally, with your starter motor constantly needing a helping hand. There were mornings when she was actually aware of her ankles, if she had done a lot of walking. A pointer to arthritis? And every time she forgot something she would worry that it was early-onset Alzheimer's.

She pottered through to the kitchen and opened the cupboard door. Coffee or tea? Coffee with frothy milk smelt heavenly, but didn't always live up to it. Or refreshing tea? Tea. Even though she lived on her own, she liked to keep up appearances and have a breakfast tray. It made her feel like a fifties film star, with a satin nightie and honey-blonde curls tumbling down her back. Note to self: buy satin dressing-gown. Nightie. Such a ditsy word. What was it her mother used to giggle about? 'It wasn't the Almighty who lifted her nightie, it was Roger the lodger, the sod.' What was the earlier bit that rhymed with sod?

The kettle clicked off and she warmed the bright yellow pot before putting in a couple of spoonfuls of tea and filling it up. She poured some milk into a small silver jug and got out a white cup and saucer, then cut a slice of soda bread and popped it into the toaster.

On the radio, someone was talking about greenfly. It was a shame, she thought, that they caused such havoc because they were enchanting with their lime sherbet gossamer wings. A ladybird hurried its carapace across the windowsill. In her childhood, she had helped ladybirds on their way home because their houses were on fire and their children were gone, according to the nursery rhyme, but she had heard about the infestation of foreign harlequin ladybirds, which were killing the locals, and felt it was her duty to cull them. She peered closely. Yes. It was pale with dark dots. Grimacing, she squashed it and flicked it on to the floor.

The toast sprang up. She spread a dollop of butter over it, took a bite and put everything on the tray, which she carried back to the bedroom, before clambering under the duvet.

There was a text from Alex on her mobile when she turned it on, suggesting brunch at a brasserie in Holland Park. How delicious. Her stomach tightened with butterflies in anticipation.

And there was an email from Jack. She opened it greedily and raced through to the end before reading it again more slowly. He was a joy. An utter joy. Intermittent though his communications were, he always managed to imbue them with such energy and humour that it was as if he was in the room. I made a fine one there, she thought, with pride, reading it a third time and then going back to Alex's text. **Fine. See you there. X.** she wrote.

With the radio softly playing Classic FM, she sipped her tea and contemplated the outfit. Pale pink T-shirt, jeans and denim wedge sandals. And enough time to titivate and make it look like I haven't tried again, she thought.

The brasserie was busy as Miranda approached, and for a moment she wondered whether they shouldn't have booked. Then she spotted Alex at an outside table, in a pale green shirt with the sleeves rolled up, and a pair of cut-off combat trousers. She smiled and gave a small wave, her heart lurching. He really was incredibly handsome, with his dreadlocks tied back loosely and his luscious lips forming a smile in return.

'Hi,' she said breathlessly, as though she'd been running instead of sauntering to the venue. She gave him a full and lingering kiss, which was swoon-inducing and on the verge of embarrassing.

'Well, hello. You look very nice.' He grinned.

'Why, thank you kindly, sir. And may I say you don't look so bad yourself? Not many men can get away with a leather sandal. Have you been here long?' she asked, gesturing to his empty cup.

'They were very swift with my coffee. What do you want to drink?'

'Coffee would be most welcome.'

'Anything to eat?'

'Are you hungry?'

'Are you?'

'Shall we carry on asking questions?' asked Miranda, raising one eyebrow (a skill she was fond of exhibiting).

'Is that what you want to do?'

'Do you?'

He laughed and picked up the menu. 'Now, it says here that they do a selection of comestibles of a brunchian nature.'

'Does it really?' she asked, her eyebrows knitted.

'What do you think?'

'No, no, no. No more of the questions. I am going to take it that there is a selection of items, but not that they're described as comestibles of a brunchian nature. Since (a) I don't believe "brunchian" exists in any dictionary, and (b) I don't believe they would use the word "comestible". "Combustible", yes – it's what you do after an enormous brunch.'

'Well, aren't we in Dictionary Corner today?'

'No more questions will be answered until food has been ordered,' said Miranda, looking down at the menu, then firmly putting it back on the table. 'I will be having scrambled egg and smoked salmon.'

'A very presentable girl's order, if I might make so bold,' Alex commented. 'Not a hint of a chap at all. If I was here with my male friends, they'd be having food with one syllable. Pie. Meat. Chips. Fried eggs.'

'Instead of which you'll be having ...?' The eyebrow went up again.

'You know, I'm very envious of that trick,' he responded. 'I'm going to have an *oeuf Florentine* and a herbal tea, I think.'

'Herbal schmerbal,' she said disapprovingly.

When the waiter had disappeared, Alex took Miranda's hand, and bit his lip. 'Miranda,' he said seriously.

Oh, God, she thought. Is he going to propose to me? In which case how hideous because I hardly know him. And oh, no, oh, no. Yet still her tummy was curiously fluttery.

'Um. I think you have your T-shirt on back to front.'

She looked down and held it out to check, then giggled. 'I think you may be right. I'll be back in two shakes of a lamb's tail. I did think it was a bit high on the neck.' Regretfully letting go of his warm and wonderful hand, she fair skipped to the Ladies to swap it round.

'Much better,' he pronounced solemnly, and she leant forward to press her lips against his. 'You, Ms Blake, are being very naughty,' he muttered on to her cheek, as they drew back. 'Poor Samantha, having to witness this teenage behaviour.'

'You know, I'd forgotten about her for a minute. Where is she?' she asked, looking around. Alex indicated where his bodyguard was drinking lemon tea to one side of them and Miranda gave a chirpy salute.

'What are you up to today, by the way?' he asked. 'I thought we could go and have a walk through Holland Park and Hyde Park, wander down to the Serpentine Gallery. Maybe go and watch a film.'

'I am doing *rien de tout* all day. That sounds like a delectable way of spending a Sunday.' She lowered her voice. 'And I quite like having Samantha around. It's almost tempting to get mugged to see her in action, isn't it?'

'You're in a very minxy mood today,' he said.

'Is it surprising? You're responsible. Thank you for a ...' she searched for the words and could only come up with '... a ravishing evening. I haven't had so much fun since I don't know when.'

They stopped talking for a moment and indulged in another bout of what Miranda would have called French kissing when she was at school.

'Has anyone told you what heavenly green eyes you've got?'

'Has anyone told you what beautiful blue eyes you've got?'

'Yes, you. On our first date. At Zuma?'

'We seem destined to be answering questions with questions today, don't we?' He smiled.

The waiter came over with the coffee and herbal tea. 'Your food is going to be a few minutes,' he said.

'Cheers,' said Miranda, and chinked her cup with Alex's.

The street was busy with people enjoying the sunshine, parents with pushchairs, friends out shopping, children on silver scooters. There were snippets of conversation: '... amazing what he can do with a chilli ...'

'… if you do that again, you'll have no sushi for the rest of the week …'

'… vile fuckin' oxygen thief …'

Miranda had closed her eyes for a moment to enjoy the soft, warm air, but they flew open at that and she immediately found the source. 'I say,' she said, in a posh voice to Alex, 'that's not very Holland Park, is it?'

'Think she's having a row with her boyfriend.'

'Why do I never come up with those expressions when I need them? I fall back on the same old shit ones like "knobhead" or "twat features".'

'So, if nothing else, this breakfast has enriched your vocabulary – or your phrases of profanity,' Alex said, as they continued to watch and listen.

The boy had patently had enough of being harangued. He poked the girl in the chest and shouted, in a thick accent, 'Yer block up ma jobbies. Now fuck off,' then turned on his heel and strode down the street away from them.

'Your *oeufs Florentine* and smoked salmon with scrambled egg,' said the waiter, emerging from the interior of the restaurant.

'Perfect timing,' Miranda commented, as he put the plates on the table.

Later, their bill paid, they strolled off for a walk, with Samantha right behind them. A woman who had been browsing at the antiques shop opposite put her small camera away and decided she had done enough for the day.

* * *

The view across palm, lemon and olive trees to the jagged peaks in the distance was one that the ex-army captain never tired of seeing. Just fifteen miles away, the fish-and-chip shops and red plastic bars of Benidorm declared their wares in big, shouty letters, but here at Casa Olivos, all was tranquil. The swimming-pool could be glimpsed beyond a low wall. The track to the house was bumpy and discouraged random strangers, while two Dobermans signalled any visitors.

Jon Wallis had completed his daily ten-kilometre run round the property and a strenuous workout with weights in his gym. He was now standing on the terrace, cooling off and surveying the scene. The two dogs, Chief and Baffle, sat quietly next to him. Chief had a habit of leaning on him while Baffle liked to contemplate the property, his silky black ears twitching. The housekeeper, Dolores, had laid out a late breakfast of coffee, cheese, bread, meat and olives, and Jon moved to the table to pick at the food. He poured a cup of thick coffee and added a spoonful of sugar to it.

Some things in life are priceless, he thought, as a soft wind stirred up leaves that had fallen from a lemon geranium, given to him by Dolores after he had bailed her family out of debt. The scent reminded him of his mother, and the lemon soap she would buy for herself while the rest of them used Palmolive.

He loved the silence. Nothing but birdsong and the rustling of the breeze through the trees. And the freedom to do as he wished. So many people were bound up with families or were cash strapped and having to do things they abhorred to make ends meet. Here he was, living the dream, as some of his mates in the army would describe it – usually when they were head down in some ditch and being shot at.

It had its disadvantages. He was short of proper friends and he couldn't even begin to imagine the complications of having a woman in his life at the moment. Which wasn't to say that he didn't have women in his life, just nobody to share it in a more permanent way. But it wouldn't be long before that was possible – he was even thinking that it could be as soon as the end of the year. He would miss this house, though, with its terracotta flagstones and cool interior. He would miss the summer nights with the cicadas setting up a racket as the sun went down and the frogs chirruping to each other on the lily-choked pond.

Where would he go when this was all over, he wondered, as he sauntered into the house for a shower, the dogs trotting behind him. He was a Spanish speaker, and South America always appealed, particularly the Andes Mountains straddling Argentina and Chile. The world was his oyster. That was the wonderful thing about being solo.

Clean and fresh in a thin T-shirt and baggy linen trousers, he sifted through his encrypted emails and clicked on one from La Inglesa. Pictures of a couple kissing at an outdoor café. A handsome man with dreadlocks and a stunning woman with the palest copper hair and eminently kissable lips. He studied the pictures for a long time. If everything came together, this would be a job he could see he was going to enjoy.

'Does she have to be quite so close?' Miranda whispered, into Alex's ear, as they strolled through Holland Park, stopping periodically to snatch a kiss and watch the fat grey squirrels harassing the pigeons for scraps. It made her melt every time his lips touched hers.

'I should imagine so. She's said that she tries to be as unobtrusive as possible. I suppose there are a lot of people around, easy access points, et cetera. Do you want me to ask her?' He spoke quietly into her ear, sending shoots of lust through her groin and making her neck prickle with excitement.

She turned his chin round with one finger so that she could kiss him again. 'I'm so glad I made that random decision to do something constructive with my life,' she murmured, against his mouth.

'So am I.' She felt his mouth smiling in return.

He took her hand and they carried on walking. 'Did you say you were going to get a proper job?' he asked.

'Mm-hmm, I did. I am. Well, I hope I am. A friend of mine has put me in touch with someone who has a PR company and I have a meeting with her tomorrow.'

'What would you be doing?'

'No idea.' She shrugged her shoulders. 'In my head, I'll be having long lunches with clients and then going back to the office to dash off a press release. But more likely I'll be offered a post as general dogsbody – if I get offered anything. You don't need me to do PR for your soups, do you? No. Didn't think so,' she rattled on, as he shook his head. 'Can you imagine? That would have been good, going in tomorrow with a new client. I suppose if you're in Waitrose, though, that's enough. They have their own PR. You know, I make a spectacular fish pie – could you put in a word for me?'

He laughed. 'Course I will. What do you reckon – could you deliver a couple of fish pies a day or a few more?'

'Yes, I do see that might not be sufficient.' She pretended to give the matter some thought. 'Maybe I could slip in a few pots of marmalade, too. And I've got some chutney left over from Christmas.'

'I think you've got something there,' he said. 'A kind of summer hamper. Has anyone ever told you that you look like a gorgeous Botticelli painting?' he asked, crushing her to him and taking her breath away.

'Do you think we could go and examine the art in my house now, instead of going to Hyde Park and the Serpentine Gallery?' she panted, her bones having turned to liquid.

'A fine idea. But Samantha may have to come and sit in the kitchen,' he breathed.

'She can sit where she bloody well likes as long as it's not at the bottom of the bed.'

A large plane tree cast a shadow over the house as they walked through the front door.

'How blessedly refreshing after the heat outside,' he said, looking around at the light and airy interior.

'What a lovely house,' Samantha said pleasantly.

'Thanks,' said Miranda, who was as much in love with her home as it was possible to be with an inanimate object. 'Do you want something to drink?'

She poured Samantha a glass of water and, with an enquiring flourish at Alex, brandished a bottle of chilled white wine from the fridge. He gave his mute assent and she plonked it on a tray with two glasses.

'It's this way.' She gestured. He followed her upstairs. 'God, it feels funny with her there. It's like having your mum and dad in the house,' she whispered, as they went into the bedroom.

'Does that make it better or worse?' he whispered back.

'Just weird. Like we have to be really, really quiet.' She bit her lip to stifle a giggle. 'As though we shouldn't really be doing this. Instead of being in our … you know … erm … grown-up,' she ended, to avoid mentioning her age again. The previous night, there had been a little silence as they had both digested the fact that there was a thirteen-year gap between them. Miranda had discovered that he was only seven years older than her daughter.

It was a very different prospect being in bed with a man so much younger during daylight hours, and she was overcome with a shyness she hadn't known since she was at school, having to get naked in the communal changing rooms before swimming. At least then everyone had been in the same boat and – apart from a girl called Susie Beigh who was always up for showing her muff – they'd kept their eyes on the mouldy tiles.

When Lucy used to complain about changing in front of other girls, Miranda had always told her, 'Everyone is naked under their clothes. Even the Queen has a bottom.' But, secretly, she felt much the same way and still had a horror of gyms where women would wander about starkers, even bending over. And she couldn't help but bloody look!

So here she was, nervously about to get on down and dirty without the benefit of soft lighting. Alex appeared to have no such qualms. He was stripped to his briefs and opening the bottle of wine while she was fannying about aimlessly tidying. 'I'm just going to nip to the bathroom,' she said, annoyed that she sounded apologetic. Once in there, she did what her mother would have called a flannel bath – washing the bare essentials – then cleaned her teeth, and put her clothes back on, glad that she was wearing pretty underwear again.

'I am going to do a quick nip, too,' Alex said as she came back into the bedroom, grabbing her as she went past and giving her a deep kiss, which brought her up in goose bumps.

The curtains were closed, but it was a light room and there was no way it could be darker. Miranda arranged herself on the bed in what she hoped was an alluring pose. She was feeling extraordinarily self-conscious. And without the concealing night, she was acutely aware of how her flesh was showing its age. How when she lay on her side, her breasts no longer held their shape. It was shallow, she knew, but she also knew how men were turned on by pornography … and generally not pornography involving middle-aged women. Pah. That word again. Middle-aged. Get it out of your head, she admonished herself. And then Alex reappeared and there was no need to worry because he was all over her like moss round a stone, enveloping her in his strong arms while the wine warmed and the sun lost its heat, finally giving up on the day.

CHAPTER TEN

It was as though Walt Disney had decided to turn Miranda's life into a film. Whatever she touched seemed to work. Or that was how it seemed. In fact, it was more that everything was imbued with a glow of romance, enchantment, lust, making a crisis into a comedy – a well of despair into a pond of plenty.

She got the job in the PR agency, and although it didn't pay very well she enjoyed having to get up early three times a week. Through nights of unbridled passion, she lost weight and her skin was luminescent.

Then Lucy met Alex, and it felt like Alfred Hitchcock had moved into the sitting room. Miranda had been wondering when to tell her prickly daughter about her new lover, and had been hoping to camouflage it with the delivery of Nigel's books. But she had turned the house upside-down and not found them, merely discovering that she was hoarding an awful lot of memorabilia for her children.

Unfortunately, she had chosen to phone and tell Lucy this on an evening when her daughter happened to be in the vicinity and, despite her best protestations, Lucy had arrived on the doorstep a few minutes later, barely giving Alex time to get his clothes on.

It had not been comfortable for any of them.

Miranda had thrown on a long dress and tied her hair back before running down to open the door. Alex was still on the stairs as Lucy took in the scene. 'Hi, Mum,' she said, giving her a cursory kiss and looking over her mother's shoulder. 'And you are?'

'Alex,' he said, coming forward to shake her hand.

Lucy pretended not to notice it, and he let it fall. 'Mum?' she asked, with a fake smile.

'As he said, this is Alex. And he and I ... And we are ... um ... erm ... seeing each other.'

There was a silence as the statement hung in the air.

Miranda was annoyed at how apologetic she had sounded. Alex was also annoyed at how apologetic she had sounded. Lucy was just horrified. Then she noticed Samantha sitting in the kitchen. 'And who are you?' she asked belligerently.

Miranda came to herself and said with a firmer voice, 'Lucy. Please. Manners. You're in *my* house and these are *my* guests.'

Lucy bristled, but her voice was smoother as she approached Samantha. 'Hello,' she said. 'I'm Lucy Blake.'

'Samantha Kane. Alex's bodyguard,' she said, shaking the hand that was offered.

'Bodyguard? Mum, what's going on?'

'Nothing's "going on" in the way you make it sound, Lucy,' said her mother, acerbically. 'Shall we go through to the sitting room and have a civilised conversation?' She led the way.

Alex immediately saw that the idyllic cocoon was about to be smashed. He observed the play between the two women and knew enough about families to sense that Miranda would be the one to crack. Lucy was being sarcastically polite. 'How old are you, Alex?' she asked pointedly.

He wanted to tell her that it was none of her business, but was aware that Miranda was desperate to avoid a full-on confrontation. 'As we know, age is a state of mind, not just a number. I'm a very old thirty,' he replied.

'So, seven years older than me, hm? And out of interest – because I've never met anyone with a bodyguard before – why do you have one?'

'My father is in business and there are complications.' He kept the explanation short.

The meeting was brief because Alex decided his presence was prolonging the agony and chose to leave with Samantha, giving Miranda a warm hug on the doorstep and telling her it didn't matter, they would deal with it together. He felt a gloomy foreboding as he walked along, Samantha dogging his footsteps in silence.

In the house, Lucy was taking her mother to task. 'How could you? He would have been seven when you were having *me*. He's only two years older than *Andrew*. It's beyond the pale. It's awful. And he's got dreadlocks. And a bodyguard. Which means he's involved in something appalling. Or his dad is. And that means you might get caught up in it and …' The diatribe went on, until Lucy burst into tears.

Miranda shuffled over on the sofa to give her a hug, and felt her daughter's stiff, resisting body succumb to her mother's warmth. The love she would always have for her child washed over her, and weakened her resolve to tell Lucy that she had her own life and would live it as she wanted to.

Maybe it would be for the best if she and Alex cooled it. Maybe it would be for the best if they left it until the danger was past.

'And I don't know how I'm going to tell Dad about those books either. I think he was banking on them.' She sniffled, pulling away from Miranda and blowing her nose.

'Well, if he cared about them that much, he should have taken them with him, shouldn't he?'

'He says he mistook the others for them. You know he can't tell one leatherbound book from another.' Lucy gave her a watery smile. 'I'm sorry, Mum, for being horrible earlier. Sorry.' She snuggled up to her in an unaccustomed display of affection. 'But it is ... you know ... isn't it?'

And Miranda, her heart sinking, felt all her insecurities resurfacing, and knew that it was.

No longer was Miranda convinced that Britain was the best place in the world to be. No longer was her little patch of London the gateway to a sparkling life. The fizz had gone now that she was alone again. It *had* felt right to end the relationship with Alex. She could never have been happy with a man her daughter detested. She was lucky, she told herself, that she hadn't gone in too deep. Although that was a lie.

Amanda had told her to stand firm, but it was the double whammy of Alex's youth and Samantha the bodyguard that had decided it. Lucy had gone on so much about the possibilities of being caught up in some awful scenario that she had been genuinely scared.

And Alex, gorgeous, meltingly handsome, kind Alex, had understood. Or said he understood. Had held her close one last time, then walked away as she had sobbed her heart out.

After she had divorced Nigel, Miranda had gone through a lot of soul searching. She had realised one major truth: that the end of a serious relationship was always going to leave you bruised, battered and bewildered, but you would survive it. And if you could survive that, you could survive anything. She also realised a lesser truth: that you would probably never give as much of yourself as you did to your first love. That, essentially, breaking up would get easier because of the knowledge that life went on. You got over things you thought you never would. And you also saw that some things were insurmountable: that it was better to end something than to stagger on wounded. The death knell having been dealt to her relationship with Alex, she went out with Amanda and got tragically drunk.

The next day at work, Amanda's friend had taken her to one side and suggested she have a holiday.

'Just a week. It'll do you good. Go on a retreat. Go hiking. I know what it's like when you come out of the first big relationship after a divorce,' she had said.

It was the last thing she fancied doing, but in the way that biting an ulcer dulls the pain, she took a grim pleasure in going on to holiday websites featuring smiling, happy people and feeling as if she was dying inside.

Tearfully bashing the keys, she typed in the words: 'sad single holidays'. 'Don't be sad,' said one.

'Yeah. Right. That makes me feel *much* better,' she said aloud, then adjusted the Google search to 'single holidays'.

The first few sites appeared to show women of a certain age smiling gamely as though they were advertising glue for dentures. There was a holiday trekking with tigers, another white-water rafting, a third hiking the Inca trail. People whose cheeks glowed with health, happiness and achievement.

For a short while as she typed and surfed, she could forget the loneliness. Then it would thunder straight back and all she could see was Alex's green eyes, his wiry body, while feeling his hands on her body. Single. Single. She hadn't cared that much about being single before. But now?

She sighed and concentrated again. Yoga. Maybe that was what she needed. She had been meaning to try it for ages. She could hang out in pyjamas and learn to do the lotus position. People said yoga was amazing, and she was almost certain she had read somewhere that it made your skin look younger and your hair look thicker.

Having found a plethora of websites offering retreats, she narrowed it down to three and then, concerned that she might spend the entire time crying into her mouth in a headstand, she sent emails with the details to Amanda, Hannah and Sophie – with whom she'd shared excellent weekends away.

> I'm thinking of doing this next week. You know why. But then I looked at what's on offer and wondered whether you might want to come too. It could even be fun, and I promise not to drone on about what's happened. Maybe we could all go? The fab four. What do you reckon? I'm going to book it tomorrow, no matter what. xxxxx

Miranda lasted precisely one day on her yoga retreat. She had flown out to Alicante on a charter flight with a scattering of people in leisurewear smelling faintly of cigarettes. There had been a moment of drama when the airline had tried to charge her for excess baggage, but she had pulled out clothes from the heaviest case and put them on until it was down to the required weight, causing sniggers from some of the other passengers.

It did seem mean when there were some huge great heffalumps getting on board with big bags. Much fairer, she thought, if you were weighed with your bags, if it was about how much extra petrol the plane needed to get off the ground.

The drive to the hotel in a minibus was beautiful, up into the hills behind the city. She was surprised to discover that, considering how small the retreat was, there was another woman from the flight who was going there. She was somewhere between plain and pretty, with pale brown hair and brown eyes. There was something familiar about her, but Miranda couldn't quite put her finger on it. 'Sorry for staring at you,' she smiled as her eye was caught, 'but do I know you from somewhere?'

'I don't know,' the woman said, frowning. 'Do you live in west London?'

'Yes, I do. Notting Hill. You?'

'Holland Park. Maybe I've seen you about the coffee shops on Holland Park Avenue. Do you ever go to Lidgates?'

'Who doesn't?' Miranda nodded. 'Although not on Saturdays. The queue's a mile long. I've passed off their meat pies as my own on many occasions. The meat is so good there, isn't it? And I like the fact that it's mostly organic and locally sourced. Oh, God, I'm sounding like an advert. Locally sourced, indeed. I'll be talking about ethical farming and genetically modified ingredients next.'

'Or e-numbers and what they mean,' said the other woman, pleasantly, and they lapsed into silence.

'Do you know? I'm not totally sure I do know what e-numbers mean, except that we shouldn't eat food with them in,' Miranda sparked up.

'I think the "e" stands for "European". And that's about the full extent of my knowledge. Oh … although I know that some are bad, some are less bad and some are okay.'

'A friend of mine always says preserved meat should be a treat – as in sausages, bacon, pastrami, that sort of thing. Not that I'm into sausages much, anyway.'

'Me neither. My name is Lola, by the way.'

'Miranda.'

'I doubt we'll be getting sausages at the yoga retreat,' Lola said, as they mounted a hill towards a small town.

'This is such a pretty area, isn't it? Have you done a lot of yoga?' Miranda asked.

'Yes, it is, and no, I haven't. Just fancied getting flexible and eating well. You?'

'Nope. Never. Had to go and kit myself out.'

'Me too. I wasn't quite sure how hot we'd be getting, so I've got short and long trousers, T-shirts and vests,' said Lola.

'And do you wear underpants when you're twisting yourself into unusual shapes? It's just that pants often ride up, don't they?' laughed Miranda, but wanting to know the answer.

'They should give you a list, really, shouldn't they?'

The hotel was very sweet, with comfortable beds and a peaceful courtyard where they did yoga early in the morning and at dusk.

At seven o'clock the next morning, Miranda decided that what she really didn't like was yoga. She hated everything about it, apart from the lying down in corpse position at the end. Sun salutations were the worst. It was like making a tent out of yogurt … It was wet, laborious and pointless. Her thong kept cutting into her and making her wince as she was stepping forward into warrior pose, and it didn't help that as she was panting in dog position someone was patently breaking wind nearby. She found it almost impossible to stand on one leg without wobbling until her knee hurt, and she had an almost uncontrollable urge to giggle during the chanting.

Lola had either lied about her prowess or was a natural, curling herself into competent knots on the mat and solemnly omming along with the teacher.

After a shower and breakfast, Miranda went to find someone in authority to see what her alternatives were. She was pleasantly surprised to find that she could transfer to a sister hotel on the coast and, for a supplement, learn how to sail. 'No point in having money if you don't enjoy it, eh?' she said to the manager, as she filled in forms and handed over her credit card. 'And luckily I've got a swimming costume, goggles and a jaunty scarf, so I shouldn't need any specialist clothing. Although I might need a peaked cap and white shorts – and possibly a stripy top.'

The manager handed her back her card. '*Claro, señora*,' he said. 'All those are very important when learning how to sail. I hope you enjoy. Do you want me to organise a taxi for you?'

Miranda immediately felt at home in her new hotel. Before, it had been all stripped wooden floors, Buddhas, water features and stones. Now it was marble, luxury towels, a bar and leather seats.

She unpacked both suitcases, put up the framed photograph of Jack and Lucy laughing on Brighton beach, and lined up the dozen pairs of shoes on one side of the bedroom.

With the rest of her possessions safely stowed, she put on her swimming costume and a sarong, then threw a towel, a book and some sun screen into her straw bag and went to the beach. 'Mad dogs and Englishmen,' she muttered to herself, as she hired a sun-bed and an umbrella from a man who appeared to have been rolled in hair.

It was glorious sand, soft and white. She ran it through her fingers. It was like flour. Beaches always stirred memories of holidays when she was a child. Building sandcastles, burying herself and friends under mountains of claggy golden scoops and trying to find their toes with the spade. Always a hat – her mother's obsession.

For a while, she surveyed the scene. Britons with patchily burnt skin and muffin tops oozing over their swimwear. Locals with their dogs. Children with various items to keep them amused or safe in the water. She watched with interest as a spherical girl of about six had her rubber ring, in the shape of a turtle, squeezed over her swollen stomach. 'You're going to need a bigger ring,' Miranda said, under her breath, echoing *Jaws*, with which Jack had been obsessed.

The child was fed a packet of crisps before she waddled down to the sea to join a number of her party, who were bobbing in the gentle waves wearing straw hats. Like a tea party before a *tsunami*, thought Miranda, as she pulled out her book and, with a sigh, sank back on the sun-bed.

It was no good, she couldn't stop thinking about Alex, and she realised she had read about twenty pages without paying any attention. A swim was what she needed – but who was going to look after her belongings? Was there anyone she could leave in charge of her wallet and phone?

She considered the options. Hmm. The family with the fat child was ruled out because she couldn't see them running after a thief in any meaningful way. There were a couple of likely lads with ribs like xylophones and spots on their backs, eyeing up the totty. Nope. Maybe it was worth risking a little dip if she swam facing the beach and tied her bag to the sun-bed somehow. She got up and crouched down to see if there was any viable way of doing it. Bugger. She wished she hadn't brought her wallet and phone now. Could she be bothered to walk back to the hotel and put them in her room? No. She took her sarong from the bag and slotted it through the plastic slats before putting her wallet and phone in the material hanging underneath. Then she did as many reef knots as she could to tie it up, put her towel back on the top and surveyed the result. Not bad, even though I say so myself, she thought, popping her book and sun screen on the lumpy bit.

She sprinted to the sea and went in sideways to keep an eye on everything. As soon as she was in deep enough to swim, she did a few strokes one way and then the other. And then, just as she was relaxing, she saw a thin man with snug-fitting yellow trunks and a grey T-shirt saunter towards her sun-bed and start to move back the towel. '*Oi!*' she shouted, attracting the attention of those around her, but nobody on the beach. 'THAT MAN. STOP THAT MAN. THAT MAN IN YELLOW. STOP. HE'S STEALING MY BAG!' she yelled, as she waded to shore. But no one moved a muscle as the man calmly sliced through her sarong with a knife and made off at a fast pace towards the road.

No one, that was, apart from a man in a blue shirt and cream trousers who appeared from nowhere and sprinted after the thief as Miranda made it out of the sea and ran to her lounger.

She couldn't believe it. She had been in the sea literally five minutes. The horrid little yellow shit had obviously been watching her tying up her belongings. Fuck. Damn. Bollocks. An afternoon at the sodding police station, then trying to sort out her cards using the hotel bloody phone. Her life was in error. Everything was falling apart. She groaned. The fat family looked on with interest, their daughter struggling to unpeel her rubber ring. It eventually came off with a sad *flup* and began to deflate on the sand. '*Muuuuuuuumy!*' the child wailed.

Miranda felt like joining her. Being an adult wasn't always as good as it was cracked up to be.

It was her fault. If only she had left her phone and wallet at the hotel. If only she had trusted the fat family, who were now clustered around the child, like an enormous pile of amorphous raspberry ripple as she continued to scream in an undulating *wahwahwah*. The rubber ring was turning into a wrinkled condom, with the grimacing head of the turtle gradually shrinking in on itself until its eyes stuck together and collapsed on its airless body.

Miranda was turning round aimlessly and stuffing things back into her straw bag while trying to spot any sign of the possible hero of the hour. If only she had stayed at the yoga hotel. If only she had waited and gone on holiday with a friend. The if-onlys had reached 'If only I'd never met Nigel' when a slightly out of breath and, as she now saw, seriously attractive man strode swiftly up to her and held out her purse and phone. 'These are yours, I believe,' he said, with a smile.

* * *

141

Her answering smile was everything he had hoped for. Her corn-flower eyes sparkled and she flashed even white teeth between full lips. Nice one, he thought. The squaddies in his old regiment would have called her a cracker.

'Oh, thank you *so* much. That is *so* brilliant. I was contemplating an afternoon of statements at the police station and being patronis-ingly told not to leave my things unattended on the beach. Thank you. Thank you. You cannot know what a relief it is. Well, you probably can,' she corrected herself, 'but ... anyway ... erm ... thank you. You've restored my faith in human nature.'

'Happy to help. I was passing and happened to be glancing this way when I saw that guy attacking your poor *kikoi*.'

'*Kikoi*?' Miranda queried.

'Sarong. Another name for a sarong. I hope he hasn't extracted anything from your purse. I don't think he would have had a moment, with me hard on his heels.'

She opened it and made a cursory check. 'No. I don't think so.' At this point, she wondered whether she should offer money. How did one do that? Should she hand over a twenty-euro note? Was that too paltry? Hand over the lot, since she would have lost it completely if he hadn't rescued it? How much had she got there?

'Here,' she said, thrusting a bundle of notes at him. 'For your trouble. He could have used that knife on you. And I would have lost my phone with all my numbers, which I haven't backed up, and my cards – and I don't even know which ones I've got or anything ...' she ended limply, as he shook his head.

'Really. It's nothing. I merely did my civic duty,' he said, holding up his hands.

'Can I at least … I don't know … buy you a drink?' she offered hopefully. He wasn't Alex, but he was ridiculously handsome.

'That would be much appreciated,' he assented, 'but, sadly, not now. I'm on my way to a meeting. Maybe later if you're not busy.'

'Yes. That would be fine. Excellent, erm … Good.' Oh, heavens to Betsy, she thought, I'm stumbling around in a synonym bog. She staggered on. 'Brilliant. Wonderful.'

He looked amused. 'What time would you like to meet up?'

'Whenever. Early evening? I'm not doing anything. I'm in a hotel just up the road, which is lovely. And it has a lovely bar …' Bloody hell, she thought, I've actually run out of words. He was probably married with children or a gigolo preying on single women or an actor or a mad axe murderer. She should at least lie about which hotel she was in. 'Or wherever. It doesn't have to be the hotel. A bar. In fact, a bar would be better.'

'How about I meet you at El Tabarro further along this beach road?' He gestured up the road. 'At about six? Does that suit?'

'Yes. That's fine. Excellent. Good …' Now I can see a synonym triangle being introduced, so I'll stop right there, she thought.

'I should introduce myself.' He smiled, the corners of his blue eyes crinkling as he shook her hand. 'Jon Wallis, erstwhile captain in the British Army and here to serve.'

He had a firm grip, and nice nails, she noticed, as she looked down. 'Miranda Blake. Here to make a clot of myself by tying my belongings to a sun-bed and getting them nicked.'

'Easily done,' he said. 'I shouldn't beat myself up about it. Nine times out of ten, these gambles pay off.'

He lifted back a cuff and moved his Rolex into view. 'Listen. I'd better get off or I'll be late for my meeting. See you at El Tabarro.'

'You bet,' she said gaily, then cursed herself for sounding like a middle-aged idiot trying to be cool.

She gazed after him as he strode away. Outstanding arse, she pronounced internally, feeling only moderately guilty about her shallowness.

Within the space of half an hour she had gone from dejection to elation. Although there was the small niggle about safety. She usually had a reliable gut instinct, but she was well aware that holidays were wont to send the compass spinning. It was fortunate that she had managed to button her lip on where she was staying. She could always hoof it back if it looked suspect.

While pondering, she had been walking back to the hotel, and as she went through the door, she suddenly transferred her attention to what she was going to wear for her meeting with Mr Jon Knight In Shining Armour Wallis. She metaphorically thumbed her nose at the carry-on luggage brigade. At least she had a wide selection of outfits to choose from and a veritable cornucopia of footwear.

Amanda had been right. A holiday was exactly what she had needed to take her mind off the aborted romance with Alex.

As Miranda happily contemplated the evening ahead, ex-Captain Jon Wallis was meeting a woman she might have recognised as Lola.

CHAPTER ELEVEN

Driving to his house in the country, Alex had one ear on the radio and heard a line that made him laugh out loud: a comedian talking about being at school where the headmaster had told the children that whatever their expectations of life were they should lower them.

When Alex was little, he had wanted to be a cowboy. Everything about them seemed glamorous – the leather hats that you would push back from your sweaty brow when you were thinking, the suede chaps with fringing, the galloping horses and the saloon bars with swinging slatted doors. For about five birthdays and Christmases in a row, he had been given books, videos, outfits and sundry paraphernalia relating to cowboys. He was going to live on a ranch in Virginia with two guns that he would slip into his holsters every morning before riding out to survey his huge herds of cattle. And he was going to change his name to Red, because obviously nobody was called Alex in the Wild West.

He went through a phase of so hating his name that he insisted people call him by his surname, and luckily nobody batted an eyelid. At home, he would stride about the estate in his Stetson and chaps, whipping out the gun and pretending to kill squirrels while shouting, 'Take that, you varmint.' He had no idea what a varmint was, but knew it wasn't something you aspired to become.

One of his books had offered up the sterling phrase: 'Never squat with your spurs on.' It had gone 'global' at school, as they called it. You would hear little boys shouting it, with bad American accents, as they went into the toilets. 'I'm not squatting and I ain't got no spurs on.'

His parents, in a rare moment of accord, had sent him to a liberal public school and he had begun to shine in maths, chemistry and sport. By the age of thirteen, he had set his sights on solving Fermat's Last Theorem, and garnering world-wide plaudits. Long into the night, he would sit over his books, which were covered with equations, his head hurting at the possibilities. Luckily, it was finally solved – to all intents and purposes – a few years later, thus narrowing the field of opportunity for the Big One. And, anyway, by then he had decided to go into ethical, ecologically based business ... partly to spite his father.

The A40 ground to a halt, putting a stop to his musings as he considered whether to divert. He switched to the local radio station to see if there were any traffic updates and happened to tune in just as they were talking about a crash involving a lorry and a van. He crawled along to the next exit and pulled over to consult the map. His phone rang: Samantha. 'Hi. You know I don't do this normally, but if you've pulled off because of the traffic, do you want to tell me the postcode and I'll tap it into the sat-nav? That way I can direct you from behind, as it were.'

'Thanks. Actually, that would be good.'

He ended the call. He couldn't work Samantha out. She gave off zero interest in him, yet she seemed to like him. Also, it wasn't as though he was complaining exactly, but he was bored with having someone else around all the time. He missed Miranda. She'd made him laugh and she had a fabulous figure – amazing to think she had two grown-up children. The benefit, he supposed, of having them young. He hadn't warmed to her daughter for obvious reasons. He thought she was a spoilt brat – he recognised the symptoms from boys at his school who had also suffered from the condition. There was an arrogant, almost lazy disregard for other people and what they might want or feel or have to do. They expected things to happen just for the asking. They had tuck boxes from Fortnum & Mason, spent winters skiing near holiday homes in Switzerland, summers in the Caribbean and had Christmas crackers from Asprey's. Mind you, they were cracking cracker gifts. He still had the solid silver and diamond cuff links, even though he had lost touch with the friend.

Some were amazingly grounded, considering their family fortunes, and more than one was now working in the charity or environmental sector. It was their parents who were to blame. You either instilled a social conscience or you didn't. You either made the children realise that they were a citizen of the world or you allowed them to think they were the masters of the universe and that you could stuff everyone or everything in your rise to the top.

Power and money.

That was it for some people.

It was such a shame that, unfortunately, some women out there were only interested in marrying rich men – or divorcing rich men and taking as much as they could before moving on to the next one. That was one of the things he admired about Miranda. She had ditched a man who was obviously dripping in lard, as it were, and not taken him to the cleaners.

'The thing about elephants is that they're big,' he heard on the radio.

'No shit, Sherlock,' he said aloud. 'Tell me something else I didn't know.'

His phone rang again. 'Hi, Samantha,' he said, into the microphone hanging from his ear.

'Wondering if you needed to stop on the way and get anything for the house? Tea, coffee, milk, whatever.'

'No, it's fine. I'll get it from the village if I need to. I know the way from here, by the way, so you can tell your sat-nav it can sit down and take the weight off its feet.'

'Cheers.'

Buying a new home is always exciting. But walking into your new home when the builders, plasterers, plumbers, electricians and decorators have left is even more exciting, he decided. The smell of it is a thrill.

Hours later, surrounded by boxes with their contents spilling out, he kind of wished he had someone else there, not only to help but to share memories with. He couldn't really ask Samantha – she could hardly be said to be guarding him if she was lugging great big boxes around. And since she'd grown up in Zimbabwe, she wouldn't know about Geoffrey and Zippy in *Rainbow* or Toad the Wet Sprocket and their seminal song 'All I Want'. He could see her prowling round the garden now, checking for whatever bodyguards checked for. Easy access points. Weak security. Questing voles.

With an easy lope, he crossed the sitting room and opened one of the double doors. 'Do you want a cup of tea?' he shouted.

She swung round. 'Yes, thank you, I would. But let me make it,' she said. 'I assume that you've put the teabags, kettle and cups in a handy box?'

'What do you take me for? An utter cretin?' He shook his head, as though saddened by her lack of faith. 'You'll have a cup of tea in your mitt in a jiffy,' he said, and hared off to the camper van where he swiftly made a brew.

'Cheat.' She laughed as she took the steaming mug.

'That's the problem with you keeping an eye on me,' he said ruefully. 'I can't do anything without you noticing.'

'Are you finding it a chore?' she asked sympathetically.

He nodded. 'Uh-huh. I'm used to going off and doing my own thing, and to be honest, I feel a bit like Paul Newman in *Cool Hand Luke*, when he's chained to another prisoner. No offence,' he added.

'None taken. If there's anything you think I could do to make it seem less arduous, then please let me know. But it's never going to be easy.'

Alex's mobile rang and he glanced at the number. Unknown. 'Sorry,' he said apologetically. 'Better take it just in case … Hello.'

'Well, hello and how's the new home?' asked his father, cheerily.

'Excellent. Getting things sorted slowly but surely. Having a quick cup of tea with Samantha.'

'And how's that going?'

'Slowly but surely,' Alex said smoothly. 'Did you want a word with her? She's standing right here.'

'No. But give me a run-down when she's not. I want to make sure it's enough protection. I'm considering having a bit of back-up, after a consultation with the Spanish police.'

'No, Dad. I can't. I know you want me to be safe, but there is a limit. One's enough.'

'How about in London? I could have someone you might not notice. Will you at least consider it? Apparently there's been some movement with the drugs cartel and it looks like they're planning something.'

'Like what?'

'Well, if they knew that, they'd tell me, wouldn't they?' was the acerbic riposte.

'If I see a man wearing a matador's outfit carrying a leg of ham and a small glass of sherry, I'll be on red alert, never you fear, Dad,' said Alex, rolling his eyes at Samantha, who was obviously listening with interest.

'That's the nice thing about people who think nothing of maiming and killing in pursuit of wealth. They always go around in fancy dress. Promise me you won't dismiss it out of hand. Discuss it with Samantha ... She knows I'm considering it and she's fine either way. Actually, of course she's fine either way. I pay her to be fine either way. Will you at least talk to her?'

'All right. Obviously. And I do know you're not doing it to piss me off. In fact, thanks. I'm being a twat. I'll talk to Samantha and let you know. Anything else?'

'When's your soup out in Waitrose?'

'Couple of weeks. They'll see how it goes, then maybe roll out my other ideas for quick organic lunch boxes and juices.'

'Sounds great. Start slowly and build up to an empire.'

'Before you know it I'll be launching a range of earthy perfumes. A sort of Alan Titchmarsh for Men – a subtle blend of Old Spice and celeriac.'

His father let out a bark of laughter, and added, 'Dusty Miller – a scent of flour mill with a hint of hat.'

'That's surprisingly funny for you, Dad,' said Alex, appreciatively.

'Try my best. Now, give that other issue some thought and let me know, will you?'

Alex ended the call.

'Well?' asked Samantha, her nose wrinkling attractively. 'Will you say yes to another tail?'

'What you may not know about my father is that he's an autocrat who'll do it anyway. He pretends to ask me, but the other "tail" is probably wagging its way to west London as we speak.'

She nodded, smiling, having guessed as much.

'Look, I'm hungry. That cup of tea has reminded me that I haven't eaten anything since last night. Shall I rustle up something for both of us?' he asked.

'Um. That would be great. Do you want any help?'

'Nope. I've been finding my way round a kitchen since I was a nipper. Mum was the worst cook ever. She'd put the food on the table and we'd all be sitting around guessing what it was – it was like that game Twenty Questions where you start off by asking whether it's animal, vegetable or mineral. In Mum's case, there was always a mineral compound – charcoal. Luckily, Dad made money and we then had a housekeeper who kept us stuffed to the gills with suet puddings.' He stopped. What was it about Samantha that made him feel like he was rambling when he was trying to be pleasant? He smiled tightly.

'I'm going to pop out into the garden and get some lettuce for a salad. And I noticed that there were some courgettes in the undergrowth of the vegetable patch and a few broad beans. I'll whip up a frittata.'

He went outside, grabbed some pots and utensils from the camper van and made busy in the kitchen.

'You'll make someone a wonderful husband,' Samantha commented, as he served up a delicious repast. 'I didn't know lettuce could taste this good, and the frittata is wonderfully fluffy.'

They lapsed into silence, and he eventually cleared the plates into the sink.

'Not the dishwasher?' she asked.

'It uses a lot of water, so that's for when I've got loads of people here. I'd better get back to the unpacking or I'm not going to be sorted before it gets dark.'

He wandered through to the sitting room and stood with his hands on his hips, debating the next step and thinking involuntarily about Miranda. They had agreed that the break should be clean, no communication, and since they didn't have mutual friends, he had no idea what she was up to.

He could see the next few years stretching out ahead of him, with only the disappointing Angelina Jolie lookalike by his side. 'Be careful what you wish for …' he said out loud, to the echoey room.

As the sun was throwing its long, languid rays across the Oxfordshire countryside, the heat on the eastern coast of Spain was still intense. Miranda was sitting on her hotel bed in deliciously cool air conditioning, surveying her clothes and wondering what would be comfortable at a bar in the evening, and whether there would be mosquitoes. If there were, she was going long-sleeved top and trousers.

Her phone buzzed and she clicked on to an incoming email. Jack. Bless him. What now? She read that he had been in a bus crash in a remote area of the Philippines. There were about four hundred people on a twenty-seater bus, he said, and they had overtaken on a blind bend. But he was okay apart from a few cuts and bruises. It could have happened anywhere:

In fact, me and Luke reckon that with so many of us on the bus, it saved us from a worse fate because we were surrounded by flesh. A sort of soft landing. And now we're having a wonderful time on a beach north of Manila. So don't worry, Mum. As usual, I have the luck of the devil – like you always said.

I'm going to hike up to some caves tomorrow, which are apparently magnificent. Just a little bus ride to get there! Well, they say you have to get straight back on the horse, don't they? Lots of love xxx

She did try not to worry, but it was impossible not to imagine all the terrors that were out there. And another bus ride after he had been in a crash. Her heart was racing as she re-read the email.

There was a complimentary bottle of red wine in the room, which she had planned to save until later, but she cracked it open and took a long swig. That's what's so brilliant about Jack, she reminded herself. He's adventurous but not stupid. The likelihood of being in two bus crashes in one country is minimal. So far he had narrowly missed a mudslide, an earthquake and an uprising. He had been struck by lightning and had had to go to hospital where they tried to keep him in overnight but he couldn't cope with the rats.

There was part of her that wanted him not to tell her about what had happened. She would write him a long email tomorrow.

Right now, she needed to start getting ready. The bathroom contained the most enormous shower head she had ever seen. She wasn't sure she liked showers where you had to get your hair wet every time unless you leant back in a ridiculous way to keep your head out of the water – and they didn't always seem that efficient in getting rid of the soap suds in difficult areas.

She gave up and washed her hair, lathering an enormous quantity of almond-smelling conditioner on it and getting it in her eyes as she put the bottle on the floor.

With the white hand towel wrapped in a turban round her clean, fragrant hair, she switched on the vanity light over the magnifying mirror near the bathroom sink. 'Hmm. Not as bad as I thought,' she said to herself, noting that she had caught a little colour out on the beach, even though she had been under the umbrella for most of the time. Apart from when that yellow-trunked turd made off with my possessions, she thought, although if he hadn't, I wouldn't now be dressing for dinner. She caught herself. Dressing for drinks with the hunky hero. Her eyes sparkled.

To blow dry, or not to blow dry, that is the question … whether 'tis nobler to go forth with straight hair or suffer the slings and arrows of curls, she pondered.

Suddenly she noticed the time on the bedside clock and the decision was made for her. She scrunched in some mousse and put the hairdryer to the roots before throwing on a floaty red top and white trousers and heading out.

* * *

Captain Wallis was at the bar, waiting for her. 'Good evening – you look wonderful,' he said, in a warm voice. 'I'm almost grateful to the would-be thief.'

She smiled. 'Why, thank you. But I am beyond grateful to you because, without your prompt action, I wouldn't be standing here. I'd probably still be in the police station, or emailing and phoning various banks and racking my brains to try to remember what else I had in my purse.'

'Hm. If I know women, you have at least one store card, a supermarket loyalty card, a book of stamps, a nail file and a sewing kit.'

'Definitely no loyalty card,' she said categorically.

'What would you like to drink, Miss Disloyal?' he asked, leaning forward and putting one foot on the metal pole that ran just above floor height. It pulled his trousers taut over his buttocks and Miranda involuntarily glanced down.

Very nice, she thought. Axe murderer, she reprimanded herself. Be careful. Even rapists and murderers have nice bottoms. Not all of them, necessarily, but there must be some who are blessed in the bottom department.

Jon looked round at her while trying to maintain eye contact with the barman. 'Do you have a drink in mind?'

'A glass of red wine, please. But I should be buying this for you. Let me get it—'

'I'm afraid that's impossible … *Una botella de Baron de Chirel rioja por favor, Xavier y dos vasos … gracias …*' he said to the barman, then added to Miranda, 'He wouldn't let you pay for it. He's a friend of mine and he knows that no lady pays when they're in my company.'

'I do want to thank you in a more concrete way, though,' said Miranda.

'Okay. How about you take me to dinner?'

Now that he had articulated what she was hoping for, she found it a bit 'fast', as her mother would have called it. Or maybe it was the implication that he brought various ladies to the bar. It was maybe … what was the word? … sleazy.

He noticed her hesitation, and guessed the reason. 'I have sisters who come to visit,' he lied, 'and I wouldn't dream of having any of them pay for a round. I can assure you that I'm not some wolf in, erm, sheep's clothing. Or even in wolf's clothing. And I totally understand if you would prefer to have dinner on your own without some random stranger waffling on. Really. I can point you to any number of restaurants where you can sit all alone. There'll only be a few people pointing at you and laughing while a waiter fawns over you, dripping his moustache sweat into your soup. There's El Pollo Ridiculoso a short step away – but beware Manuel and his moulting chest. And, of course, Los Dos Diablos, where for fifty quid you can have fish and chips and ogle the owner. Although I should warn you that they're not his own teeth. He'll be all over you like a dog on a trotter. Remember to take floss …'

'Stop – stop!' she cried. 'Enough. Do those places actually exist?'

'They most certainly do. Perhaps not the colourful members of staff. But, really, I'm nothing if not a gentleman. If it puts you at ease, I can give you references. My old sergeant major would give you a glowing one – and he could probably shout it from across the Med. I think he peaked at about the same decibels as Concorde.'

'No. It's all right. It does go against the grain, though, to have dinner with someone I've just met, and have no idea about. I spent years telling my children not to talk to strange men …' She tailed off, clearly somewhat embarrassed.

'And here is a strange man, and you're talking to him,' he finished, then gave her his biggest, widest, most innocent smile. 'Tell you what, why don't we stay here? It's close to your hotel, and you can slip off whenever you want to.'

She looked at him suspiciously. 'How do you know it's close to my hotel?'

'Ah. It's all in the clues,' he said smoothly. 'The spot on the beach is not far from here. You walked in tonight wearing high heels and not wincing. There was no taxi. Therefore you're staying not far away. It's an army thing, sorry.'

She gave a brief laugh. 'Hmm. Not a bad summation. And when you put it that way, it makes sense. So, yes, let's stay here. Do they do food?'

'They do bloody good tapas. What do you like to eat? Meat, fish, cheese, eggs?'

'All of the above. I'll let you order, since you know your way around the menu.'

The dishes arrived in small earthenware pots and each one was delicious. Jon kept her entertained with descriptions of the local characters and what happened during and after the tourist season. 'So what do you do actually do here?' she eventually asked, reaching forward to pick out another anchovy.

'One of those jobs that's hard to put into words. I kind of facilitate. Ease the passage of businessmen who want to trade here.'

'Company director is what you'd put down on an insurance form, I suppose?' She swallowed the fish and peered at what was left, opting for a slice of tortilla.

'Something like that. What do you do when you're not getting robbed on a beach?'

'I have two children so I used to be very busy. Then I divorced their father, and I live on what came to me in the settlement.'

'A lady who lunches then – or dines with old soldiers?' He raised his glass.

'To quote your earlier statement, something like that. I did recently get a job in PR and I have dabbled in voluntary work.'

'Is that a euphemism for a sponsored walk?' Jon grinned and poured out more wine.

'No. I helped clear out a canal. And very hard work it was too,' she admonished.

'But it must have been fun or you wouldn't have done it. I have to say, I didn't have you down as a tree-hugger. You look far too clean. Did you have to wear waders and yellow rubber dungarees?'

'I had to buy something called a wicking shirt and various other items of clothing I'd never heard of. I may do another when I get home.'

'You'll have the bargees of Britain raising their standard to you, if you're not careful. Miranda, queen of canals. I see a television series. A range of tea towels.'

'Towels – what they call owls up north,' she quipped.

He laughed. 'Did you make that up yourself?'

'No,' she acknowledged. 'I heard it on the radio and it stuck. Every time I hang my towel on a towel rail, I imagine a row of small owls clinging on by their fingertips.'

Jon drained his glass and glanced at his watch. 'Well, I've had a wonderful evening,' he said, 'an unexpected bonus on a night when I was planning to do paperwork. But I have an early start tomorrow. You're here for a week, you said. If you fancy meeting up again or you need any information, give me a ring.' He handed her a turquoise business card, which had a small logo of crossed swords on it.

'Thanks. And I'm staying at the Serena Hotel,' Miranda said, throwing caution to the wind.

'I shall walk you to the door, then.' Jon stood and waited for her to lead the way outside.

Like taking candy from a baby, he thought, as he gently slipped his hand through her elbow and steered her along the esplanade. It was so satisfying when a plan came together – and with such little effort. It helped that he found her bloody sexy.

CHAPTER TWELVE

The Mediterranean Sea is almost completely enclosed by land and touches three continents – Asia, Europe and Africa. It connects three-quarters of the globe. It's linked to the Atlantic by the Strait of Gibraltar and becomes saltier the further east you go. The fishermen hunting for swordfish, sardines, mullet and hake were well out to sea by the time Miranda stretched and wriggled herself to full consciousness in her king-size bed. She rubbed her eyes briskly to wake herself up before remembering that every magazine article said it was the most delicate skin on the face and shouldn't be rubbed if you wanted to avoid wrinkles. If only her mother had told her to relish the brisk eye-rubbing she had enjoyed as a child, she thought. Why were so many of life's pleasures tainted? Drinking cocktails till dawn: wrinkles and crêpey skin. Playing in the sun: wrinkles and cancer. Laughing and having fun: wrinkles and broken bones. Having children: wrinkles, frown lines, fallen arches, high blood pressure, broken relationships.

Right. She was *not* going to think about Alex today. What was done was done. It was postponed, not over. They had said that. Neither of them believed it, but that was what they had said.

She swung her legs over the side of the bed and stretched again. Was there anything but gorgeousness in stretching? It was one of the few things in life that was both unadulterated ecstasy and good for you. It was a shame that yoga combined two terrible traits, being both difficult and boring; otherwise it would be perfect. Maybe she should try Pilates – any exercise that involved lying down, then sliding up and down a moving bed had to be better than panting away, trying to get your ankles up round your ears. Who wanted to look like Madonna anyway? She was like a collection of hand-knitted steel ropes.

Miranda cleaned her teeth, examined her gums and turned on the shower. She had read somewhere that too much bathing stripped the natural oils from the skin and gave you wrinkles. Yet another enjoyable occupation blighted. Well, bugger that for a game of soldiers, she thought belligerently. She was going to go for the full loofah job and rummage up some more spare skin to hang round her elbows in future.

Half an hour later, fully covered with body lotion and sun screen, she was ready for an early breakfast before her first day of sailing.

Miranda felt a frisson of excitement and nervousness as she headed to the beach, hoping that her outfit of white shorts and lilac polo shirt would fit the bill.

She needn't have worried. Of the five others who were on the course, only one had made any effort – a girl with enviably lissom legs and long blonde hair called Becky.

The instructor was Brian, a leathery Englishman in his sixties with bright blue eyes, a crew-cut and stubble. She would bet he'd been a right *roué* in his youth.

They sat in the wooden hut to have the basics of sailing explained to them. It all sounded fairly straightforward. Feel where the wind is coming from and make it go into the sails. And if you're heading *into* the wind, tack and jibe, which meant zigzagging. Then there was the trimming of the sails – or essentially making them smaller or bigger. Actually, she wasn't quite sure how you could make the boat go forwards if the wind was coming from the front, but how difficult could it be? One of Nigel's friends, who was basically a moron, sailed a yacht, which she had been on numerous times. Weirdly, he had a very nice wife. Maybe they didn't have sex. Or talk to each other. And essentially led separate lives. Or had a mutual love of something esoteric like … tapestry. Although *he* looked more like the dogging type … Now, where were we again?

Brian had had long experience of teaching holidaymakers and patiently went over everything a number of times to check they all understood. He had a model of a dinghy and a sail on the desk, with a fan to demonstrate.

'What's the worst that can happen?' asked Miranda.

'You head out to sea and are never heard from again. Your half-eaten carcass washes to and fro in the minimal tides until it fractures and becomes sand,' Brian answered. There was a pause. 'Any other questions, or shall we go aboard?'

'Yeah,' piped up Becky. 'If we acksherly do start heading out to sea, and we can't turn round, do we just drop the sail and start swimming? Is that the default position, as it were?'

'I don't think there's any danger of you heading out to sea today. It's an onshore breeze so you're more likely to keep bumping into the beach. It's an excellent morning for practising tacking, which is the most difficult part of learning how to sail, since any fool can put up a sail if the wind is blowing directly behind it and making it go forwards. Shall we?' he asked, standing up and gesturing to the row of dinghies.

Miranda chose one next to a man who introduced himself as Bill, a builder from Basildon. 'All the Bs, eh?' she said jovially. 'I'm Miranda from Motting Hill. In London.'

He gave a pained smile and bent to the task of taking his dinghy on to the water, his burnt paunch protruding under his life vest like a nesting puffin.

Once on the water, Miranda swiftly discovered she had an aptitude for sailing, balancing the mainsail and the jib. Whether it was all knowledge gained by osmosis from trips on various craft, or simply natural inclination, she found that she instinctively knew what to do and was whipping over the waves with gay abandon while Bill and one of the other men were either going nowhere with sails hanging like limp bingo wings or heading for shore at speed with sails ballooning.

Brian zipped up and down with those who were furthest out to sea, and at one stage shouted over to Miranda, 'You didn't say you were a member of the British racing team!'

She yelled back, 'I'm thinking of nipping over to Algeria for coffee and a shish kebab, if you want to come!'

He smiled, and manoeuvred towards Becky, who had capsized and was struggling to get back on the boat.

It was a stunning day. The sky was rich blue with one stray cloud scampering across towards La Mancha as Brian called out to them to make their way ashore to stock up on liquids and reapply sun screen.

In the now stifling hut, they sipped ice-cold water and chatted.

'You're a natural,' Becky said to Miranda, passing her a biscuit.

'No, thanks.' She shook her head. 'I'm too excited to eat. That was brilliant. I don't know how it happened – I've never taken to anything like this before. I love it. How about you?'

'I could have done without turning the boat upside-down and having a panic attack stuck under one of the sails. Until that point, I was feeling quietly confident. At least I wasn't as bad as Bill and Mark,' she whispered.

'Bless them. They did seem to be struggling. Mind you, you should have seen me in the yoga class I was in a couple of days ago. My goodness, it seems like ages since I arrived here. A lot's happened in forty-eight hours. Anyway, I did this yoga class and people were quietly doing poses with strange names while I was huffing and puffing like a steam train with my arms and legs wobbling about like a frog on a hotplate.'

'Ha-ha. I went to Morocco last year with my boyfriend to learn how to ride. I just could not get the hang of it. I was scared of the horses with their big teeth and rolling eyes, and unless they were walking, I had no control at all. I was pinging up and down on the saddle and I swear the horse was laughing at me. And trying to get me off his back. We cantered one day and the frigging thing bolted with me. Up until then, you could hardly get him to a trot, even if you dug your heels through to his kidneys. Then off he goes, head down, tail up, sniggering fit to bust. Bastard.'

Miranda nodded sympathetically. 'Where's your boyfriend today?'

'Oh, we split up a couple of weeks ago. We couldn't get the money back, and since he was the one who did the dirty on me, I said I was taking the holiday,' she said.

'That's a bore.' Miranda glugged down the last of her water as Brian gave them each a pointer for the next session.

'And then we'll wrap up. We don't like to overdo it on day one. You'll all ache tomorrow, particularly your backs, and obviously your hands will be sore from the ropes. It'll ease up throughout the week, though. Some of you may be feeling a bit battered and bruised now.' He nodded at Bill, whose knees were already showing signs of having been bashed about on the sides of the dinghy. 'You may want to go and have a swim at the end of the session to stretch out the muscles, and when you're back in your hotels or villas, have a soak in a hot bath, or rub on something like Deep Heat or whatever. By the way, the award for the first head-butting of the boom goes to Mark. Well done.' He nodded to Mark and raised a thumb. 'And first capsize obviously to Becky. Nice one. We'll *all* be capsizing during the week because you need to learn how to get back on board. So I'll be making you capsize, to get the hang of the technique. But I don't expect you to be able to do it without practice. Before you go today, I'm going to be giving you a bit of reading material, which you can keep – it's included in the price of the course. You need to learn it if you're to get your RYA certificate at the end of the week. And, as I explained earlier, that's what you have to show to be able to hire a dinghy anywhere in the world. Okay. Let's get back on the high seas,' he finished, and they ambled out into the fresh air.

'I don't know whether I've got the oomph to get back after a capsize,' said Becky, as they walked to the dinghies. 'I was exhausted.'

'I know,' said Miranda. 'All well and good for him to say that you just stand on the centre board and hang on to the gunwale until it swings upright before jumping on. Oh, yes, and release the mainsail. But you can bet your bottom dollar I'll do a better impression of drowning.'

Brian made sure they had their life jackets on and sent them out again, with words of encouragement.

'The breeze has picked up, so you should find it easier.'

Miranda only realised her hands were hurting when she started pulling on the ropes, but the exhilaration of sailing kicked in and she forgot about everything as she gave in to the thrill of it.

A couple of times, Bill and Darren – a young lad from Essex – looked in imminent danger of colliding with her, but she managed to steer herself out of the way.

'I wonder if we use the expression about things being a breeze because of sailing,' she panted to Becky, as she dragged the dinghy on to the beach at the end of the session. 'I'm pooped, as my mum would say. It was nice and steady, though, wasn't it?'

'If you say so. My knees were hurting too much for me to notice.'

'Do you fancy a drink afterwards?' Miranda asked, as they padded up the soft sand to the hut.

'Yeah, I could kill for a cold glass of dry white wine,' Becky said, taking possession of her manual from Brian. She flicked through it. 'Friggin' 'ell. Navigation. Rules of the sea. Mooring. Tying knots. Buoys and what they mean. Tidal stuff. Man overboard. This is like A-level physics or something. If Shithead was here, I'd have to do this, or have him lording it over me at every opportunity. But since he's not …' She left the sentence hanging.

'Since he's not, we're both going to get A-stars. That's what we're going to do,' said Miranda, firmly.

''S all right for you, Brian's blue-eyed girl. You're like Captain Birds Eye on the water.'

'Look on the bright side! You're not as useless as Bill or Mark.'

'What do you think of Darren?' asked Becky, checking over her shoulder to make sure he wasn't behind them.

'Aha. Methought there was an exchange of flirtiness. Do we fancy him?'

Becky blushed.

'He seems very nice. Quiet. But, then, still waters can run deep,' said Miranda.

'Or he could be as boring as fuck,' Becky pronounced.

'Well, you've got time to find out, haven't you?'

They sauntered to the nearest bar and ordered a bottle of Rias Baixas on the recommendation of the waiter.

Miranda swilled it around and sniffed it, then sipped and announced it to be an excellent choice.

When the waiter had left, Becky leant forward. 'You know when you do that swirling stuff and smelling, what is it exactly that you're doing and how can you tell if it's good? Because Spudface did it all the time and sometimes the wine was shit.'

'You're mainly checking that it's not corked,' Miranda said. 'And you can certainly tell if it is.'

Becky raised her eyebrows and held up her hands to indicate she didn't understand.

'Corked is when there's a musty taste to it,' Miranda explained.

'Well, Shit for Brains used to say that musty was good.'

'Hmm. I suppose it is sometimes. Maybe I mean tangy. It's like a damp dog or mouldy newspapers. It's difficult to describe unless you've got one in front of you. In really good restaurants, you can ask the waiter to have a check, and they're usually pretty on the ball.

And you can send the wine back if it's corked. The strange thing is that if you carry on drinking it, somehow the tang goes away.'

Miranda's lecture was halted by the appearance of the previous night's dinner date.

'Well, hello, fair maiden.' Jon pretended to bow. 'I was hoping I'd bump into you.' He turned to Becky, who was watching with interest. 'Good afternoon …?'

'Becky,' she said, raising her hand to him a fraction.

'Becky,' he echoed. 'As I was saying, I hoped I'd see you today, Miranda. I have an invitation to a party on a yacht on Friday night. And when I say yacht, I mean an enormous yacht. More like a floating palace. It's a 340-footer with a helicopter on the top and a sixty-foot dining table. There's a charity auction for women in Africa dying of drought or pestilence or HIV or whatever. Apart from that, it should be very jolly. Do you fancy coming with me?'

'Well, I don't know … um …' Miranda was flustered. 'What time would it be on Friday? And I don't know if I've got anything to wear. Or …'

'Oh, go on. Sounds brilliant,' said Becky, her eyes shining.

'All right. Okay. Yes. Thank you. Thank you for inviting me. What time did you say?'

'I didn't. Things kick off at nineteen hundred hours, so if I pick you up from the hotel at, say, eighteen thirty?'

'That would be fine. And the dress code?'

'It's a black tie do. But if you don't have an evening dress stashed in your luggage, just wear something smartish.'

Miranda was feeling all of a dither, her mind racing ahead, thinking about the clothes and shoes she had packed. The lull in the conversation brought her back to the present. 'I'm sorry,' she said.

'Where are my manners? Would you like to join us for a glass of wine?'

'No, thanks. I'm on my way to a meeting. See you Friday, if not before,' he said, pointing a finger at Miranda. 'Nice meeting you, Becky,' he added, before disappearing back on to the street.

Becky waited a moment, then exclaimed, 'Phew. He's a bit of all-bloody-right.'

Miranda gave a cheeky smile. 'I know. I haven't done badly for an old bird, have I?'

'No, you have not. And you don't look like an old bird, neither.'

'You are too, too kind. But I'm old enough to be your mother.'

'Yes, but that doesn't matter, does it? And you look well fit. Plus, you don't *seem* like anybody's mother, and that's also it, isn't it? So tell, tell.'

'Tell what?'

'How you met him. Who he is. What he does for a living. Where he lives.'

'I'm not sure I know where he lives. Presumably somewhere near here, since we met after he chased a bloke who stole my things from a sun-bed while I was having a quick swim.'

'Oooooh. What a hero,' breathed Becky.

'Yes. He was. And he caught the thief and brought back my stuff and then we went for a drink so that I could say thank you.'

'And did you kiss?'

'No, we did not,' Miranda said primly. 'I don't do that sort of thing with a man I barely know.'

'Oh, I would,' pronounced Becky, nodding frantically. 'There's nothing like a snog to round off an evening out.'

'Yes, well, I was married for a hundred years, and I haven't really gone out with anyone since I divorced a couple of years ago. Eighteen months ago,' she corrected.

'Eighteen months without a shag? That's exceptional,' exclaimed Becky.

'Is it? Well, actually, it's not entirely accurate. There was a brief relationship before I came here. In fact, that's why I'm here. To get over it. But before then, I was having a perfectly okay time. It was quite pleasant and unburdensome, if that's a word, doing what I wanted to do. Not worrying about whether I'd shaved my legs because nobody was going to tell me that I looked like a lesbian. Some days, I didn't bother to get dressed – just lolled about in my nightwear.'

'Who's the bloke you had your fling with, then?'

Miranda ordered another bottle of wine and told Becky the sorry tale of Alex, the bodyguard and her daughter. She ended, 'And that's why I came on this holiday on my own. Originally, as I said, I planned on having a yoga holiday. Now it's a sailing course, as you know.'

'Well, it's a bleedin' shame, I say,' said Becky, downing her glass and standing up. 'Oooh. I feel a bit squiffy. I'm going to the toilet. The *baños*, I think they say here. Or is it *toilettas*? *Excusi, señor*, where is the *baños*?' she asked the waiter.

'The toilet is down the stairs and first on the left,' he answered, in impeccable English, and watched her make her way unsteadily to the loo. If he had not been expected at a family dinner that night, he would have had a pop at her. English girls were renowned for being an easy lay, particularly after a couple of bottles of *vino*.

The sun had sunk beneath the horizon and the first stars were beginning to appear as they left the bar. 'Are you going to be all right getting back?' Miranda asked. And then, because she would have been worried if it had been *her* daughter, she took Becky's arm companionably and walked her back to her hotel before hailing a cab to her own.

She yawned her way through a shower and flossed her teeth before falling into a deep and dreamless sleep at about the same time as she used to put the children to bed when they were at primary school.

CHAPTER THIRTEEN

The days unfurled in glorious azure and yellow, with Becky and Miranda beetling over the waves in ever-increasing confidence. Brian had been impressed with their dedication – they were the only two who had swotted up on the manual and could answer the questions he posed without thinking too hard.

'What are you going to do with your new-found knowledge back in Blighty?' he asked Miranda.

'Hmm. I was wondering that myself,' she said thoughtfully, 'since originally I was on a yoga course! But I've really enjoyed myself – *am* enjoying myself. And I'm considering maybe doing something like crewing on a yacht. Learning and earning. And impressing my children – because impressed they would be. My daughter was stunned when she discovered I'd cleared a canal with a bunch of green people.' She stopped. 'Green as in ecological, environmental-type people. And as for coming on a yoga holiday, which I was doing originally, she thought I was one stop down the line from Barking. At least sailing is something I've done before – albeit hanging about in a bikini on deck and wondering where my next rum punch is coming from. My son, on the other hand, wouldn't bat an eyelid if I took up nude sky diving. He's the type who thinks you're mad if you haven't tried as many of life's options as you can,

and that the worst thing in the world is to be described as "safe".
Hey. I've just thought. *That*'s what I'm going to do. Sail round the
world single-handed!' she declared.

'You are *not*!' gasped Becky, her eyes alight. 'That is *well* cool.'

'Yeah. Okay. Perhaps not. But it's an exciting thought,' Miranda
said perkily. 'Let's look at the scenario, though. Would I manage on
my own for weeks on end while sharks circled and a twenty-foot
wave hovered off the starboard bow? What would I do if my mast
sheered off and I was left with essentially a surfboard? Could I live
without the possibility of an ice-cold gin and tonic at the end of the
day and a nice hot shower? All of a sudden, it's sounding like hell.
On the plus side, I do love the idea of telling my children … and I
may still do that.'

'Keep them on their toes, eh?' Brian raised his eyebrows.

'It would be nice not to be thought of as boring old Mum.'

'I think you're what they call a yummy mummy, aren't you?'
asked Becky.

'Thanks, Becky. I knew I liked you. Should we be back out?' she
asked Brian.

'You're an eager beaver today,' he commented, noting the air of
anticipation.

'I know. It must be the party I'm going to tonight, making me
over-excited. It's some sod-off big yacht and there's going to be an
auction and loads of glam people and, er …' She tailed off.

'And a glamorous man? Or are you going with Becky?'

She laughed. 'Yes. And a glamorous man – I've only met him a
couple of times but he seems very nice. Muscles in his earlobes. I
reckon he could do one-armed press-ups and rip a ship from its
moorings while mixing a martini.'

'Do you think you're going to be able to stay awake past eight, then?' He'd heard about her early nights.

'I'll knock back a double espresso before I go out. Maybe have a run round the block.'

She noticed his expression. 'Yes. Definitely a double espresso,' she said.

He grinned. 'We need to get back on the water. Don't forget to do up your life jackets.' He pointed at Miranda's, which was hanging loose.

'What are you going to wear tonight, then?' asked Becky, as they walked down the beach.

'I bought a cracking red halter-neck dress with diamanté round the neckline at a boutique yesterday after we finished. It's a bit short, but it looks great with the red high heels I brought with me from England. And I'll wear a stout pair of pants so that I don't feel exposed.'

'I hate the word "stout",' said Becky, 'And 'specially when it's to do with knickers. Frilly. Sexy. Satin. Twinkly. That's what you want with knickers. Just in case you get lucky.'

'You are incorrigible,' Miranda grunted, pulling the boat out.

'Hair up or down?' Becky bent to pick up her dinghy rope.

'Down, I was thinking.'

'Lovely. But it'll be all over the shop in the wind, won't it? Gluing itself to your lipstick. Getting in the way if you have a … snog,' she said, with a glint.

'Get thy boat out to sea, young doxy,' said Miranda, peremptorily, stepping into her own. And while she learnt how to retrieve the boat from a capsize, she debated the question of her hair, eventually concluding that merely for elegance – and nothing to do with the possibility of kissing the devilishly attractive captain – she would put it up.

At the end of the day's sailing, they all retired to a café for revivifying beer and coffee.

'I wish I was coming tonight,' Becky said. 'You're going to have such a cool night. And I'm going to be sitting on my ownsome, like some saddo, playing Angry Birds on my iPhone and doing Facebook.'

'Nonsense,' said Miranda, crisply. 'You've been out every single night you've been here. And no doubt you'll succumb again and be found wandering about half-cut with some Spaniard trying to seduce you.'

'Oh, yeah. Now I remember. I've arranged to meet up with a few girls. But it won't be as much fun as your evening. It sounds epic.'

Miranda laughed. 'I must admit, it does sound pretty bloody great, doesn't it? I get a bit of a tingle when I think of it.'

'Like being sixteen all over again.'

'God, what an appalling thought. I don't think I could do sixteen again if you paid me. If it wasn't for the lines on my face, I'd rather like to stay the age I am now.'

'You're hardly a prune,' said Becky. 'Talking of which, do you fancy some olives?'

'Let's have those ones that come with manchego cheese.' She raised her voice to include the others. 'Anyone else up for a snack?' Then she noticed the time. 'Oops. Actually, I'd better go. I have things to do before the evening's festivities. See you tomorrow for a debrief.'

'Is that 'cos you won't have any briefs on, then?' Bill asked.

Miranda sighed and rolled her eyes. 'You can always be trusted to lower the tone, eh? In the worst-case scenario, I may have a sore head. From alcohol,' she added, to scotch any riposte. She waved a gay goodbye as she left to go back to the hotel.

It was her favourite time of the day, when it was still warm but not punishing. There was a balmy breeze and the waves lapped softly at the beach. Miranda was suddenly reminded very vividly of a holiday romance she'd had in Greece. She had been exactly that age she'd sworn she never wanted to revisit – sixteen. He was an eighteen-year-old from Cardiff, about to go to university. He smoked roll-up cigarettes and had an irresistible swagger. Bad boys. What was it about bad boys? She had obsessed about him for months. It would be interesting to see where he was now. See if he had made something of himself. Engineering. Or was it bridges? She couldn't recall what he was going to study but felt sure it had been something her parents didn't approve of, with the whiff of an oily rag. I bet he was a darned sight more interesting, no matter what he ended up doing, than Nigel, she thought finally, putting an end to the reminiscence.

'*Buenas tardes.*' She smiled at the hotel receptionist as she went past, her flip-flops slapping noisily on the tiled floor.

Her phone burst into life, barking like a dog. She scrabbled about in her bag, the noise diminishing and ascending as it moved around. With moments to spare until it rang off, she snatched it up and pressed the green answer button.

'Amanda,' she said breathlessly.

'Have I caught you at a bad time? Are you, as we say in polite circles, on the job?'

'Of course I am. Hold on a second, while I move this expanse of hairy flesh to one side … frigging Norah, that sounds disgusting. Let me start again. Of course I'm on the job – excuse me while I put this man down. Nope, that sounds like I'm having him exterminated. Here we go … once more.' She drew breath and said, 'No, I am not on the job. I am walking up to my hotel room.'

'Good. Glad we got that sorted. How's it going? Are you now as bendy as a pipe cleaner, and cleansed in mind and body?'

'No, I'm not. That's because I changed after one lesson, and am now doing a sailing course – and I *love it*,' she fairly shouted down the phone.

'Well, it's a bleeding good job that I didn't get a flight to come and join you, then, isn't it?' said Amanda. 'I can't stand the sea – it makes me bilious. It's full of fish pooing, great big jellyfish out to sting you, sharks waiting to take your leg off. Salty water. Give me a swimming-pool, a lilo and a G and T any day.'

'As you say, good job you didn't come and join me. I'd still be up on the hill realigning my *chakra*s and trying to do a half-paralysed dog with a hat stand.'

'That, I'll have you know, is my absolute favourite yoga position,' Amanda declared.

'Of course it is. Of course it is,' Miranda said, opening the door to her room.

'Are we repeating because I might be hard of hearing now? I repeat. Are we repeating—'

'Did you phone for anything in particular?' Miranda butted in. 'Only I need to get ready for a humdinger of a party, which I'm going to with a rather handsome chap called Jon Wallis, ex-captain in the British Army.'

'Is that hyphenated or double-barrelled?'

'Indubitably.'

There was a pause. 'I don't really understand that answer.'

'Well, I'm not totally sure I understood the question.'

'Is he one of those posh army types?'

'No. But he *is* a James Bond type. Looks like a cross between Daniel Craig, Brad Pitt and George Clooney. He's got that dirty-blond hair and the most incredible blue eyes. And a most excellent pair of—'

'Testicles,' Amanda interrupted.

'Buttocks,' corrected Miranda. 'Like I'd have seen his bloody testicles.'

'You could sort of see Daniel Craig's in those tiny blue Speedos.'

'No, you couldn't.'

That was odd. She was sure she'd put her watch in the safe. How weird.

'Where's this party, then?' Amanda asked.

'On a whopper of a yacht. There's an auction and dancing. That TV presenter Katie Fisher's hosting it.'

'The one who got sacked from breakfast television for being too old?'

'Yes. Now, you can be the final arbiter. Hair up or down?'

'Down. Nobody looks young with her hair up. Very ageing.'

'What about the wind?'

'Take charcoal tablets.'

Miranda laughed and flicked on the television screen, pressing the buttons for Sky News.

'I meant the windy nature of being on a boat. Hair all over the shop.'

'But that's sexy. You could always take a scrunchie for an emergency tie-back.'

'Shush a minute … Are you watching the news?'

'No. Why? What's happened?'

Miranda watched the television. 'That is incredible.'

'What is?' asked Amanda.

'They reckon they're going to gestate a mammoth inside an elephant.'

'Why?'

'I dunno. Cos they can, I suppose.'

'It'll be like that film, *Jurassic Park*. Velociraptors left, right and centre. Feeding the dinosaurs one moment, being scoffed by them the next. Ridiculous.'

'Unless we eat them. Mammoth animals would deliver mammoth chops,' said Miranda, going through to the bathroom and turning on the shower. 'I can just see Nigella marinating a mammoth steak.' She put on a deep, sexy voice: 'Pour on seven gallons of extra virgin olive oil. Chop up thousands of juicy red tomatoes. Marinate for a week. Roast in a large pan for a week. Serve with chips.'

'How old is he?' Amanda asked.

'What – the mammoth? About ten thousand years old.'

'Your ex-army captain, you cretin,' laughed Amanda.

'Late thirties, early forties.'

'Excellent. Well, it's a shame I'm not there to hang on to your coat tails and cramp your style. I'll be at the boring ballet watching boring ballerinas prance about on pointy shoes and being all drapy. I demand that you phone me tomorrow and tell me all about it. And I'm glad you're having a good time and not crying into your paella.'

'Seriously? I would prefer to be going out with Alex. As you know. But with things as they are … And in the meantime …'

'And in the meantime, you're having a good time,' finished Amanda.

'Exactly. I'll phone you tomorrow,' Miranda said, and ended the call, slipping off her sweaty top and shorts and gratefully stepping into the shower.

As she let the water cascade over her head, she contemplated the evening. A small part of her antenna was suspicious of a man who lived and worked in Spain, inviting a woman he hardly knew to a high-profile party. Surely, the antenna reasoned, he would have any number of girlfriends to choose from. Young, stunning girlfriends, not ancient old biddies like her. She mentally shook herself. Not old. Not middle-aged. 'I … am … bloody … gorgeous,' she said loudly to the shower head, massaging a goose-egg-sized portion of conditioner into her hair and grabbing the loofah.

By six fifteen she was as ready as she was going to be. She sent a quick text to Lucy and an email to Jack before putting a comb, a tissue, lip gloss and some mints into her evening bag. With a final critical look in the mirror and a slight adjustment to her hair, which she had pushed back with a diamanté clip, she made her way to the reception area.

Jon Wallis felt a stirring in his loins as he caught sight of her through the doorway. She was handing in her key and smiling at the receptionist. She reminded him of a voluptuous Farrah Fawcett. He couldn't decide whether it was a help or a hindrance that he found her seriously attractive.

'All's fair in love and war,' he muttered to himself as he strode in, coming to an abrupt halt and clicking his heels together before bowing.

Miranda fought an overwhelming urge to curtsy – not succumbing because she was aware that her short dress might reveal more than she intended. Instead she beamed at him and held out her hand. He looked at it quizzically. 'You may kiss it,' she said imperiously.

So he did, with a flourish and a naughty smile. 'Madame,' he said, 'your carriage awaits.' He gestured to the black Mercedes outside, with a driver visible through the passenger window.

'Thank you,' she said, her heart missing a beat as he put his hand to the small of her back and ushered her out.

It was a clear evening, and she looked up at the stars before bending her head to step into the car. 'It's funny, but no matter how much I try to remember the names of the constellations, I can only recognise the big Plough, the little Plough and Orion's Belt,' she said, as he slid in to join her on the back seat.

'Orion. The hunter,' he said. 'They say that one of the stars in the constellation – Betelgeuse – is so large and old that it may explode and disappear within a few thousand years, which means that if you can hang on till then, you'll see the fireworks.'

'My eyelids would be down to my ankles. I'd have to use bulldog clips to hold them back.'

'An agreeable image,' he said, in his pleasant baritone. 'Back to the heavenly spheres … The Plough, or Dipper, is a very useful guide to night-time navigation. You can find Polaris, or the North Star, by imagining a line from the bottom of the big Plough's cup or ladle, as it were, to the top of the cup and extending it. And that's due north. Only in the northern hemisphere, though.'

'Coo,' said Miranda, peering out of the window and straining to see the sky. 'I love that stuff, imagining the sailors of yesteryear setting their course by the moon and the stars. And not just at sea. When you see a moon as bright as this one tonight, you can imagine them being really happy that they were going to a ball or travelling to see friends. You can see the road like a silver ribbon when the moon is on full beam.'

'And where does your fancy take you when it's a cloudy night?' he asked, amused.

'Ah. Then it's a highwayman's moon. The road clear and then obscured,' she said huskily, dramatically. 'A cloaked figure sits on a panting horse and hears a coach rumbling along the packed earth. He keeps to the shadows before putting his spurs to the trembling flesh …'

'And, with a cry of "Hi-ho, Sylvia," he relieves them of their fripperies,' Jon finished, with a flourish.

'Hmm,' she said. 'I was thinking more in the line of thrusting a pistol into the carriage and threatening the occupants with their money or their lives.'

'You have a very romantic nature,' he stated.

'I'm the victim of a childhood spent reading romantic fiction. Although I reckon there are loads of us – that's why films like *Zorro* are so successful. A dark and handsome stranger, his face partially hidden. A beautiful girl falls in love with him, not knowing he's an outlaw. He saves her from being married off to a cruel and unyielding man …'

'And then they have children, get divorced and bicker over the house,' he said, before leaning forward to the driver and speaking in fast Spanish.

'I wish I spoke another language,' she said wistfully.

'I thought you did,' he said. 'I'm sure I heard you speaking to the waiter when I saw you with the blonde girl you've been doing your skipper training with.'

Her eyebrows came together. 'How did you know I was doing a sailing course?' she asked.

'I'm a spy,' he announced. Then he looked at her and smiled. 'Elementary, my dear Watson. You were both wearing T-shirts and shorts, and when you scratched your upper arm, you revealed a suntan line. No woman goes to a sunny place and has what they call a trucker's tan unless they have to. Second, my lady, there was on the table not one but two manuals with the RYA logo on it, which stands for the Royal Yachting Association. Plus, your hands looked roughed up and you had bruises on your knees. And that's the case for the prosecution.'

'Wow. You're good,' she proclaimed, sitting back in the seat and peering out of the window to avoid coming over all unnecessary looking at him. It was bloody sexy, she thought, when a man noticed so much about you. I'm a mother of two and should know better, she remonstrated to herself. If this was Lucy, I'd be advising her to be careful and to limit her alcohol intake. And possibly to make sure she'd brought a condom.

'What?' he asked, as she took a sharp breath.

'Nothing,' she said, hurrying on to cover her confusion. 'How much further is it?'

'About ten minutes. Just a few miles further down the coast. Are you bored with my company already?'

She heard the smile in his voice. 'Of course not. Tell me more about yourself.'

And he told her his story – only it was a story his family would not have recognised … but, then, they wouldn't have recognised his name either.

CHAPTER FOURTEEN

The yacht *La Maritana* was twinkling like the Orion constellation itself, white lights draped along its length as it bobbed and swayed in the inky sea. The night air carried the sound of guests chatting and laughing, with the clink of glasses cutting through the hum.

A large gaggle of people milled on the quayside, waiting to get past the twisted red silk rope and on to the gangplank. Very slim women in short satin slips jostled with ample-bosomed matrons in well-upholstered dresses. Men smelling of aftershave, with slicked-back hair, ushered their lady friends forwards as others pressed large-denomination notes into palms.

There was a buzz about the evening, which was infectious.

'How many people are they going to be able to fit on this boat before it sinks?' whispered Miranda, as they edged towards it.

'I seem to remember seeing the guest list running on for a fair few pages. And then there'll be the determined gatecrashers.'

'How on earth could anyone get past those men? They're like ship containers with feet.'

'You'd be surprised,' he said wryly. 'Never underestimate the power of money.'

'But if you've got loads of money, why would you care about being invited? Have your own party instead.'

'Ah. But you wouldn't necessarily have the great and the good turning up. There'll be celebrities, rich entrepreneurs, European royalty … You were talking about highwaymen – if I was a modern-day pirate, I'd corral this boat. It's going to be wall-to-wall diamonds and bling.'

'Could you do it?' she wondered.

He cocked his head to one side. 'I'd probably have to ask my friends in the Special Boat Service for some pointers. But I wouldn't think it was that difficult. Most important thing would be to remove it from the dock. Isolate it. Then you'd need a getaway boat.'

'That's quite exciting. That you could do it. How many high-seas men would it take?' she enquired jauntily.

'Is that the ocean-going version of highwaymen?' he teased. 'Well, since you ask, I'd reckon on five at most. You don't want too big an operation because the more people who are involved the more likely it is to get leaked.'

'And that's the last thing you'd want on a boat – a leak.' She nodded sagely.

'Are you thinking of going into piracy?' he asked, gesturing to one of the bouncers as they moved forwards.

'Well, I must say, it does sound tempting. Leaping aboard with a cutlass between the teeth and a shout of "Your money or your life!" Although I don't think I could go through with that part. Killing them to get their dosh does seem to be a step too far. I'd never sleep at night.'

'There are those who can and those who can't,' he said, as he manoeuvred her deftly through the crush and up the gangplank.

'That was impressive, Captain Wallis.' She laughed over her shoulder.

He felt a small pang in the region of his heart as her blue eyes twinkled into his. She was a pocket rocket in her sexy little red dress. He wanted to pick her up, throw her over his shoulder and march off with her to ravish her on the beach. And yet he also had an urge to protect her – an urge he was quashing furiously. It was not the plan, not the plan at all.

Miranda was finding him just as electric. There was something about a soldier. It was how she had felt about boys on motorbikes when she was growing up – they flirted with death, they were dangerous, intoxicating.

It was amazing that, in the space of a few months, she could go from having no prospective men in her life, to two very contrasting characters. One with corded forearms and biceps bigger than a watermelon (she assumed), able to snap a man's neck like a pencil. The other – she thought of Alex – with surprising strength in his lithe body. She had a vision of him wielding a chainsaw as they tidied round the canal.

She snorted.

'What?' asked Jon, putting his hand in the middle of her back to help her up the final feet of red carpet and on to the boat.

'Sorry. An expression I was thinking of which sounded like a euphemism for a, erm, a …'

'It's okay. Whatever it is, I've almost certainly heard it. Press on,' he encouraged.

'For a bikini wax. "A tidy round the canal"?'

He grinned. 'Yes, it most assuredly does. What on earth made you think of that?'

'Something to do with water, probably – you know how your brain rambles off …'

'I know how some *women's* brains ramble off,' he said.

'Rogue.' She tapped him playfully. Really, she thought, I'm behaving like a coquettish twenty-year-old. Grow up. Mutton. Lamb. She took a glass of champagne and gazed about the yacht, taking in the expensive décor. 'Jiminy Cricket!' she exclaimed.

'Thought you might approve,' Jon said, guiding her towards the back of the boat.

'How do you get enough money to buy something like this?' she asked.

'Money-laundering. People-smuggling. Gambling. Piracy,' he said promptly.

'No. *Really.*'

'Finance mostly. Which some people would describe as daylight robbery. If you want to have a mosey round, I'd do it now before the place gets too crowded.'

'I most certainly do. I wish I'd brought my phone so I could take pictures. I didn't even think about it,' she said regretfully.

So that was one thing he didn't have to worry about, he thought. With a command to him not to move an inch, she walked away, her hips swaying provocatively.

He leant forward on the ship's rail, sipping his drink, and saw the small dinghy flash its light three times. Good. He adjusted his position slightly so that he could observe the arrivals.

A while later, he gave a barely perceptible nod to a slim, dark-haired man in a well-cut dinner jacket who was sauntering up the gangplank. He pulled back one crisp white cuff and checked his watch. As in any operation, his brain had switched gear and was now fully synchronised with his team. One more piece had to slot in, and they were set.

'Did you miss me?' Miranda asked, coming up behind him.

'Every minute felt like an hour,' he joked.

'I've decided I need to get into finance,' she said chattily. 'This is incredible. And you're right, it's awash with bloody great diamonds and small men with big watches that are so blinged up you can't tell the time. Strange that while the rest of the expensive stuff gets smaller and smaller – like tiny mobile phones and computers the size of clutch bags – watches are enormous.'

'Since you've done a recce, where would you suggest we stand for optimum viewing of the evening's delights?' He straightened as he spoke.

'Near the bar,' she said promptly.

'Lead on, then,' he said, putting his empty glass on a waiter's silver tray, and following her inside, where small halogen lights gleamed from the wooden ceiling while picture lamps illuminated sea scenes.

A plush carpet covered the floor, and was so thick that Miranda found she was walking like a dressage horse. If she owned the yacht, she would make sure it looked more seaworthy. Somehow, carpet didn't seem right when you thought of waves crashing over the deck. It was more a show home than a yacht capable of crossing thousands of miles of deep and turbulent ocean.

They found a space and Miranda leant against the corner of the highly polished wood and brass bar.

'What can I get you?' Jon asked, attracting the attention of a passing waiter.

'Another glass of champagne, I think. It would be rude not to,' she said, her attention wandering to a woman in a silver dress and staggeringly high heels. She was sure she had seen her before. Her brow cleared as she suddenly put the name to the face.

'Hey, Lola,' she called, surprised.

Aha, thought Jon. The final piece of the jigsaw.

Lola sashayed over to them. 'Well, hello … Miranda, isn't it? I wondered where you'd got to. One yoga lesson and then we never saw you again. We thought you must have gone home.'

'No. It wasn't my thing, I'm afraid. I arrived with high hopes, but I was hope*less*. Even sitting cross-legged at the beginning gave me pins and needles. I suppose that means I'm absolutely the sort of person in need of yoga but, really, I have to have something to work towards. It's too depressing to be the worst one by far. It's like being the dunce at school.'

'Except if you're at the bottom the only way is up,' said Lola.

'Hmm. Sometimes you just carry on bumping along the bottom. This is Jon Wallis, by the way.' She indicated the man lounging nonchalantly at her side.

'Hello, Jon. I'm Lola.' She stretched out an elegant hand and smiled.

He raised one eyebrow and bowed infinitesimally.

'Have you met before?' asked Miranda, catching the look between them.

'I would most certainly never forget the face,' Jon answered, then asked, 'Are you two friends from England or friends from here?'

'I met Lola on the bus going up to the yoga hotel,' Miranda explained, 'and, as we know, I was shit and she was a million times better than me.' She looked enviously at the other woman's perfect figure, outlined in the clinging dress.

Lola smiled apologetically. 'I don't think I told you that I've done yoga for years. Not regularly, but I'm lucky enough to be flexible in the right places. And, as you say, it's easier to improve if you feel you have an aptitude for something. So, where have you been since you scarpered?' she asked, with a knowing look and a flick of an eye to Jon.

Miranda blushed slightly and tried to pretend it wasn't happening. It'll go away in a minute if I ignore it, she thought, going redder and redder. 'I've been doing a sailing course down on the beach near the hotel – a sister hotel to the one you've been staying in. Or should I say that *we* were staying in? Until I left, of course,' she gabbled, hoping vainly that Lola and Jon would not notice the tell-tale stain spreading to her neck. 'It finishes tomorrow, and I've had the most fantastic time, because I've discovered I do have an aptitude for sailing and, funnily enough, I told them I was going to sail round the world single-handed after this, which would surprise everyone at home because they're more used to hearing me talk about shoes and children and clothes and, erm, you know, obviously really important world events,' she ended lamely, having run out of words and not succeeded in reducing the pinkness.

'Phew.' Lola nodded, her mouth turned down in fake grudging approval. 'Well, that beats my achievement into a cocked hat.'

'What was that?' asked Jon, with interest.

'I can now do a crow into a handstand – if that means anything to you?'

'Can you really?' breathed Miranda, impressed. She wasn't totally sure what a crow was, but turning anything into a handstand sounded pretty darned cool.

'Well, I only did it once, but it'll keep me going for years, I can tell you,' said Lola.

The music suddenly turned up a notch. A small group of dancers threaded their way through the guests to an area that had been roped off and the event kicked off properly.

A spotlight illuminated a woman with auburn hair and flawless skin wearing a glorious green Hollywood glamour dress.

'Bloody hell, that *is* a stunner,' Jon uttered, in a gravelly voice.

Katie Fisher would have been gratified by the comment, had she heard it. She had spent most of the day being primped. She had never been more uncomfortable in her life – and that included the time she had slept on a pile of stilettos at a friend's house after a night of evil cocktails. Every time she drew breath, there was some kind of metal thing puncturing a hole in her ribcage. But she had needed the job and had shown the organisers a photo of her in the outfit that had been taken on a shoot for *FHM*. It had clinched the deal. She had not shown them the other photographs where she was half naked and looked like a hooker.

'Good evening, and welcome to the beautiful yacht *La Maritana*, moored off Alicante and the venue for a hugely important auction, which is going to be helping women and girls in Africa. For those of you who don't know, the money is essentially being given for education and health and there is a lot more detail in the brochures. If you don't have one, there are girls in gold and silver circulating who are desperate to give you one,' Katie said, with a smile at the double-entendre as a few titters could be heard.

She had been impressed by the auction items, one of which was a fortnight's holiday on this very yacht, with the crew included. God knows how much that was worth. And there was a raffle with such cracking prizes she was tempted to have a go herself, although she couldn't remember the last time she had ever won anything. A bottle of ginger wine on the tombola when she opened a garden fête in Dorset – *and* she had had to give it back. The organiser had made it clear that she'd been more than adequately recompensed by having her picture in the local newspaper eating a cheese straw. Among the top prizes tonight was a pink diamond the size of a marble. No wonder the tickets were five hundred euros each. She had seen one man buy ten tickets without flinching, and handing over a wad of crisp notes that looked newly minted. Maybe they *were* newly minted. She was sure there some rum customers here who were no stranger to the wrong side of the law.

Katie noticed a restlessness among the partygoers and pressed on with her spiel. That was the worst thing about dos like this one: her speech had been written by committee and was what she would describe as 'muddy'. She had done her best to perk it up, but they had insisted on thanking Uncle Tom Cobbley and all before she got to the auction.

'Right,' she said. 'The moment you've all been waiting for. The auction. If I could have the lights as bright as possible, so I can see the whites of your eyes, I'll start with lot number ten, a walk-on role in the next Bond film. It doesn't say here whether that includes walking near 007 himself, or getting your hands on any of the equipment …' There was a snigger from some of the women

– 'Settle, girls.' Katie smiled. '… but you'll be as close as most of us are going to get to the most famous spy in the world. Who'll bid a thousand euros?'

'Are you going to bid for anything?' Miranda murmured to Jon, the heat from his body making her feel light-headed. Or was it the champagne?

'I don't know. Is there anything you fancy?' he murmured back, his warm breath in her ear sending shivers down her back.

Her stomach did a flip. That was very suggestive. 'I haven't studied the list,' she said breathlessly, and admonished herself for getting overexcited. He'd probably meant nothing.

He turned round to the bar and picked up a shiny laminated programme, which he handed to her before returning to studying Katie Fisher. She was his kind of woman. Confident, sexy, with a slightly husky speaking voice. There was something vulnerable about her too. And she had a body you just wanted to roam over.

'You can have a pair of shoes made for you by Manolo Blahnik,' Miranda whispered to him, having looked through the brochure. 'I didn't know he was Spanish. Apparently you go to his place in London and he designs something specially.'

He didn't answer, instead raising his arm to bid for a day at a racetrack with a Formula One driver. He was rewarded with a warm smile from Katie Fisher. 'Five thousand euros from the handsome gentleman by the bar,' she said, before asking for more bids.

Miranda couldn't help but swell with pride. The handsome gentleman … who was standing next to *her*.

In the end, the lot went to a small fat man wearing a suit stretched to fit, making him look like a killer whale.

And then it was the raffle. The winner of the diamond was a woman so thin she could have been used as a pipette. As she walked forward to collect the prize, Miranda thought she had rarely seen anyone uglier. Her crotch appeared to be the biggest part of her, the only bit with flesh on it, outlined in a clinging pair of oyster-coloured trousers.

'And to those who have, more shall be given.' Jon spoke into her ear, sending golden flecks of ecstasy along her veins again.

'Who is she?' she whispered back.

'Christina de Dolares. Married to one of the richest men in the country, and not short of diamonds.'

'It should have been me,' Miranda wailed, *sotto voce*.

'Did you buy a ticket?' he asked.

'No. I suppose that'll be one of the reasons it wasn't me.'

'You have to be in it to win it, don't they say?'

'Yes, I think they do,' she said.

Katie Fisher made a shushing sound into the microphone. 'Just before I let you get on with the party, can I say a huge thank-you to all of you for coming along. I've done a rudimentary adding up and – bearing in mind my maths is so bad that I still reckon I'm thirty-seven – I think you've raised in excess of one million euros tonight. Which is not bad. You might be a small crowd, but you've got big hearts and you will have changed lives. Thank you, and goodnight. Enjoy the rest of your evening.'

When the applause had died down, a band struck up. 'Shall we?' Jon asked, gesturing to the dance floor.

'Don't mind if I do,' Miranda responded, feeling a little giddy. She tripped along gaily and almost fell into his arms.

'Are you all right?' he asked solicitously.

'Umm … Think so. I feel a bit woozy. I shouldn't have had that last champagne. Maybe I need a sit-down or a breath of fresh air.'

'I know somewhere you'll be able to have a rest,' he said, nodding over his shoulder to Lola, who began to do a provocative dance with another woman, which ensured most eyes were focused on them.

Anyone watching would have seen what looked like an amorous couple finding a sheltered spot to get more intimately acquainted. Instead Miranda was led down a flight of steps where – by now completely unconscious – she was bundled on to a dinghy and quietly whisked away under a highwayman's moon, by two men in dark clothing, their faces obscured by balaclavas.

CHAPTER FIFTEEN

'And then, as if my week 'adn't been bad enough, I got sent a male girdle. A mirdle! My life is over,' said the man on the radio.

Alex switched channels.

'The problem with quantitative easing is that we still don't know …'

'Whether it's as effective as other pile cream,' Alex finished, and pressed another button on his digital radio. He liked to have some kind of noise when he was concentrating on paperwork, but it needed to be the right kind. Already he had wasted time by checking out a group he had heard on one station, which had an interesting rock-folk vibe going on, and then wasted more time by downloading it on to his iPod.

In fact, he was aware that a large part of the problem lay in an overriding urge to procrastinate. It was a sunny Friday and he wanted to be outside. Or have a beer in the pub. He pressed a few more buttons truculently, then gave in and grabbed his phone. 'Matt,' he said abruptly, 'what are you up to?'

'Not a lot. I should be writing a script for the new series of *Ashamed*, but Tracy says she's got a bug.'

'In the computer or in the bloodstream?'

'Fuck knows. Either way, she ain't coming out to play, so I'm sitting in the office on my lonesome, playing computer games and trying to get motivated. I never write well without someone else to bounce ideas off.'

'Fancy a beer at the Cross Keys?'

'Too right I bloody do. Get 'em in,' shouted Matt, and Alex could hear the sound of a computer being slammed shut.

The pub was a breezy place, tucked away in a back-street. Its court-yard was a riot of hanging baskets and pots of flowers, but its main attraction to Alex and Matt was the selection of real ales and the many varieties of crisps.

Alex was propping up the bar when Matt arrived in a flurry of bonhomie. He flirted with the barmaid, gave Alex a hearty punch on the arm and ripped straight into the Hot English Mustard crisps.

'And you'll be having?' smiled Alex.

'What have you got there?' Matt asked, gesturing at the pint.

'Adnams.'

'Do you know, I think I'm going to have a cider. I might move on to ale, but I'm going to start with an aperitif. A clear pint of your finest Weston's,' he addressed the barmaid, with a charming grin. He turned to Alex. 'Made in Much Marcle, I seem to remember from a ridiculously shit pub quiz in Herefordshire. Or was it Hertfordshire? One or the other. Much Marcle. Never forgot it – one of those names that sounds like it's straight out of an Agatha Twistie tale. Or *Midslaughter Murder*. Cheers,' he said, crunching a crisp. 'God, these are good. Seabrook. Never heard of them. I'm going to order a box of them, goddamnit, you see if I don't,' he said. 'Here, take this credit card, if you please, young lady. I have a feeling we're going to need something a lot more substantial than flimsy bits of paper with random heads on them.'

'I think you'll find it's the Queen's head,' Alex said, giving Matt a patronising look.

'Not her head I was talking about, you twat. The ones on the other side. Name one.'

'Sir Christopher Wren.'

'Actually, that's not a bad offer. Let me have a look.' He took out a ten-pound note with a flourish. 'Ha. Charles Darwin 1809 to 1882. That makes him seventy-three when he snuffed it. A good age. Considering he was living on a diet of Galapagos tortoises, crispy finches and a squeeze of lime. Or had they finished with the limes by then? And let me have a look at the twenty. Hmm. Never heard of him.'

'Who is it?'

'Guess.'

'No. If you've never heard of him, how am I supposed to guess? You can't give me a clue.'

'First man, crossed with a crisp.'

'First man. First man ...' Alex mused. 'First man?'

'The name of the first man allegedly on earth.'

'Oh. Adam. And a crisp, you say? Adam Walker. Adam Pringle. Adam ... Seabrook?'

'Adam Smith, 1723 to 1790. Do me a favour and put in a search on your thingumajig there and tell us who he is while I hunt through the fat wallet for a fiver.' He rummaged as Alex typed, then pulled out a five-pound note. He looked at the back. 'Elizabeth Fry 1780 to 1845,' he declared. 'Who the fuck is she? This is ridiculous. I'm going to speak to my MP about it. Ludicrous. We're talking about the very stuff of life – the stuff that allows us to eat and drink in this here hostelry. It should feature massive beacons of excellence and we've got a bloke who discovered beagles, a chap related to a crisp and a woman in a bonnet who is delightful and possibly Turkish.'

Alex looked up questioningly from his BlackBerry.

'Fry's Turkish Delight?' Matt said helpfully.

Alex groaned, then read out, '"Adam Smith. A Scottish moral philosopher and a pioneer of political economics. Author of *The Wealth of Nations* – one of the most influential works on economics." Blah-blah … callous business activity, blah. Do you need any more information?'

'Sorry. I'd dozed off. What about this Elizabeth Fry woman?'

'"English prison reformer, social reformer, Quaker, Christian philanthropist." Um … Now that's interesting. Her mother Catherine was part of the Barclay family, who were among the founders of Barclays Bank.'

'So. We've got a turtle scoffer, a bloke who's responsible for the mess we're in, and some bird who banks at Barclays. Not what you'd call a stellar cast, is it? I mean, if you want to impress the neighbours. We're not talking giants of the Western world here, are we? It's not like sticking George Washington on a dollar bill. Adam bloody Smith. Elizabeth bloody Fry. I ask you.' He swigged his cider.

'Feeling a bit better now, are we?' asked Alex, amused.

'Yup. As I said, I hate being on my own all morning with no one to talk to. Hey, I might use some of that stuff in the next episode. Interesting who we choose to put on notes, eh? I'd have Isambard Kingdom Brunel because we all know who he is and the Clifton Suspension Bridge is still a good bridge.'

'As opposed to other bridges, which are always on the verge of falling down and the like,' Alex said drily.

'As opposed to loads of other bridges we don't even know the names of because they're boring. Serviceable, but boring.' Matt pressed on: 'And I'd have Tolkien because Gollum is a slam-dunking baddie, simultaneously pitiable and revolting. He'd have to be on the fifty-quid note because it's the biggest denomination we have at the moment. And, hmm ...'

'Egbert, King of Wessex,' prompted Alex.

'Who?'

'The first king of England. Or was it Alfred the Great? He might have been first.'

'How do you know that guff? Well, I wouldn't have either of them. That's the point I'm trying to make. We need people we've heard of. Alfred the Great ... we know he burnt some cakes, full stop. End of knowledge. If we're going to have royalty, let's have someone with a proper story. Henry the Eighth. Elizabeth the First. Oliver Cromwell. It'd be good to have him on one side and the Queen on the other. Ha-ha. No! I know.' He pointed a finger. 'James Dyson! Best vacuum cleaners on the planet. And best hand driers. I actually dry my hands if there's one of them in the bog, instead of wiping them on my jeans.'

'Oh. You wash your hands? Now there's one for the books.'

But Matt was unstoppable. 'Deffo Dyson. And maybe Bobby Charlton, because wherever you are in the world, he's the first foot-baller everyone mentions. I was in some godawful shitty place in India – the middle of nowhere – and this boy, can't have been more than five, runs up and waves his skinny little arms, shouting, "Bobby Charlton, Bobby Charlton,"' and Matt waved his arms in the air, almost taking out the barmaid, who was carrying two glasses of wine to a couple in the corner. 'And Manchester United is probably *the* most famous team in the *world*. So that's it. Bobby on the fiver, Dyson on the tenner, Brunel on the twenty, Tolkien on the fifty.'

'No women, I notice,' commented Alex.

'Hmm. Yeah. Judi Dench, then. Everyone knows her.'

'But will they know her in a hundred years?' Alex asked.

'Doesn't matter. We'll be using small chips embedded in our fingers to pay for things by then. It'll be immaterial. Or we could have J. K. Rowling instead of Tolkien. If we must. But I don't see why we should have women if they're not as famous as men. It's their fault. They should get out more. Another pint?'

'It would be rude not to. And can you get some olives?'

'You're *sooo* middle class with your nasty tree fruit. I'm getting some more crisps, so you can cock off.'

The afternoon slid by, with neither of them in a particular hurry to get back to their work. Samantha, at a table on the terrace, nursed a glass of soda water and some cashew nuts, while the other body-guard who had been employed by Alex's father was sitting in a car outside the flat.

'She's not bad-looking, your bird,' Matt said, after their third pint.

'Yep. I'll give you that. She looks great. No sense of humour, though.' Alex nodded at Samantha, who raised her hand slightly.

'Doesn't fancy you, eh? Bummer,' Matt said, dragging his eyes back to his friend.

'She's all over me like a cheap suit,' Alex contradicted him. 'Have to pull her off.'

'You don't do that to girls. Or if you do, you're doing it all wrong.'

'Yeah. Right. No wonder I never get anything done.'

'What happened to that other girl you were seeing?'

Alex had a flash of Miranda laughing up at him from rumpled sheets, her glorious hair tumbling over her shoulders. He shrugged it away. 'Woman. Miranda. Off the scene. All sorts of complications. Daughter who didn't approve. Samantha dogging my every foot-step. It was getting difficult. So we've cooled it. I dunno. There's part of me thinks it might be easier if I … oh, y'know … if I keep myself to myself until this deal that Dad's doing is all sorted. Bodyguard – sounds sexy, she *is* sexy, but it's just not. It's weird. I can't describe it. Imagine having an audience for everything you do.' Alex rolled his eyes towards Samantha.

'I'd quite fancy that, actually, mate. Be like having a kinky three-some. Know what I mean?'

'You could get it on with someone when there was another person there who was totally uninvolved?'

'"Get it on with someone"? What sort of language is that? It's like talking about "having it off".'

'What would you say, then?'

'Copping off. Bashing into. Making the beast with two backs. Humping. Knobbing. Boning. Boring senseless with your worthy organic eco-shit bollocks.'

'Thank you for enlightening me. They say it's good to talk. And sometimes it is. On the other hand, sometimes … it isn't.'

'I bet you want a crack at Samantha, though, eh? You'd be mad not to. She'd crush you between her thighs like a nutcracker. In fact, you'd have your nuts cracked. Those are some muscles. What d'you think? Fake tits?'

Alex laughed. 'I'm not surprised you've done so well with that series of yours,' he said. 'You're like a cross between *Viz* and *Maxim*.

Allegedly a grown-up, but still in your dirty teens with a stash of porn and a crunchy sock. No, I do not fancy a crack at Samantha. Well, maybe I do,' he admitted grudgingly, as Matt did a fake jaw-drop, 'but when I'm sober all I can see is a nightmare scenario. And then Dad would furnish me with a different bodyguard. Oh, okay. Yes. I'll get on the case. How can she fail to succumb to my organic eco-shit nonsense, eh?'

Matt changed the topic. 'I see whatchamacallit's nose has dropped out through overdoing it on the Colombian marching powder,' he commented, gesturing at the celebrity on the front of the newspaper that had been flung on to the seat next to them. 'Must have done shedloads. That is one helluva state to get into. He'd look quite good as a Norman soldier wearing one of those helmets with the long flat nosepieces.'

The conversation rambled on until suddenly Matt sprang up with an exclamation. 'Fuck. It's six o'clock. We're supposed to be going to the theatre tonight. I've got to get home, get changed and get out. Bugger. And it's your round too. Shit bollocks. You owe me. See yers.' He stood up, drained his cider and, with a 'Don't let the bastards grind you down', he was gone, dragging newspapers off tables and leaving a trail of wobbling glasses as he went.

Alex nursed what was left of his pint and contemplated the evening ahead. He couldn't decide whether to stay in the pub, go to see a film or go home and watch television. Or go to his house in the country and potter about. He was going there tomorrow anyway. *Or*, and this was the big *or*, finish the paper-work. It was at times like this that he wished he could throw it all to someone else, but that was what running your own business was all about.

With a sigh, he stood up and went out to Samantha. 'I think I'm going to have a wander round the park before going home. Do you want to walk with me or around me?'

She smiled, understanding the frustration of always having someone in tow. 'Whichever you'd prefer,' she said. 'If you want to talk, I'll walk with you. If you want to ramble and think, I'll stay out of your way. It really is up to you.'

'If it's all the same, then, I'll ramble. And try not to make your job too difficult.' He set off at a smart pace and before long was lost in thought in the centre of Hyde Park. The leaves on the trees had begun to get their fine summer dusting of smut, the grass had lost some of its spring, the birds seemed less polished. If he had to pick one time of the year as his favourite, it would be that brief moment between spring and summer, when nature was clean and fresh.

A couple rode past him on shiny lightweight bikes.

'So they were paying him about four hundred K a year,' said the woman, whose bottom spread over her saddle.

'Well, if you pay peanuts, you get monkeys,' brayed the other.

It would be nice to be out on a bicycle, he thought, down on the towpath by the Thames. Cycling to Richmond. He must get round to buying another to replace the last one, which had been stolen. Correction: most of it was stolen. The frame was still there. Bike pillagers should be hung from lampposts, in his opinion – or from the frames they left behind.

He walked past families out with footballs and went towards the pond, where birds scrapped over pieces of bread. It was strange how birds and fish ate bread. The universal loaf. A group of men and women in their twenties, with American accents and baggy clothing, was playing softball. A rotund man, his shiny running top stretched over his pimpled stomach, was gruntingly jogging. A skinny woman puffed past in black Lycra, her bony bottom moving like a sad greyhound's. Skinny women really were ugly, he thought. What must it feel like to have sex with a woman whose hip bones were razor sharp? And yet their legs always looked great. A dichotomy.

He cast a sneaky look at Samantha, walking a few feet away. Her body really was perfect. Strong and supple. Womanly but firm. Were her breasts real? They looked it, but you couldn't tell these days unless you got your hands on them. Shame they couldn't have sex just once, so he could stop thinking about it.

He stopped walking and turned.

'Do you fancy a drink?' he asked, with a light in his eye.

She had wondered when this would happen. It always did with single men and it was always irritating. And, in Alex's case, she had honestly thought he was made of sterner stuff. She fought back the urge to sigh, and gave him her standard response, which she had now honed to a few pithy sentences.

'No, thank you.' She smiled. 'For a start, as you know, I don't drink on duty. And with you, I will always be on duty. Second – and I may be speaking out of turn here, and excuse me if I've got the wrong end of the stick – I'm gay. Very gay. Not playing gay to get you interested. Nothing would bore me more than a man trying to come on to me.'

Alex tried to keep his face noncommittal, but his reaction was written all over his face. He had gone from a standing start to being excited and then ... well, he had to confess ... crushed. 'It was just a drink I was offering, not anything else,' he lied, sounding unconvincing to both of them.

'Well, as I said, I'm sorry for mistaking your intentions. I apologise.'

'No offence taken. And I'm sorry if that's what I appeared to be doing. It's a lovely evening and I was merely thinking it would be nice to sit outside and have a few jars. But obviously …' he tailed off. Well, that was all bloody embarrassing. Lesbian, eh? He couldn't wait to tell Matt.

They walked on in silence, Samantha a few steps behind, a small smile playing about her lips.

Alex stopped again.

Here it comes, she thought.

'Listen, if you ever want to bring a girlfriend over to while away the hours, I wouldn't mind at all. I can see how dull it must be day after day, night after night, watching my back,' he said.

She grinned. 'No. It's fine. Honestly. I keep my private life very private. But thank you for offering. If you do want to keep me happy, you could take me to the cinema tonight. I'm desperate to see *Inception*, and it's on at the Odeon.'

It was the oddest way of seeing a film. Samantha sat halfway down the auditorium in a seat against the wall, and insisted he sit in front of her. It was also weird how you viewed a film, he thought, when you knew the person with you was probably checking out the girls in the same way as you. Life. You thought you had it taped, and then it threw you a googly from silly mid-on.

CHAPTER SIXTEEN

The atmosphere on board *La Maritana* was at mercury-bursting-out-of-the-thermometer point. Fuelled by champagne and heady after the auction, the dancing was turning into a riot. It looked like a collection of bean bags being thrown about, with flailing arms and people suddenly disappearing from view.

There was something about being on a boat that brought out reckless behaviour. Already one woman had flounced off threatening divorce: her husband had been found with his naked bottom pressed against a porthole, dancing the light fandango with a blonde girl in orange fringing.

Katie Fisher was enjoying herself. She liked a party. And because she was working, she was just the right side of silly, spacing her cocktails with large glasses of sparkling water. She was being whirled around the dance floor by one well-heeled man after another, flirting gaily with all and sundry. She was engaged to Bob Hewlett, a landscape gardener, whom she described as 'fit as a robber's dog' – so she was feeling confident and excited, a thrilling combination. 'I can understand why sailors used alcohol as an anaesthetic when they had to have their legs lopped off,' she bellowed, to the man she was jiving with. 'I can't feel any part of my body.'

'I bet I can,' he shouted back, and pulled her towards him in a sweaty embrace, from which she had to extricate herself – not least because his wife was throwing her daggers. How awful to feel so vulnerable about your marriage, she thought. That's the problem with really rich men – they don't feel they have to behave themselves. 'Thank you very much, but I really do need to go and get a drink,' she puffed, after cavorting round the floor, and went off for a breather, leaving him to face the music.

She wound her way through the throng and went outside, finding a space on the lower deck where she leant on the railings and gazed out to sea. It was such a beautiful night: the stars were like white tea lights on a navy velvet carpet and the moon was luminous.

She sensed a man next to her, putting his foot on one of the metal rails. 'A stunning evening,' he said, in a deep, pleasant voice.

She half turned, and caught a glimpse of a chiselled jaw and blond hair. 'It is, isn't it? The right side of warm, a slight breeze, and a host of stars. The sort of night that makes you feel small. Here on Earth, kept on by gravity, while planets whirl in space to infinity.'

'Oh dear. Too much champagne?' he asked.

She smiled and fully looked at him. Fuckaduck. If she wasn't with Bob, she'd be in danger with this one. He was gorgeous. 'Katie Fisher,' she said, holding out her hand.

'Jon Wallis,' he said, taking it in a firm grip.

'Are you having a good night?' she asked, turning back to contemplate the view, focusing this time on the twinkling lights along the bay.

'Extremely. You did an excellent job of bumping up the auction prices. They must be very happy with you,' he said.

'I hope so. They said they were, but you can't always believe them. Sometimes you think you've made a hash of it and they're ecstatic. Other times you work really hard and all you get back from your agent is that they were expecting more.'

'Difficult when you work in a field where it's nigh on impossible to measure success.'

'Hmm. It's like those questionnaires you get given to fill out about the service you've had at places like banks or on planes. Were you satisfied, happy, very happy, not happy, dissatisfied? And you want to draw another box, which says, "Well, I was expecting what I got. I veered from ecstatic to depressed and if I had any other option, which didn't involve a lot of bother, I would use some other company." Or maybe I put too much thought into the question-naires I fill out.'

He laughed.

'So, can you measure what you do for a living?' she asked.

He thought for a minute, a muscle going in his jaw, then fixed her with a devastating smile. 'Possibly in monetary terms. I've done very well. I used to be in the army, but now I'm a facilitator. I work with a number of people in this area, and I think we've got a good business going – well, they keep coming back for more, at least. Come to think of it, it's difficult to quantify most businesses unless it's on the money side. There are those who have products to sell where they either work or don't work. But people still have choices. You could be making the best cars in the world, but unless people buy them, you're not a success. Now, you appear to have no drink. Can I get you something? Would you like one of those devilishly fine martinis they're offering upstairs, or champagne ... or water?' he asked, taking his foot off the rung with a ding.

'Thank you, I'd love one. A martini, please,' she said, her voice rising at the end of the sentence. She observed his muscular form as he strode away and up the stairs. He walked like a cat, she thought. Quietly, purposefully, lithely. She opened the locket she was wearing round her neck and smiled at Bob. It's okay, she said silently to him. No one can make me laugh like you. I'm window-shopping, just like you do. That was the brilliant thing about their relationship, she thought. The trust. They knew that they could have others but they chose not to. And why would you throw away giant boxes of memories for a brief scratch of an itch? It did help that he had the best hairy chest in the world and smelt heavenly. Heaven. If religion hadn't been invented, would we have a word for Heaven?

At that point a glass was handed to her, with a quizzical look. 'You were miles away,' he commented, in response to her mute query.

'Oh! Oh, yes. Yes, I was,' she said. 'I can't think how I'd got on to it, but I was thinking of Heaven.'

'Because Heaven isn't enough for you?'

'No. Yes. No,' she said briefly.

He smiled, clearly thinking she had been daydreaming about him, and not unhappy about the prospect.

She narrowed her eyes to try to bring an image to mind. 'Didn't I see you with a woman earlier?' she asked. 'I've just recalled seeing you with a woman in a lovely red halter-neck dress while we were doing the auction – you were bidding for something.'

'Yes, I met her on the beach recently. I hardly know her at all,' he said smoothly. 'I think she's left already. Said she wanted an early night.'

The band was playing an Abba song, and both infinitesimally moved in time to the beat.

'They're good, aren't they?' she said, after a moment.

'Mmm. Fancy a dance? Shake the fidgets out of your legs?' Jon asked.

'Maybe later. Enjoying this martini and the fresh air,' she said, sniffing the air and tasting a salty tang on her lips from the sea spray.

He sipped his drink. 'The guy on the bar is a gifted martini maker. He used to work at one of the top hotels in London. He's married to a Spanish girl and is now a freelance mixologist, working most of the big yachts and houses round here. Yes, that is the term. I know – we would have called them barmen and been done with it,' he said wryly. 'Life moves on, and so does the terminology. How long have you got out here?'

'Flying back on Tuesday. I thought I'd take the opportunity to have a mini break. Not that I really deserve it – I haven't exactly had a hard year, work wise. You get to a certain age in television when, unless you turn into a caricature or do something mad, like marrying a Premiership footballer or taking up with a cross-dressing trapeze artist, the opportunities dry up. Although, having said that, I do keep on getting asked to appear in "celebrity" shows.' She sketched speech marks in the air with her free hand. 'But then you're invariably described as a Z-lister by the newspapers, and the producers try to make you look as idiotic as possible. I did say yes to one of them and, to my eternal shame, yes to another. Then, to my eternal shame *again*, they decided to go with someone else.'

He chuckled. 'Never good to be rejected when you deign to offer yourself. A salutary lesson. Unfortunately it usually happens when you're desperate.'

'And then it makes you feel more desperate,' she said bitterly.

'Oh dear. What have you signed up to now?' he asked, standing back and cocking his head on one side.

'I can almost hardly bear to articulate it. I am … tsh!' she exclaimed. 'I'm doing an advert.'

'An advert for what? It's okay. You can tell me – my lips are sealed.' He did the zipping motion with one hand.

She shook her head as if to dislodge the response. 'Urgh. Laxatives. I know,' she giggled, 'but laxatives are big business. Oh, stop it,' she said, as he started laughing. 'The thing is, I know loads – and I mean loads – of women who only go once a week. Really. Obviously, they should eat more roughage and stop drinking, and take more exercise, and then they would go more. Honestly, I can't believe we're talking about this. But … they were offering a lot of money.' She balanced her martini on the rail and put her head in her hands. 'You're right. I should have said no. And it will probably accelerate my demise in the world of television. Next year, I'll be advertising incontinence pants, haemorrhoid cream and the walk-in bath.'

'And the big red button that says help is coming.' He nodded. 'The advert for assisted living for the elderly.'

'Money,' Katie pronounced savagely, 'most definitely *is* the root of all evil. Not that an advert is evil, *per se*. But I would be just *so* good if I had loads of money. I'd make sure that lots of it went to charity.'

'Of course you would,' he said soothingly. 'You'd be benevolently helping people in need while having your toenails painted.'

She threw him a cheeky look. 'Yes, exactly. I'd live in a modest house, with a modest car and a modest pension, and then I'd write out cheques and give the rest away.'

'You *say* that …' He left the sentence hanging.

Katie drained her martini and smiled. 'No doubt you're right. I'd be as much of a wanker as the rest of 'em, up to my ears in Fendi bags and gilt-encrusted chocolate buttons. Let's go and shake up the dance floor.'

It was late on Saturday morning that Alex woke up after a restless night, his head feeling as if it had been squashed between two enormous breasts made of Play-Doh and conkers. That, he thought, was why you shouldn't drink alcohol without bubbles. Or on your own. He had a fuzzy recollection of listening endlessly to a Morrissey song on repeat while getting through glasses of whisky. Classic. Maudlin music under the influence. How unoriginal.

He padded carefully to the bathroom and stood naked in front of the medicine cabinet. He moved his eyes slowly along the row of bottles and packets, so as not to disturb his brain. Eventually, he reached out for some co-codamol he had been given for a broken wrist, and looked at the instructions. It appeared to be well out of date. What was the worst that could happen? He could barely see, anyway. He downed two and left the rest out in case he needed fortification. And then he remembered he was supposed to be driving to Oxfordshire. He read the label again. 'May cause drowsiness.' *May* cause drowsiness. Well, he could wait and see whether that happened. He read on: 'Not to be used when there is pressure inside the skull.' Cock off. That was why he was using it. Oh. Due to injury. His head was hurting from the act of reading. What he needed was coffee. And juice. A fried egg. Ketchup.

He trailed through to the kitchen, only briefly wondering whether either of his bodyguards would have their binoculars trained on him. Well, let them. He honestly didn't care if they could see his garden vegetables. He smiled as he used the expression, which had been coined by one of his friends and picked up for general use. Then he stopped smiling because it activated his ear muscles, which was not pleasant.

How was it possible for everything to ache because of what had been essentially a coma?

He opened the fridge and bent as little as he could to get the coffee and milk. Standing up, he got a rush of blood to the head and stood there hanging on to the plastic egg indentations like a rock climber.

This must be how it feels to be very old, he thought. Shuffling about and lurching from upright object to upright object, but without the option of improvement.

An hour later, his stomach full of egg, beans, coffee, juice, milk, toast, nachos and chunks bitten straight from a lump of Cheddar, he was feeling much more in tune with the world. He had just demolished a small army of zombies on his iPhone and was frantically negotiating his way out of a cul-de-sac full of flesh-eaters when he was irritatingly interrupted by a phone call.

When he had heard what his father had to say, he was amazed to discover just how angry he could be with the very world he had felt so in tune with.

CHAPTER SEVENTEEN

For many of those holidaying on the Costa del Sol, Saturday was their last full day of sunbathing. They were going back to jobs that started on Monday and they were determined to be as brown as possible. Everywhere bodies were sizzling, some already striped by previous encounters with the blazing heat.

On the sea, the small school of dinghies bounced on the waves, the face of one girl looking concerned as she went through the motions. Becky couldn't help but think that they should have put more than a cursory phone call in to Miranda at the hotel. It was the last day of the course, and she had said that she wouldn't miss it.

'She'll have overdone it at that party last night,' said Brian, putting on his life jacket before the day's sailing. 'I heard it went on until five this morning. She'll have unplugged the phone.'

'But surely she would have left a message with Reception,' said Becky.

'More likely she'll have left the Do Not Disturb sign on the door by mistake,' Brian reasoned.

And Becky had to make do with that.

At the end of the afternoon, they were all handed their RYA certificates.

'This is the best,' said Becky, giving Brian a grateful hug, which made him flush. 'I haven't had a certificate since I went swimming up and down the pool for life saving. I love it that I can now go and rent a dinghy at home. My mum and dad are going to be well chuffed. This is so cool.'

'Ta, mate,' said Bill, briefly, with a firm and hearty handshake, while Mark left it at 'Thanks. Great job. Really enjoyed it.'

Darren immediately flicked on his phone, took a picture of the certificate and sent it to a friend of his back in Britain. 'He said I'd never do it,' he explained. 'Said I was the sort of wanker who'd end up in 'ospital wiv me 'ead smashed open. This'll learn 'im.'

Brian went to a small cupboard and brought out a bottle of wine, which he opened in celebration, pouring it into plastic beakers. 'Well done, all of you, you've been a great group. It's a shame Miranda's not here, but she'll still get the certificate. I hope you all carry on sailing, and that you've enjoyed yourselves,' he said.

They murmured their thanks, and after what she thought was a decent interval, Becky asked what would happen to Miranda's certificate. 'I'll send it to the address she's given me,' Brian told her. 'Why?'

'Oh, I was going to mosey on past the hotel and see if she was around. I could drop it off to her. If she's not up by now, we ought to be worried!'

'I would give it to you, but under the rules, I have to send it to her at her home. It's safer that way – just in case she isn't at the hotel. She may have stayed elsewhere. Or gone back to Britain early. You never know. But you're all old enough and ugly enough to decide whether to come or not.'

'Oi, 'oo are you callin' ugly?' Bill narrowed his eyes in mock anger.

'And I'm not old,' said Mark, who was in his sixties.

'You might be, but your bird isn't, is she?' asked Bill, giving him a nudge. 'You've got a twenty-year-old, 'aven't yer?'

Becky grimaced. She actually believed that Mark had a twenty-year-old girlfriend. Probably bought off a website. Strange how men could do that and not be embarrassed. If she ever thought that someone was only with her because of a passport, she'd drop them quicker than a hot spoon. 'I think I'll head off.' She put down her beaker, and included them all in a general goodbye. 'And thank you again, Brian. I haven't enjoyed myself so much for years. I can't wait to show off when I get back home. Good luck with the next lot.' She waved and set off up the wide pavement that ran the length of the beach.

Now that she was out in the sunshine and without the cooling breeze, she felt uncomfortably sticky and windswept. She tried to run her hand through her hair but it came to a halt in a mass of knots. A cleat hitch and double reef knot, if I'm not much mistaken, she thought proudly, disentangling her fingers and checking to see how much hair she had pulled out.

The hotel was further than she had thought, and she was parched by the time she walked into the deliciously cool reception area. 'I was wondering if you could call Miranda Blake's room for me, please,' she asked the young man, whose name badge proclaimed him to be Manuel Roya.

She could hear the phone ringing, and they both waited, looking at each other expectantly. He raised his eyebrows as the ringing went on for longer than anyone could possibly need to answer.

'Hmm. She's obviously not there,' said Becky. 'Do you know if she came in last night?'

'I'm sorry, señorita, but that would have been my colleague. He's back on duty tomorrow evening.'

Becky bit her lip. 'I suppose she may have spent the night elsewhere,' she said, echoing Brian's comment. Right this minute, Miranda might be having a late lunch with Jon Wallis.

In some ways, Becky was right, Miranda was having a late lunch.

As the deckchair attendants on the beach were putting away umbrellas and counting up their earnings, Miranda was waking up to unfamiliar surroundings. With her eyes still closed, and feeling sleepy, she stretched and was aware that the bed was narrower than the one she had been sleeping in. Odd. She opened her eyes and saw a ceiling that was pale blue instead of white. She sat up with a jolt. Where was she? And why didn't she remember getting here, wherever here was?

She was wearing an unfamiliar thin blue cotton caftan, and she could see her toothbrush and toothpaste on a shelf in the bathroom, which was directly opposite where she lay.

Curiouser and curiouser. She swung her legs out of bed and stood up. There was a small window with a view across to the sea in the distance. She couldn't open it, but from what she could see, there was a steep drop directly beneath.

Miranda decided that there was no point in trying to sort out anything until she had proper clothes on. Her mind whirling, she ran a shower. There was soap and a small plastic pot of shampoo. How annoying – no razor, no conditioner and no face moisturiser. Her hair would go bonkers and her skin would be as tight as a tick's.

She washed swiftly, while trying to backtrack over what had happened. The party with Jon on the yacht. She'd been wearing a new red halter-neck dress. There'd been the auction. And then what? Had she slept with him? Oh, God, was this his house and had she shagged the man? How bloody embarrassing to have no sodding clue. What a slapper. She caught sight of herself in the mirror looking aghast, dried herself speedily and ran back into the bedroom.

She wanted to make sure that she would be in some sort of condition to talk about what had gone on. She found her red dress in the wardrobe, along with a thin kimono and a thicker knee-length orange caftan. She dragged it over her head and, thus attired, strode to the door and turned the handle. It wouldn't open. 'Hello,' she called.

No answer. The house was eerily quiet.

'Hello,' she called, a little louder, with a mixture of awkwardness, irritation and gathering fear.

Nothing. 'HELLOOOOO! HELP! HELP!' she eventually shouted.

She heard a faint noise, then footsteps coming closer.

She prepared to smile as the door was opened, and was astounded to see a face she had not expected.

'Lola,' she exclaimed.

'Hallo, Miranda,' said Lola, dressed in tight black stretchy Capri pants and a slim-fitting black T-shirt. She shut the door firmly behind her as she entered the room, and Miranda heard the lock being turned.

'What's going on and where am I?' she asked, confused.

'Would you like to sit down while I explain?' Lola asked, gesturing to a flimsy table and two chairs by the far wall.

'I'd like some coffee and some food, as well as the explanation, if that's all right.' Her voice had sounded weak – she hated it.

Lola spoke in Spanish into a small walkie-talkie, then sat on one of the chairs, waiting for Miranda to join her. 'Where to begin?' she said, glancing at her watch.

'At the beginning would be nice,' said Miranda, acerbically, happier with her tone. That's it, she thought. Take control.

'I'm not sure it would,' said Lola, with a half-smile, 'since the beginning occurred with the purchase of an island not far from here by a man called David Miller. You've heard of him, I think. Or you've certainly heard of his son – Alex Miller?'

Miranda nodded, and suddenly she understood that what Alex had told her had been the truth. About being kidnapped. Kidnapped. KIDNAPPED. How bloody ridiculous. At my age. Oh, God, her brain was saying, round and round, as Lola continued to talk. Kidnapped. What about the flight? Lucy? Jack? She tried to concentrate. It's important to focus, she told herself. Focus.

'We've had you under surveillance since you took up with Alex at the canal. I was sitting in the beer garden at the pub where you first went for a drink with each other,' said Lola.

Miranda stared at her with cold eyes.

'You looked directly at me, and I did wonder whether it would make the continued surveillance difficult. But, thankfully, you're not that observant. The only thing I've been changing about my appearance is my hair. We considered putting a bug in your car, but decided not to when we heard that you were coming here. We couldn't believe it – right here where we wanted you. Although I did check round your car to see if there was anything useful, while you were shopping … one of the few times when you did recognise that something was amiss.'

Miranda tried not to show any emotion.

'Yes, I could see that you were confused. You thought you'd locked the car with the zapper as you were walking away. But you hadn't. All I did was simply cross that beam with a small laser, which prevented the lock activating. Anyway, as I said, we didn't really need to do anything after you told your friends you were flying to Alicante for a yoga holiday. Yes, of course we hacked into your emails,' she responded, to a look on Miranda's face. 'I bet your children are always on at you about putting a security password on your broadband account, aren't they? Mmm. Of course they are. Well, they're right. I was outside your house, reading all your emails. And then it was just a matter of booking myself on the same flight and into the same hotel.'

Miranda had a horrible sinking feeling as Lola rambled on. She was in limbo, waiting for the name to be spoken. The name of the person she was sure was behind this. What a fool she had been. Of course he wouldn't be interested in a raddled old trout like her, she thought. And then, there it was.

'… so we faked a theft from your sun-bed and Captain Jon Wallis became your hero, returning your belongings to you and inveigling himself into your affections.' She paused to allow the words to sink in. 'And don't pretend that he didn't.'

There was a crackle on the walkie-talkie.

'*Sí, sí. Un momento. Y no esta demasiado caliente? Bien,*' she said, walking to the door and unlocking it, to allow in a man carrying coffee and some toast. He was tall, thick-set, with a shaven head, and one arm entirely tattooed with snakes.

Miranda watched him with a jaundiced eye.

'I warn you. Ees not hot, zee coffee. So no point srowing it on Lola,' he said, pre-empting one of the thoughts that had crossed her mind. Then he left and the door was locked again.

'And what happens now?' Miranda asked, sounding belligerent.

'Well, there's the thing. This house is built like a fortress. Toughened glass. Double door locks – that's why it all sounds so quiet. And, essentially, you're being held here until there's an agreement that we can continue to use the island for what it's been used for over the years.'

'Which is?'

'Which is as a staging post. We facilitate activities on the mainland.'

'What does that mean?' Miranda asked caustically.

'You don't need to know. But, suffice it to say, it's important to our business. And you are the means to that end. You won't come to any harm as long as Mr Miller plays ball.'

'And why the hell would Mr Miller play ball with someone his son has known for a few months and doesn't give two hoots about?'

'Oh, I think you underestimate your attraction, Miranda. I've spoken to a friend of Alex, a man called Matt. As you know, most men are susceptible to a woman's flattery, and I can be very persuasive. *In vino veritas*, they say. He told me that Alex is very keen on you. That it's the fault of your daughter and his bodyguard that you're not together. Now, if this situation is wrapped up as quickly as we all feel it will be, you'll be out of here in a few days. If not … well, we may have to come up with something else. This island, as I said, is extremely important.'

'And I bet the police know all about it, and where you are,' said Miranda, taking a sip of the lukewarm coffee and trying to sound braver than she felt.

'The police. Yes. Well, the police who know about it are taking a cut, so they're unlikely to get involved. And we've strenuously urged the Millers not to inform the authorities. We've already sent a small token implying that it would be a very bad idea. Just the end of an index finger from a woman of your age – don't worry, she was on her way out anyway, after a drugs overdose. We have a friend at the hospital. I must go. I've left some of the books you brought with you over there, and I'm sorry, but you're going to have to make do with them for company for the moment. See you later.'

Lola left without a backward glance, and Miranda heard the sound of the lock being turned.

She ate the toast and drank her coffee, although it tasted like ashes. All she could think about – apart from how absurd it was – was how she could get a message to Jack and Lucy. On the off-chance that she had missed something, she went round the room with a fine-tooth comb. No. It really was as sparse as it looked. She roamed up and down, trying and trying to think of anything she could do to help herself.

In all the thriller films she had watched there had always been an air-conditioning vent that the captive managed to escape along. Or they broke up a piece of furniture and hit the jailer on the head with such force they knocked them out. Did she have the might to do that if the man mountain came in? No, it was laughable. And judging by the light coming in through the window, she had eaten nothing for about twenty-four hours, apart from the small pieces of toast, so any strength she did have would be vastly diminished.

They obviously didn't think she could do anything, or they would have put her in a smaller room and left her with nothing to break up and use as a weapon. Which made her so angry, she took a tentative swing with one of the chairs, then felt silly and put it down.

She wondered what Alex would make of the news. She knew what Lucy would say. That she had warned her of the dangers. That she should have known she shouldn't get involved. But she was Miranda's daughter and she would do whatever was needed. Had she given anyone Alex's number? Had she given Alex any of her family's numbers? No, of course she hadn't. Mind you, it wasn't exactly complicated to track anyone down, these days, with Twitter, Facebook, Google Earth, and satellites beaming down images everywhere, she thought. Maybe that was what they would do, Alex and his father. Find her with images taken from space. Or did such things only happen in that American series *24*?

In some ways, it would be better if Jack wasn't told. Bless him. He'd want to get involved in the rescue operation. If there was a rescue operation. How did these things get sorted? Or was Lola right, that David Miller would agree to let them use the island and she would be out in a few days? And would anyone think to tell the PR company that she wasn't going to be in?

Suddenly she had an idea. Becky would know she'd gone missing – it was the last day of the sailing course and they were going to pick up their certificates. She would alert the authorities. And then what? Or would Becky just assume she'd gone off with that bastard con-artist Jon Wallis? She doubted he had even been in the army. He was a smooth-talking thug. How could she have fallen for his patter?

She lay down on the bed and racked her brains, rubbing her forehead as though she could make a useful contribution leap out.

The patch of light at the window grew darker, turning from sky blue to purple and Miranda continued to lie on the bed, her mind in turmoil.

CHAPTER EIGHTEEN

Some pieces of music are unhelpful when you're in a moving vehicle. The insistence of a harpsichord in classical music when you're trying to park is guaranteed to make you hurry it up and accidentally bump into the kerb. Rap music in slow-moving traffic is to be avoided if you don't want a coronary. Priests chanting when you're attempting to navigate a series of sleeping policemen can only end in disaster.

Alex couldn't settle on the music he needed to listen to in his camper van while racing – inasmuch as anything that rattled and shed metal parts beyond fifty miles an hour could race – to his father's house for a meeting about Miranda.

Knowing his father, Alex felt that his own contribution would be minimal and anything he said would be discounted. He had to be there because Miranda was his 'fault'. He expected to be read a lecture, but that was the least of his worries. He wanted Miranda safe – and as soon as she was, he was going to … he was going to … What was he going to do?

She had wormed her way into his affections without him realising it and he had been on the way to falling in love with her when Lucy had put a spanner in the works. He wondered if maybe he actually did love her. Perhaps that was why he hadn't been able to concentrate on anything since they'd split up.

He fiddled with the knob on the radio again and found a song by the Smiths that fitted his angry, belligerent, impotent mood.

The worst of it was that, before this had happened, he had thought his father was overreacting. After all, people built hotels on disputed bits of land all over the place and nothing happened. New York, for example: he had read about the Mafia there, but that didn't stop new buildings going up, did it?

The next fifteen minutes went by in a blur because he was having fantasies about rescuing Miranda. About finding out where she was being held and then going in wielding a gun. Knives. Grenades. He would throw the whole bloody lot at them. They deserved to be slaughtered. Kidnapping was a heinous crime. Taking innocent people and holding them for ransom. What sort of men did that?

Samantha's sleek car followed him through the gates to the big house, but she didn't come in with him.

Belinda opened the door. 'A nasty business,' she said, shaking her head, 'and I know as it's not nice to say so, but I'm glad you're safe, Alex. Your father's in the library.'

Two men wearing dark suits and the sort of haircuts sported by ex-military types stood up as he came in.

'Alex,' his father said gravely, inclining his head as a hello. 'How are you?'

'You know,' said Alex. 'Not brilliant. Obviously.'

David Miller had been through rough patches in his life, and he had no doubt this obstacle could also be surmounted. He had not told his son, but he had considered kidnapping insurance before this had happened, and had then discounted it because he was damned if he was going to give way to thugs.

'These men here are from the security firm that employs Samantha,' he said, 'and they're hopefully going to be tracking Mrs Blake down and … ah, facilitating her return.'

Everyone nodded.

'And I assume we're getting the police on to this straight away?' Alex asked.

'At this stage, no. We have it on good authority that there are a number of police in this area of Spain who may have connections with those involved in this drugs operation, so we're going to attempt a discreet rescue.'

'Discreet rescue? What does that mean? Sneak her out through a side door when they're not looking?' Alex asked, his lip curled. 'And are we really going to be trying to rescue Miranda and risk God knows what in the process rather than negotiating?'

The three older men gave him a sceptical look.

'It generally doesn't work like that in a case where money is not the object. If it was money, then, yes, we could negotiate.'

'But you can offer them a deal, Dad. Get her freed and then renege. What's wrong with that?'

'Because that would leave us open to another attack and perhaps swifter and more unpleasant action from this gang. We do need to get the police on our side eventually – and this is definitely going to clear out the bad apples.'

'I'm confused. I thought you said you weren't getting the police involved.'

'Not at this stage, because we don't want the gang to know what we're doing through the police who are in their pay. But later on, when it's too late for them to move her, when we're basically close enough to see the whites of their eyes, we *will* include the authorities. Then they'll have to clamp down – and put these drug-runners in jail.'

Alex sat in the leather chair, mulling over what he had been told. The three men were silent. 'So … it seems to me,' he said slowly, 'that in fact you wanted someone to get kidnapped. Obviously not me. But someone else. And then you could get the police to do something about this gang. Otherwise, how would you be rid of them once and for all, with the crooked police helping them?'

His father stood up and walked over to the side table where a silver jug of iced water was gathering condensation. 'Would you like some?' he asked Alex, who shook his head.

'Am I right, Dad?'

'To a certain extent. It's true that we need something radical to sort this out. We did *not*, I repeat *not*, expect Mrs Blake to be the person who—'

'Can you stop calling her Mrs Blake?' Alex finally burst out. 'Her name is Miranda. Or Ms Blake, if you must.' He didn't know why it was important, but he wanted them to stop making it sound as if he had been having an affair with a married woman. She was the ex-Mrs Blake.

David Miller sipped his water, the ice tinkling in the crystal glass. 'As I was saying, we did *not* expect Miranda to be kidnapped. In fact, we've only just discovered that – unbelievably – she went on holiday to the very spot where these men operate. Alicante. Did you know that?'

Alex shook his head.

'Which is probably why she was targeted. She was a gift. The right place at the right time. And she was alone, apparently.'

Alex could only imagine the terror of being kidnapped. Struggling. Trying to get away. Stuffed into a car boot fighting for air. Your hands and feet tied. Blindfolded. He was overwhelmed with an anger so strong he felt he could have moved mountains. 'What's going to happen? I want to be involved, whatever it is.'

'Of course you'll be included. But possibly more in an advisory capacity. No, before you ask, you're most definitely not going to be involved in anything else. You might do more harm than good. Please sit down again, Alex, and let these gentlemen explain the most likely scenario.'

Many men, as they get older, start to resemble women, particularly if their hair creeps over their shirt collars. The firm jaw-line is lost as the jowls start to droop, the chest becomes shapeless and starts merging with the paunch. A certain Widow Twankiness descends. Already Nigel Blake was starting to exhibit some of those characteristics, no more so than now when he was quivering with irritation and anger.

His bloody ex-wife had been bloody kidnapped. As if his life wasn't bad enough, spiralling out of control. Andrew Flight was not returning his calls – burying his head in the sand – but something had to be done, and done fast, or both of them would go under. He was going to have to get into Miranda's house, somehow. He couldn't believe that a whole box of books had gone missing. She obviously hadn't looked hard enough. His source at Christie's had told him they were worth a mint, and without them … well, without them, it was unthinkable.

When Lucy had phoned him in tears, it was all he could do not to rant down the phone about how it was not a good time for him to be having to deal with her stupid mother. Unfortunately, Lucy was his only hope of getting the books, and he was going to have to leave it at least until tomorrow to broach the subject. It didn't help that Lucy had tearfully asked whether between them they could raise enough money to pay a ransom if there was one.

'This man David Miller says that it isn't about money,' she had said. 'It's about these drug people on his island. And they want him to leave them alone to get on with it. And he isn't playing ball. Which means Mum might get killed, Dad. And I don't know whether I told her I loved her last time I spoke to her.' She sniffed and blew her nose. 'But what else can we do? And what about Jack? I don't know whether to tell him. What can he do, because he's so far away? Should I go out to Spain? Is there any point in that, Dad?'

'Look, pumpkin, I'm sure this chap has got it all under control.' Nigel had tried to calm her while rage at his ex-wife surged through his veins. 'And I honestly can't see any point in going out. None at all. You're of more help here.'

'What can I do here, though, Dad?' she had wailed. 'What help can I be? I'm just sitting here imagining Mum being beaten and in a cold cell with broken fingernails and no one to look after her and no food. Chained to a radiator. Huddling next to the wall. Filthy. And all alone …' She sobbed.

'Lucy, Lucy. Sssh. You're making yourself sick. Now, stop it. You're thinking of hostages in very different situations. These are not people who want your mother to be in a terrible state. Listen to me. Shush. These are people who are using your mother as a bargaining tool. A gambling chip. They'll be keeping her in a house somewhere, not a dungeon. They'll have taken away her phone and some of her stuff, and that's it, I'm sure. And as for Jack – hmm, I don't know either. I think it would be unfair not to let him know. Do you want me to write to him?'

He could hear Lucy blowing her nose again, and when she spoke, she had lost the edge of hysteria in her voice. 'Can you, Dad? Thank you. And I wish I knew where Andrew had got to. He hasn't returned my calls, and if I wasn't so worried about Mum, I'd be worried about him. Well, he has texted. But he sounds strange. Anyway, I'm sure it's nothing. I think it's just that I'm a bit jumpy.'

Nigel had calmed his daughter, but inside he was gnashing his teeth. He took a long time composing a careful email to his son and then sat, as the daylight faded, contemplating how easily one's life could come crashing down around one's ears like a pack of cards.

Miranda was also sitting in the gloom, unable to make her limbs move to switch on a light. She had been overcome with severe lassitude as each idea of escape died in its infancy. It was pointless. There was absolutely nothing she could do. She lay down on the bed and tried not to cry.

Eventually, she heard the locks turning and light flooded in from outside. She couldn't judge whether it would be better or worse for her captors if she did or did not co-operate, so she closed her eyes to delay the decision. 'Ah, Mrs Blake,' came the gravelly voice of Jon Wallis. He flicked on the light. 'I know you aren't sleeping. I can tell from the shallowness of your breaths and you've got your eyes tightly screwed shut. No one does that when they're asleep. You might as well sit up,' he said.

Her jaw tightened, but she did as he said, rubbing away the wetness on her cheeks and annoyed that he had seen her do it.

'I thought you might want to know the circumstances of how you came here,' he said, 'and I wanted to assure you that from the moment you drank that drugged champagne, you were in – how shall I put it? – safe hands. And it was Lola who – er – tended you when you got here. Just so you know that at no stage did anyone take advantage of you, as it were.'

He paused. She tried to give him no encouragement, feigning indifference, while wondering if there was any way of using him to get out of here. She looked at his face and no longer found it attractive. It was the face of a duplicitous man who had kidnapped her because of his rotten drugs empire. He was evil, immoral and weak. She loathed him. But what was it her grandmother used to say? 'Sugar catches more flies than vinegar'? Maybe if she was pleasant towards him, he might relax his guard. Or had she read too many novels … seen too many films? He was an ex-soldier. He probably knew every trick in the book – and she only knew one. And it involved a handkerchief and a fake thumb. It was amazing, she thought, how even in the most serious situation her brain could be frivolous.

'I know it doesn't seem like it,' he said, 'but you'll be well treated while you're here, and I don't anticipate it being a long stay.'

'Well treated?' she burst out. 'Well treated? Stuck in a room with hardly any furniture and three books to read – one of which is bloody unreadable?'

'The James Joyce, I assume?' He seemed to choke off a smile. 'But then I never did like novels, and thick ones like that … well.' He made a dismissive noise. 'Anyway, we can always get you a different book if that would make it more comfortable.'

'And what about my family? I have no phone, and they're going to be worried. Can I send a text to them? Or an email?'

'No, I'm afraid we can't allow you to do that. There are people out there who can trace these things, and it would be better for all concerned if you were to stay here. Otherwise, we would have to move you to more ... erm ... uncomfortable lodgings. Can I just give you a few tips while I'm here? As you've probably noticed, there is a steep drop outside the window – just in case you were contemplating tying clothing together and attempting to escape that way. And, also, the glass is specially toughened, so it would be nigh on impossible to break it in the first place. I'm only telling you so that you don't spend your entire time wondering how to do it. Lola has already informed you of the soundproof double doors through to the main house, which are locked from the outside. She has a black belt in karate, and God knows what else. And Bam has withstood stabbings and shootings, so he's well able to deal with a tiddler like you.'

She bridled at the word 'tiddler'.

'Finally, I'm going to apologise in advance for the food and drink. I'm afraid it has to be tepid to avoid any possibility of you throwing it at Lola and Bam and trying to get out that way. A bit like the window, the likelihood of it having any effect whatsoever is very slight, but we like to cover all eventualities. Oh, and sorry about the paper plates and cups, but that's for obvious reasons – glass can be very sharp. I'm sure I don't need to tell a mother of two children that, do I? Right,' he said, standing up. 'Unless you have any questions, I'm going to take my leave of you.'

'Questions? Of *course* I've got questions. What is all this about?'

'Oh, come on, Miranda,' he said contemptuously. 'You know what this is about. Alex Miller must have told you. How else did he explain Samantha Kane?'

She was silent. Then she asked, 'Why can't you find another island to ferry your drugs to Spain?'

'There aren't any others like it. It's the only one that's uninhabited in these waters and is in a very handy location. And, we were here first.'

'Does my family know what has happened to me?'

'I understand that Lucy has been informed. And we assume that she'll have told Jack and probably your ex-husband.'

She hated his casual use of her children's names. Lucy and Jack. As though he knew them. 'What's the penalty for drug-smuggling, these days? Whatever it is, it's a bloody shame it isn't a hanging offence,' she said. 'Now, can you please leave? You're giving me a headache.' And she lay down on the bed with one arm over her face.

'Your dinner will be along in a minute,' he said, as though she hadn't spoken, 'and if I remember rightly, it's a kind of beef stew. Dolores does a very good beef stew.'

'Bully for Dolores,' Miranda muttered, in a small voice that didn't sound like hers. Right, she thought. Buck up. This isn't getting the baby bathed. But she was finding it almost impossible to get through the situation. The word 'kidnapped' kept flashing at the front of her brain and, despite her best efforts, all she could think of was what happened to kidnap victims if the captors didn't get what they wanted.

CHAPTER NINETEEN

Swimming-pool attire differs depending on what country you're in. Katie Fisher had once been to Brazil where women wore thong bikinis as a matter of course. It had been one of the few places where her curvy bottom had felt at home, as she had told one of her close friends.

And now she was sitting cross-legged on a sun-bed, speaking to her on the phone from Alicante.

'It's budgie-smuggling country.' She spoke quietly to avoid being overheard. 'There are at least three men whose nuts and bolts I can see quite clearly through their tiny snug trunks. And one of them is wearing a virtually see-through white pair. The worst of it is, I can't stop looking.'

'Pull yourself together,' said Dee. 'Get back to your book, or whatever you were doing before he started trundling around.'

'It's one of those books you have to keep putting down because it's a bit ranty. All about nutrition and science. And I can't be bothered to go down to the room to get the other book I brought. Which is also really hard work. *Frankenstein* by Mary Shelley. Every sentence is twenty pages long. And how thick am I that I didn't know she was married to Percy Bysshe Shelley, the poet?'

There was an uninterested murmur from Dee.

'A lot of Shelleys on the sheeshore. No? And Bysshe. Really, what sort of a name is that? Anyway, it's fascinating here. It's one of those pools that's four storeys up, so it's a not-quite-infinity job. And there are men who look like their skin is stretched because they've overdone the bacon sandwiches, being oiled up by women who are falser than a false nose, with hard round breasts. Really obvious that they're fake. And with my fashion guru hat on, I'd say that frilly retro bikinis are in this year – it's all turquoise and white spotty or red and white gingham. I feel ridiculously old-fashioned in my ten-year-old, slightly snagged H&M yellow bikini with ties at the sides.'

'You're going to have to upgrade for your honeymoon, then. Go and get a retro bikini from the retro-bikini shop.'

'Bob won't care. He'd have me in a ratty old bra and pants set. That's why I love him.'

'Yes, he will care. All men secretly want to see you in something nice. Unless you end up going to a nudist colony.'

'In which case, I'll be wearing a coat. As if we'd go to a nudist colony … Can you imagine anything worse than people meandering about with their wobbly bits all akimbo? You wouldn't mind if they were gorgeous, but you can bet your bottom dollar that everyone on that holiday would be pallid, sweaty and limp. In fact, I'd fit in perfectly! Ha. Maybe I'll suggest it. Anyway, how's *Hello Britain!*?' she asked. It was the breakfast television show from which she had been sacked, but for which Dee still worked.

'Oh, fair to middling. Keera surpassed herself the other day,' she said, talking about the host of the show, Keera Keithley. 'She was talking to one of the producers about a party we'd both been to, and she said it wasn't much cop because it was full of Z-list

celebrities and then she turned to me and said, "No offence."
Honestly. She's such a beast.'

Katie laughed.

'And then yesterday I was at this polo match thing – yes, I know.
I don't know anything about polo,' she pressed on through Katie's
'huh' of disbelief, 'but I like to hang out with other massive Z-list
celebrities and you don't have to watch the polo. You can just eat
the food and get pissed. And I was wearing a long white skirt—'

'Oooh, I think I know what's coming,' interrupted Katie.

'Yeah. So I'm wearing a long white skirt – oh, and I forgot to tell
you I also had a cold sore, which was very sore and very big, so I was
already trying to hide a bit from the photographers – and I went to
the loo – you know, one of those Portaloo places. Well, the skirt
must have dragged on the ground, or drooped a bit at the back or
something, because unbeknown to me, I came out with Blue Loo
on the back of it. And I'm not talking about a small amount, either.
I'm talking about massive stains on the hem and right near my
bottom. Bright blue. And I didn't notice until the prince of somewhere European, who I was being introduced to, wrinkled his nose!
I swear I was mortified. Great big cold sore at the front, massive
Blue Loo patches round the rear. And then as I slunk off, I saw I'd
got a little bit of loo paper sticking to my foot. I wanted to *die*,' she
ended melodramatically.

'Ooo-er, I think I might be getting company,' whispered Katie.
'The bloke I met on the boat last night is picking his way past the
thongs. Speak later.' She rang off and sat up straighter, pulling her
sarong round her stomach to hide the little tummy she always had,
no matter how hard she dieted. Even if she hadn't known he was an
ex-soldier, she would have guessed at Jon Wallis having been in the

military. For a start, he had excellent bearing. But there was something else that was almost indefinable. A certain sort of self-confidence. The look of a man who would know what to do in a crisis. And a hint of what she called the cat that walked by himself, after the story by Rudyard Kipling where the other animals are domesticated, but the cat only agrees to the parts of home life he wants.

'Good afternoon,' he said, smiling. The corners of his blue eyes crinkled attractively. 'I thought I might find you here.'

'Soaking up the last rays before I go home tomorrow,' she said. 'I know it's bad to sunbathe, but it feels so nice getting the sun on your bones. Being warmed right through to your core has to be good for you somewhere along the line, doesn't it?'

'Of course it does. Chilled marrow is not nice. And it is starting to get chilly now that the sun is starting to go down. I was wondering whether you fancied having dinner tonight?'

A frisson of excitement ran through her stomach, while guilty feelings ran everywhere else because, after all, she was engaged to be married. Plus she had thought last night that he was not as much fun as Bob. However … Jon did have an enormous python-sized coil of animal magnetism. Taking everything into consideration, she really ought not to go.

'Love to,' she said, her green eyes sparkling.

'Let me see, it's coming up to six. Is it okay if I pick you up at about eight thirty?'

'That would be great. What's the dress code?'

He grinned. 'You women and your dress obsession.'

She felt a little of her balloon deflate. You women. As if there were lots of women in his life. And as though she was like all other women, instead of being a marvellously unique woman.

'You look fantastic in your bikini, so come in that,' he said, and was suddenly redeemed in her eyes.

'But, really, what shall I wear? Formal or informal?'

'If you must, then smart-casual,' he said.

'I hate that expression,' Katie said, unconsciously echoing something Miranda had said only a few days previously. 'What does it *mean*? Trousers and T-shirt? Trousers and puffy satin blouse? Sequined dress with shorts and Dr Martens? Tutu and sweater? Gingham dress, socks and plaits? Pink jumpsuit and pearls? Nurse's outfit and—'

'I'm going to have to stop you there because for one thing it's starting to get kinky, and there are better times and places.' He smiled. 'Also, I have a horrible feeling that you could go on like that for some time, and I have work to do. Wear whatever you feel comfortable in. I'll see you later.'

He had said smart-casual because he didn't want her to turn up in jeans and a sloppy top. He liked a woman who made an effort, and he had realised when he saw Katie by the pool in a tatty bikini that she might be the opposite. In truth, he liked a high-maintenance woman with a French manicure and immaculate makeup. It made the undressing later much more exciting and sexy. He was sure she would be entertaining company – he just hoped that when she appeared for dinner, she would have stepped up to the mark.

Meanwhile, at a hotel along the coast, the management was having a discussion about Mrs Miranda Blake.

Checkout time was eleven, but by three in the afternoon, she had not made an appearance. Señor Gomez, the duty manager, had been contacted by the head housekeeper, saying that no effort had been made to pack anything in the room, and the safe was still locked. It was one of the minor irritations in running a hotel that there were always people who were prepared to do a runner, but gut instinct told him that Mrs Blake, whom he had met on a few occasions, was not among their number. It was more likely that she had had an accident of some sort.

He looked around the room, noting that she was an orderly guest, with a staggering number of shoes, considering she was only on holiday for a week. 'Yes, I agree with you,' he told the housekeeper, who was anxious to get on and clean the room ready for the next occupant. 'We'd better get this lot packed up and stored. I'll come back to get the articles out of the safe after I've tried to contact Mrs Blake.' And then he would have to phone the police and report the case. He knew they would get on to their colleagues at the airport to stop her if she did try to leave the country. She was a nice woman, and he hoped she was not lying in a hospital somewhere, seriously injured.

After ringing her mobile which, as he suspected, eventually went to voicemail, he put through the bill from the credit-card imprint, then had to go and deal with a blocked bathroom sink in a ground-floor room, where he suspected children had been pushing small plastic animals and toilet paper down the plug hole.

Dolores's stew had been as delicious as Jon Wallis had said it would be, and Miranda wolfed it down, despite feeling very sorry for herself.

She lay on the bed trying to think of reasons to be cheerful, having very quickly come to the conclusion that the last thing she should do was slump into a weeping heap. Normally when she couldn't get her brain to settle – like when she was worried about Jack – she would listen to the radio or put on a radio dramatisation and get lost in another world. The sound of voices quieted the voices in her head. If only she had a book of cryptic crosswords and a pen, she could concentrate on something other than the situation that she was in. Instead, she decided, I'll think uplifting thoughts. First off, *Desert Island Discs*. What are my eight records?

She had to abandon that train of thought, since each piece of music was suffused with memories of her children … or of Alex. Ridiculous, I've barely known him ten minutes, she thought and yet already we have 'our song'. Elbow's 'Starlings'. She remembered the conversation.

Him: 'It's a seminal piece.'

Her: 'Why do men always classify everything they like in music as seminal?'

Him: 'What would you call it?'

Her: 'A fab song.'

When Jack had first played it to her, she'd hated the discordant brass sounds that kept breaking through the soft drumming. She tried humming the line that she could recall, 'Darling, is this love?' said with that lovely northern accent.

She wondered how she would cope on a desert island. She certainly wasn't coping that well here.

'Hardly surprising,' she said aloud, to the empty and deadened room, 'because of the rather high element of danger. Do we think that's got anything to do with it?'

She bit her bottom lip to stop it trembling. Come on, now, she admonished herself. Get back to thinking about a desert island –

going for a swim in the sea, walking around with my feet wriggling in the sand, eating fruit from the trees.

What would she do if she was marooned? She was fairly sure she could rig up a tent, or some kind of rudimentary shelter. She'd be very lonely, though.

She remembered listening to one edition of *Desert Island Discs* where the man who was to be stranded had said he needed to be with other people to see the lovable parts of himself. Otherwise he essentially slid into a Slough of Despond. No, she didn't think she had to have someone else to validate her as a person. She didn't like being on her own because she liked to laugh and have fun, and that was difficult to do on your own. On your own. Totally on your own.

She would have to coax an animal in for company. How would you do that? You'd have to make sure it wasn't dangerous … like Jon bloody Wallis, she thought. And then: Stop thinking about him.

She wished she had some knitting needles and some wool. She'd use a seriously complicated pattern and make a Fair Isle sweater, or a family of owls on an owl rail. All the trains from *Thomas the Tank Engine*. A rope-ladder. Anything to make her concentrate on something else.

Right. The desert island. She had always wondered if people who had been in a terrible incident ever slept properly again. Children who had witnessed their parents being murdered. People who had been in motorway pile-ups. Those who had seen others exploded by bombs. Shopkeepers who had been attacked by men wearing masks and carrying knives. Would you sleep soundly or would it all keep coming back to haunt you in various horrible nightmares? Would this?

Right. Getting back to the desert island. What is my luxury item? Before this had happened, she would have chosen a big comfortable bed. Or a bath with an endless supply of hot water, perfumed candles and fragrant oils. Now she realised that her luxury item would be something to occupy her brain. A piano and some books on how to play it. Or another musical instrument. An oboe. No, too high – it would probably give her a headache. A saxophone. Or a nice bassoon. She could make drum noises using the trees, like she had once seen chimpanzees do, thumping the trunks with the palms of their hands. She had an image of herself sitting down and banging them with her feet while blowing her bassoon. And then the image of herself shut in a soundless room with a few books and a small bottle of shampoo re-imposed itself into her consciousness, and despite her best endeavours, she succumbed again to a prolonged fit of crying.

It was amazing how quickly it got dark the further south you went, Katie thought. One minute she was bathing in the residual warmth of the setting sun, the next she was essentially moon-bathing. With a shiver, she lobbed everything into her favourite pink and black striped canvas bag and headed back to her room.

She loved hotels. She loved leaving the place a mess and coming in to find it all tidy and sorted. New shampoo, conditioner and body-lotion bottles – she popped them into her sponge bag with the others – and a chocolate on the pillow. When did chocolates on pillows start happening? It was an odd concept. White sheets. Brown chocolate. Mind you, it probably wasn't the worst thing the maids had ever seen on the sheets.

PENNY SMITH

First things first, tell Bob she was going out to dinner with another man. As an incorrigible flirt, it wasn't ideal, Katie thought, to be getting married to a jealous man, but everything else in their relationship was fantastic. She wished he could do flirting too, but he was one of those who believed that even kissing someone else was a betrayal – while she thought it was a frivolous and meaningless pastime. She had been asked on numerous occasions how she would feel if she saw Bob playing tonsil hockey with another woman. She had replied that it would depend on how drunk she was. She might even join in! A drunken kiss had ended their relationship once, and she wasn't about to let it happen again. But then … but then … What was it actors said? 'What goes on tour stays on tour.' She was in Spain. The likelihood of her being caught out was around zero.

Bob's phone went straight on voicemail.

'Hello my love. Me here. Listen, I bumped into this bloke last night who's going to take me to dinner. Nothing improper,' she said, her fingers crossed. 'He might even be quite useful. He's a facilitator and, who knows, he might have work for me in the future. He seems to know everyone. I'm going out at half eight, but don't forget we're an hour ahead. Love you. Ring me. No matter what time. Love you. Oh, and I'm going to have a shower now, so I might not answer. Love you.'

She put the phone down. That was a record number of love-yous. She *must* be feeling guilty.

In the bathroom mirror, she saw a woman with a naughty gleam in her eye, a pink nose and a white line on one side of her face from the arm of her sunglasses. She ran the water in the shower to let it warm up and went to choose an outfit. She hadn't brought much,

246

so it was done in a moment and she was back in the bathroom within minutes.

Jon Wallis was also in the bathroom, having gone home to check on his prisoner and find out if there had been any developments. He wasn't too concerned about the lack of communication so far, assuming that David Miller would be activating various lines of enquiry and deciding how far he could be pushed.

But there was a faint nagging at the back of his mind about Lola. He had seen a shadow cross her face when he had casually mentioned that he would be dining with Katie Fisher that night. What was going on there, he wondered.

He dressed with care, pulling out a crisp, pale grey shirt and a soft pair of Ralph Lauren trousers. Padding about in bare feet, he roughed up his hair, splashed on a dash of Vetiver aftershave and selected a slim watch. With a final glance in the mirror, he left the room, stopping only to pick up a pair of tan deck shoes.

The dogs were waiting at the front door, and he patted them before getting into his car, where he selected a radio station playing American rock music. He switched his route a number of times, but nobody was following him and he was at the hotel bang on time.

CHAPTER TWENTY

Normally on a drizzly Sunday evening, Lucy would have been happily reading the newspapers while gathering her thoughts for the week ahead. But today … well, there was nothing normal about having your mother kidnapped. She couldn't even phone her friends to ask them for advice because for one thing there was apparently a blanket ban on saying anything at all to anyone outside the immediate family – she couldn't even speak to Andrew about it – and for another, what were they supposed to say, even if she did tell them?

'Sorry. How awful for you.'

That was about it. Unless they were a member of the SAS or had access to mercenaries in Spain, it was pointless.

So here she was, sitting in front of the television, flicking through the channels and finding that an inordinate number of programmes featured women in danger. Even the omnibus edition of *EastEnders* seemed to have women screaming everywhere. Or maybe it was always like that. She zipped past the news programmes in case there was something upsetting on them, briefly pausing to marvel at a man with an unfeasibly big head on Dave.

In the end, she found herself watching *Embarrassing Bodies*, which was fascinating in a gruesome way and took her mind off the hideousness of her situation. It showed a parade of people arriving at the television 'surgery'. They would then begin their story by telling the doctor that they were too embarrassed to show their 'deformities' – as they saw them – to their nearest and dearest. They would then reveal whatever it was to millions of viewers. She assumed they did it so that they could get surgery without going through the NHS – or to Bulgaria.

It was strange what passed for normal behaviour these days, she thought. If it wasn't this, it was *The Jeremy Kyle Show*, with its never-ending selection of men who had got umpteen different women pregnant and had had sex with their mothers. Or women who had to have tests to prove their children weren't the result of a one-night stand with their boyfriend's grandfather. And everyone had spots and tattoos. She was glad she lived in a nice part of London, worked in a nice part of London and didn't have to deal with them.

Who would be a social worker? she thought. Trying to help pond life with the fallout from their animal behaviour. These were the sort of people who had sex against the bins behind Marks & Spencer or the Pound Shop. Why weren't their mothers being kidnapped instead of hers? Why did they deserve to have their families safe?

Life was so unfair.

Coincidentally, that final thought was very similar to the one entertained by her father as he broke into Miranda's house and set off the burglar alarm, which his daughter had erroneously told him was never on.

Desperate men take desperate measures, and Nigel had decided he couldn't hold on any longer to find and sell the books that he *knew* were in the house. In his head, it would be easy enough to break a section of window, climb in and look round. It seemed to be the perfect opportunity. The neighbours would be expecting Miranda back, so wouldn't be surprised to see the lights going on, and obviously she herself was not going to be disturbing him since she was otherwise engaged.

As Lucy was marvelling at the surgical removal of a haemorrhoid the size of a pink grapefruit, Nigel was dressed for redress in navy tracksuit bottoms, a long-sleeved black polo shirt and his golf shoes (for added grip), and he was approaching the rear of Miranda's home.

There was a moment of delicious pleasure as the window broke tidily with one firm tap of his heavy spanner. He reached through and opened the latch, throwing a blanket over the jagged glass. He heaved himself up and over, but landed in the deep kitchen sink where he sat with his legs sticking up, like a lamb in a bucket. Then the alarm went off, giving him such a shock that he was surprised he didn't have a coronary thrombosis. The noise was astounding. It was a high-pitched *wahwahwah* sound, combined with a long, thin shriek, such as a penguin might give as it was gutted. He stayed stock still for a moment, his eyes wide. And then he might have tried to get straight out of the window again, except that he was stuck. While he wriggled around, he decided that if the police did come he would brazen it out. After all, he had a perfect right to be there. He was Miranda's husband and they were his books.

Meanwhile, he needed to get on. Eventually he levered himself out of the sink, closed the curtains, turned on the lights and made his way to the bathroom where he grabbed a handful of cotton wool from the cabinet to stuff into his ears before heading to the top of the house. He recalled Miranda saying that the boxes were in the attic, and once inside, with the hatch closed, he found that the sound of the alarm was deadened to a workable din.

At least he wouldn't be disturbed by the neighbours – he had lived in London long enough to know that, while they might be irritated, no one would bother to investigate. He was ripping open his sixth beautifully packed box, and was half sitting on a poorly executed pottery triceratops (Jack, aged seven), when he was apprehended by PC Edward Johnson and WPC Georgia Dean on her first arrest.

In Oxfordshire, Alex was prowling around his house, unable to sit down for more than a minute. His father had told him that he would be kept informed every step of the way, but he knew that 'every step', in David Miller's parlance, meant 'on a need-to-know basis' and that he would therefore be more excluded than included.

He could understand why his mother had left. There was only so much anyone could take of being bossed about and controlled before they buggered off, if they had a choice. It was odd, though, that she had replaced one dictator with another. He could only surmise that on some level she found it easier to abrogate responsibility and have someone else sort out her life.

That was what had been so wonderful about the relationship he had had with Miranda. That he *had* with Miranda. It was not over because they had wanted it to be over. It had been forced upon them. They were equals. They had the same outlook on life. He knew he had photographs of her on his phone, but he couldn't bear to look at them because they made him feel so powerless and weak.

He needed to be there for her. He wanted to be there when she was released so that he could wrap her in his arms, protect her. Never let her go. Oh, God, he was sounding like some maudlin shit song. He needed to *do* something. He needed to get to Spain, whatever his father had said.

There was just the issue of Samantha and the other bodyguard, whom he had nicknamed Urk. Presumably they would inform their employer if he took a flight to Spain. But did that matter if it was too late? They couldn't stop him if he was at the airport, could they? Would they be able to buy a ticket there and then – get on the same plane? Did it matter either way? It would be very useful having bodyguards when dealing with kidnappers. The more he thought about it, the more it seemed like a win-win situation.

Opening a bottle of beer from the fridge, he went over to his computer and fired it up. He immediately found a seat on easyJet from London Stansted to Alicante, leaving at seven o'clock in the morning. Within ten minutes, he was clicking on the final orange icon to confirm his booking. He then sat for a moment in front of the screen, resting his head on one hand and debating whether or not to tell his 'shadows'. Surely it was better to trust that at least one would make it on to the plane with him rather than risk his father banning him from going. There was no way of finding out how full the flight was, but there couldn't be that many people going out on a Monday morning, could there?

The architect of Alex's misfortunes, Jon Wallis, was at that moment outside a restaurant having a confusing conversation with Lola, while his dinner date was musing to herself about whether or not she could have been a courtesan.

Deep in her soul, Katie Fisher felt that she would have made a very good one – although she would have insisted on the men being clean, possibly even clean-shaven. She would hazard a guess that a whole piece of toast could be concealed in a big beard – and even a small goatee might be home to a biscuit.

Jon was proving to be a very agreeable dinner companion. She wasn't exactly laughing her socks off, but there had been some amusing interludes and he was so devilishly charming that she could forgive him the lack of a silly sense of humour, which Bob had in spades.

If it wasn't for Bob, she would have been having a pop at him, no doubt about it. The strong forearms, the hint of a firm, hairy chest beneath the shirt, the deep blue eyes. And when he strode towards the doorway with his phone, there were also the muscly thighs, the tight bottom. No two ways about it, that is one healthy, handsome animal, she thought. She could see him through the window and he didn't look that happy.

She went back to contemplating the life of a courtesan. What was the difference between a courtesan and a prostitute? Did you have to make more effort to be one than the other? Courtesan. Sounded a bit like Parmesan. You probably would smell cheesy after servicing a bunch of skanky blokes, she thought, and smiled.

Jon, returning to the table, thought it was for him, and gave her a slow, sexy half-smile, which brought back the low quiver of excitement she'd felt when she'd first met him.

'You are a dangerous man, Mr Wallis,' she said, raising her glass to him.

'And you, Miss Fisher, are a very dangerous woman,' he responded, raising his own glass and taking a sip of the burgundy liquid while looking at her over the rim.

'While you were out there chatting, I was trying to work out whether I would have enjoyed being a courtesan,' she said, taking a risk that he would enter into the spirit and not hear it as a come-on. Or did she secretly want him to hear it that way?

'The lure of money or of a tight corset?' he asked, after a beat.

'No. The lure of men, I think,' she said, considering. 'Have you ever used a prostitute?'

He almost choked on his wine. 'What a question,' he spluttered.

'It's funny,' she said mildly, 'but whenever I ask men that, they always say no. But somebody must be doing it, or there wouldn't be any necessity for ladies of the night. Have you ever used a high-class hooker – that's what they call them, isn't it, if they have nice clothes and are pretty, but still want paying?'

'I have never needed to resort to paying for female company,' he said distinctly, then asked, 'Have you ever offered yourself for cash?'

She laughed. 'That's the tables neatly turned, isn't it? No, I haven't. But, as I said, I was thinking that I actually would have made a reasonable courtesan. Somehow it sounds more romantic being a courtesan than a prostitute, even though we've got these romantic visions of prostitution, like that television programme *Diary of a Call Girl*. Or films like *Pretty Woman*. The tart with a heart. Or the tart with an art.'

'Mata Hari. Courtesan or spy?' he posed the question.

'Hmm. Interesting. Both, probably. She was a dancer, wasn't she, with a made-up name? I seem to remember she just liked getting her kit off. And then she became the mistress of some high-ranking officers from both sides during the First World War, but whether she was a spy or what they would now call a sex addict is another matter. I think to be a courtesan you had to offer more than just an excess of skills in the bedroom department. Obviously you had to have honed those skills – although there must be a limit to how much honing you can do – but I think you were expected to be witty, erudite, well educated. And dance and sing. Or am I getting confused with media studies?'

'Do you have this sort of conversation often?' he asked, wondering where this was all leading, if she was going to offer to do something for cash. After all, there were precedents – that famous model Sophie Something-or-other, who had confessed to charging some staggering amount of money for sex to fund her cocaine habit.

She frowned and tried to think back to what had started this train of thought. Then her brow cleared.

'No. I don't have them often. But how I got there is like this,' she explained. 'I was thinking about how swanning about in nice clothes, like I was last night, makes you raise your game. And then I thought about the expression "on the game". And before I knew it, I was being a courtesan in Venice at the time of Lucrezia Borgia.'

'Aha. Now I get it. I would imagine it's rather like being in the army. You think it's going to be all throwing yourself down in the dust and being a hero as bullets rain over you. But it's long periods of boredom followed by long periods of absolute terror with a very small window of opportunity for feeling like a hero – and being one. You've got a fifty-fifty chance of being a dead hero.'

There was silence, and Katie could hear the couple at the next table kissing rather noisily, like two seals slapping over rocks. 'Um.

I hate to sound clueless, but where is the similarity between being in the army and being a courtesan, where basically you're just being massively rogered by someone while you try to think up new witticisms for afterwards?'

He laughed. 'I meant about the romance and excitement. I should imagine there would be tiny specks of time when it *was* exciting – like when you got given a diamond necklace by your "protector" – but mostly it was probably either boring or downright horrible. And if they left you, you had to go and find another one, even if he was ugly and old and smelt of—'

'Brake fluid,' she finished.

'You really do have an extraordinary mind,' he said, 'and on that basis, I'm going to agree that you would have made an excellent courtesan. Now, do you want dessert?'

'I don't think so. They don't do very good puddings really, do they? Just that *crème caramel* thing that they call *flan*.'

'Coffee?'

'Maybe a glass of pudding wine or a smidge of liqueur.'

He waved the waiter over and had a brief conversation with him. 'I've ordered a delicious Pedro Ximenez. I hope you like it.'

Her phone buzzed in her handbag and, with an expression of apology, she took it out to see who was calling. 'Do you mind …?' she asked, standing up.

'Of course not,' he said, and she pressed the answer button as she moved away from the table.

'Hello, gorgeous,' she said, making her way to the same spot where Jon had taken his call.

'I hope you're behaving yourself?' she heard her fiancé say sternly.

'Of course I'm not. I've got the Spanish rugby team lined up and I'm going to take them down one after another,' she said promptly. 'And the referees.'

'Hmm. It's not them I'm worried about. It's the man you're with. Some men hunt in packs, but the lone wolves are the ones I like to keep an eye on. And particularly when they're out with my beautiful, funny, witty fiancée.'

She felt a wonderful warm glow when he said that, and answered in a girly voice, 'Aw, shucks. He's not half as funny or as handsome or as charming as you are. And he's only made me laugh once,' she lied, having long since decided that honesty was not always the best policy. She didn't like people telling *her* the ugly truth, and what was the point in making him feel jealous?

'What time are you home on Tuesday?' he asked.

'I think it's around eight o'clock in the evening. I know I've got most of the day to get a thoroughly decent tan before I head to the airport and borrow someone's aloe vera gel to take the sting out of the burn. Are you going to come and pick me up, then?'

'Might do. Play your cards right.'

'Twist,' she said.

'Five of clubs,' he said.

'Twist again,' she said.

'Like we did in summer,' he said. 'And it's the Queen of my Hearts.'

'Damn. Bust,' she said sadly. 'Will you still come and pick me up, though?'

'Play your cards right …'

'Six of diamonds. Enough. My pudding will be getting cold. I'll speak to you later, or if not, bright and early tomorrow.'

'Phone me when you're getting into bed,' he said.

'You suspicious man.' She laughed.

'I like hearing from you when you're horizontal. Although normally when you're horizontal with me.'

'I'm pressing the red button right now,' she said. '*Hasta la vista*, as they say in this neck of the woods.'

'Phone me,' he said, and rang off.

She reapplied lip gloss and went back into the restaurant.

'Everything okay?' asked Jon, rising slightly as she plonked her bag on the table.

'Fine, thanks. My fiancé checking I was all right and hadn't been kidnapped,' she said.

Jon smiled at the obvious gag, while an image of Miranda flashed in his mind for an instant.

'You're right, this wine is delicious,' said Katie, licking her lips with relish.

Jon's predatory instinct had been bolstered by the obvious care with which his date had dressed that evening. When he had met her at the hotel, she had sashayed towards him in high strappy sandals and a short orange dress with her long auburn hair tumbling down her back. She looked a million dollars, and now here she was licking her moist lips having talked about how she would have been a good courtesan.

He touched a passing waitress on her arm and softly asked for the bill.

'Oh, let me get my card,' Katie said, reaching for her bag.

But he merely held it in his hand while paying with his, then handed it back. 'It was my invitation,' he said. 'Would you like a brief walk before I take you back to the hotel?'

'Actually, that would be lovely,' she said. 'It's such a starry night. And the moon is so bright.'

'The sort of moon you'd have been pleased to see if you were in a carriage in the eighteenth century, off to a ball. The road ahead clear, the coachman with his musket ...'

'How very romantic,' she said, her head cocked to one side, contemplatively.

'Shall we?' he asked, standing up and offering his arm.

She slipped her hand through and they walked outside, talking and ambling through the streets with Jon pointing out buildings of interest. Suddenly the vista opened and they were at the marina. 'Oh, look. *Lu Maritana*,' she said, surprised. 'Scene of my triumph last night. I hadn't realised it was so close to the restaurant. My goodness, it's bloody huge, isn't it?'

'One of the biggest in the world, I believe,' he said.

She could feel the taut muscles beneath his shirt as he turned to speak. There was something indefinably sexy about a man who could crush you with barely an effort. It was making her overheat. And she quickly removed her arm from his, covering the movement by walking swiftly ahead and throwing a comment gaily over her shoulder. 'I bet it never goes out to sea, though. It'd probably drown if—'

He was not to hear what the 'if' was since at that point Katie Fisher tripped over a mooring rope and disappeared out of sight with a surprised '*Whumph!*', a splash and a final wave of her handbag.

CHAPTER TWENTY-ONE

There are a number of sights guaranteed to strike fear into the heart of even the most stalwart of people.

A loo roll with only one sheet of paper.

A 'Gate Closed' sign after what you swore was a five-minute nap.

A small child advancing with a bogey on the end of its finger.

A man snapping on a rubber glove.

That was what Katie Fisher saw before she passed out again.

'I'm going to take that as a positive sign, and ring her fiancé,' Jon said to the doctor, as she was taken off for an X-ray.

'Do you know if she has insurance?' was all he said.

'She's here working, so I'm sure all the necessary documentation is in place.'

It was peculiar how he found himself uttering such archaic phrases when he spoke Spanish.

He phoned one of his contacts in the police, and by the time Katie was being wheeled into surgery, he had Bob Hewlett's number. He handed it to the doctor and let him explain what had happened. Jon left the Accident and Emergency Department as he heard the doctor talking about a dilated pupil and the need to relieve pressure because of a ruptured artery as a result of a small fracture on the side of the head.

It was not exactly the end to the evening that he had anticipated. He had done what he could – those years in the army coming in useful again as he had switched into first-aid mode when Katie had knocked herself out. He had even rescued her handbag, although it had very little in it: her mobile phone, a lip gloss, some (wet) tissues, her room key and a small travel wallet with one credit card and 30 (soggy) euros.

He would drop it off at the hotel, ask them to put it in the safe and warn them that she might not be checking out for a few days. He assumed that her fiancé would fly out and deal with packing up her clothes and paying the bill.

The car purred into life and he selected a classical music station to drive along the coast road. He loved these moon-flood nights, when the sea shone like a sheet of beaten pewter. Until Miranda had gone all lyrical on him, he had never thought about coaches in the mists of time, trundling along rutted roads taking their cargoes of girls in frills to mansion house balls. It was always about the enemy – or you – having a clear shot. Or sailing and avoiding rocks and islands. That was girls for you, though, harking back to an era that they would have hated living in, with none of the creature comforts they all craved. Or not the ones he liked, anyway. That was why he had never had a relationship with any women in the army. Deeply unsexy, he thought, a woman who can take you down in unarmed combat. Unless they were wearing a ton of makeup, high heels and a one-piece catsuit. He smiled, pulled up outside the smart hotel and went to deliver the handbag and the message.

* * *

At about the same time as Jon Wallis was turning on to the bumpy road that led to his isolated house, Alex was showering and feeling very positive. He had slept soundly, waking up fractionally before the alarm clock at three a.m. He knocked off about hundred press-ups before throwing himself under the cool water.

A beep on his phone alerted him to the taxi waiting outside, and after a final check – passport, credit cards, mobile phone – he was on his way. He turned round to look, and there was Samantha in the car behind. Good: he was glad she was on duty. He wondered, not for the first time, whether she was able to hack into his computer, whether she was reading his emails, following his trans-actions. Not that it mattered. He had once thought during an idle moment that his life could stand up to scrutiny in a court of law. Until now. Depending on what happened when he got to Spain. He sincerely hoped that he was going to draw blood and felt a thrill of excitement in the pit of his stomach.

He gazed out of the window, seeing shadowy fields and shad-owy animals – or possibly shadowy hay bales. It was difficult to be sure in this light. The clouds were patchy and ragged. He seemed to remember cumulus fractus and congestus as being fairly common clouds. Or had he read that somewhere and just enjoyed the words? Angry, fractious clouds and cold, bunged-up, congested clouds. The big comfy-looking clouds were definitely cumulonimbus. Comfy as long as you weren't in a small plane heading into a massive turbulent one. His grandmother used to subscribe to *Reader's Digest*, and he remembered one article about the incredible ferocity inside a towering cumulonimbus, which was why he never forgot the name. He would quite like to have a wind-powered astronaut-type suit and actually go inside one. Be tumbled about every which way and emerge from the top of it. What a ride.

He turned to look out of the other window and noticed a car alongside them on the dual carriageway. Urk. So … he was going to get his two bodyguards. Unless they were going to try to stop him leaving the country. Just let them, he thought.

Stansted was humming, and he was in Departures before Urk and Samantha, both of whom were carrying sizeable bags. He wondered if either of them was taking a gun to Spain, or if it was the sort of thing you bought when you got there. He shook his head. The sort of questions you begin to consider when you've got bodyguards, he thought. He imagined a Customs officer asking if he had anything to declare. 'Two bodyguards carrying fuck knows what,' he would say.

Although not now this minute. He was alone, in public, without his attack dogs. It was a secure area, and he could do as he liked – there would be no shadow. It was like being in a car on your own after passing your test. No instructor to tell you what to do. Signal. Mirror. Handbrake. *Stop when I bang my hand on the dashboard.* He had done such an excellent emergency stop that his seatbelt had virtually strangled him with its efficient tightening.

How sad, he thought. There's nothing I want to do. He meandered around the shops, picking things up and putting them down, finally buying a copy of the *Guardian*, some extra-strong mints and a travel adaptor. There were four at home, but it was the one thing he always forgot when he was packing.

'Hello, Samantha,' he said brightly, having spotted her lurking near the Mulberry shop. 'Looking for a new purse?'

'Good morning, Alex,' she said, her hands in the pockets of the snug black trousers she wore most of the time, then continued, with a sarcastic twist to her voice, 'I must say, I'm looking forward to our little trip away.'

'Out of interest, have you bought a return flight?'

'No,' she said, anticipating the next question.

'Is that because you've accessed my computer?'

'Yes,' she acknowledged.

'My God, my dad really is a … a …'

'Thorough person?'

He shook his head in disbelief. 'Whatever. I did wonder. When did you two book your tickets?'

'Shortly after you. Let's face it, Alex, you really do not want to be getting involved with these drug-runners without us. And, no, before you ask, I did not phone your father. My brief is to shadow you, not to influence you. Although I did toy with trying to talk you out of this trip. It does seem to be ridiculously foolhardy, putting yourself right in harm's way. Frankly, I can't see that it's going to achieve much, and could in fact jeopardise the whole mission. But obviously you're your own man, and I realised last night that you'd discount anything I said – as I can tell by your body language now. It isn't too late to stop this, mind you, and have a rational debate …'

He put up his hands to stop her. 'I've thought long and hard about this. I cannot sit in England while Miranda is in Spain. Dad won't tell me what he's doing. And I need to be doing something. This is what I've chosen to do. I'm sorry you think it ridiculous, but imagine if you were in my shoes.'

Samantha's face softened. 'Well, obviously your father does know you've booked a flight. And I imagine he'll call you at some stage,' she said.

'Hmm. Something to look forward to. I've had nothing for breakfast. Do you fancy a coffee?'

They walked to Costa Coffee and sat there chatting desultorily as he sipped his fruit juice, having necked a double espresso.

'Where's Urk, by the way?'

Samantha tried to look as if she disapproved of the nickname, but failed, as she always did.

'Troy is comparing electrical items in Dixons to do with television-watching round the world. Football, apparently.'

'Of course it's about football. It's all there is that unites every country on the planet.'

'I wonder how it all began – if there was one person who created the game of football, or if it happened … organically. It's interesting how, if you go out of the cities in almost any country, there'll be boys kicking a ball around while girls are playing board-game type things. You know? I was in Jordan one time and two little girls had scratched out rough squares in the dirt and were using different-sized stones to play … oh, I dunno – couldn't make head or tail of it myself. But they were so engrossed they were oblivious to the hikers who were thumping past on the way up the hill.'

'There on business?'

'Yes.'

'Nice place?'

'Stunning. You'll have seen the tombs at Petra, particularly what they call the Treasury, in one of the Harrison Ford films. *Indiana*

Jones and the Last Crusade, I think. The stone is the most beautiful rose-pink. You go down this dusty path with really steep, high walls and then suddenly – and I mean suddenly – it's right in front of you through a gap this size.' She sketched a narrow opening in front of her face.

'They say it's one of those things you have to see before you die,' he said, tapping the side of the coffee cup absentmindedly. 'Maybe I'll suggest it to Miranda once we've got her away from those tossers.'

'Out of interest, have you actually got a plan?' Samantha asked.

'Yup. I tempt them out, and you and Urk shoot them. Then I grab Miranda, throw her over my shoulder and leave while you tidy up the mess.'

She nodded, her bottom lip over her top lip so that she looked fat-cheeked and lantern-jawed. It was a habit she had when she was thinking, and he found it very endearing – if unattractive. It did give her nice dimples, though. He was partial to dimples.

'So, no proper plan, then?' she eventually said.

'Not as such.'

'Do we know where she's being held?' she asked.

'Not as such.'

'Does your father?'

'I assume he will at some stage,' he said, fixing her with his bright green eyes, 'and that's why I thought I'd come out. I want to be there when things start happening. There's no way I'm going to be stuck at home hearing about it second-hand.'

'Obviously my job is to keep you safe, and that job is made difficult if we are, as it were, in the dragon's lair.' She drained her cup.

'But, you see, I don't think they'll be after me now. They've got Miranda. They've got their pawn, if you like,' he said. 'They know he's going to be dealing with it, and that I'd be more trouble than I'm worth. Or that's what I'm banking on. Have you been told anything about what Dad's going to do?'

'I'm merely a bodyguard,' she responded.

'And a rather good one. I'll be recommending you to all my friends,' he said, with a smile. He slurped the last of his juice and leant back to stretch. 'Aw, that is *sooooo* good. I always feel like I could go on and on until I'm arched over like a crab, only I know I'd get to a stage where I'd be stuck. Now … are we ready for the easyJet scramble? And are we going to sit together or sprinkle ourselves liberally through the plane?'

'I should imagine that Ur— Troy,' she corrected herself, 'will have a view about where he's sitting, and will save a seat nearby for you. I'll attempt to find somewhere close, too. But you don't have to worry about that. As I know you wouldn't,' she added, with a grin.

They rose and walked towards the gate, where a number of people with fading early-morning pillow creases were herding. As it happened, the flight wasn't full and they easily found seats in the same area halfway down. Troy was essentially taking up two seats with his vast bulk. It wasn't that he was fat, he was just enormous.

They'll never see us coming, thought Alex, as he unfolded his newspaper and began to read.

'Would you mind if I looked at the other part of your paper?' asked the man sitting on his right.

'No, go ahead,' said Alex.

* * *

'Thanks,' said Bob, and took the sports section and G2, where he spotted an article about old phrases being brought back into use, which he knew Katie would love. What was it that the doctor had said? Subdural haemorrhage, but that she should be all right with no lasting damage. Bloody scary. Luckily, it sounded like she wouldn't have known much about it. When the doctor had talked about the brain being compressed, Bob had almost gone into shock. The idea of a head swelling. Urgh. And then the head being drilled to relieve the pressure. Poor, poor Katie.

He had booked the first flight out. He would stay at the hotel this evening and check how much it was before booking anywhere else. No point in staying at a five-star hotel with a swimming-pool and all mod cons if he was going to be spending most of his time carrying grapes to the hospital. They'd said she'd be out in about three days, and able to fly home within a couple of weeks, so maybe she might like to lie by the pool. What did people with no money do? He wondered. It's all very well having insurance, but you have to sort things out immediately, he thought, then addressed himself to the article.

Bob Hewlett was exactly the sort of man her friends had been hoping Katie would marry. He was a landscape gardener from Yorkshire who rode a motorbike and was 'fuck-off gorgeous', as Dee described him. He was the sort of man who wrapped you in his arms and gave you a bear hug that made the world right. It was impossible to feel vulnerable from within that circle.

The bag that he had packed as soon as he had finished booking the flight was full of Katie items.

Marmite. Hair masque. Lapsang souchong teabags. A Georgette Heyer novel. An eye mask with 'Sweet Dreams' written on it. *Private*

Eye. A bag of M&Ms. And a copy of *Bike*, which admittedly was his, but he wanted to show her the latest Triumph model he was thinking of getting. Since she would be the pillion on it, he wanted to make sure she approved. Secretly, he didn't care that much about her opinion, but he had to have something to look at while she was having tests and whatnot.

They had definitely said there would be no problem, hadn't they? He was sure they had last night, but now he wasn't quite so certain. Could a subdural haemorrhage happen again?

'I'm sorry?' the dreadlocked man beside him asked.

'Oh. Did I say that out loud? I do apologise. 'S been a long old day.'

The other looked at the time on his phone, which was sitting on his tray.

Bob made a small huff noise of affirmation. 'Yeah. I know. All started early this morning, though.'

'With a subdural haemorrhage?'

'Exactly. Not mine. Girlfriend. In Spain. Now in hospital,' Bob explained in brief.

'Bugger,' the young man said politely. He had a fucking girlfriend who had been fucking kidnapped, for fuck's sake.

'She's okay, though,' Bob said, and after a short pause he went back to reading the article. Interesting – there was actually a word for packing tightly. Suffarcinate. Oh, that was good: a homerkin was a liquid measure for beer. You could suffarcinate the homerkins. Jobler: one who does small jobs. He couldn't understand why any of those words had fallen out of use and were on the verge of extinction. Well, he could understand why wee-squashing wasn't doing well. For one thing, it was the most un-onomatopoeic word he had ever heard. It sounded like it was what you did when you were desperate for a pee, but meant the spearing of fish or eels by torchlight from canoes. God, that must be exhausting. He had watched a programme where they had speared alligators or crocodiles by lamplight. Seemed a thankless task.

'Excuse me,' he asked the man on his left, 'Would you mind if I kept this article?'

'Take the whole lot if you want,' Alex said pleasantly, and got out his iPod from his jeans. He had discovered that it's very difficult to concentrate on a newspaper when visions of the girl you have decided right there and then is going to be your wife keep imprinting themselves on your inner eyeballs. He had never had the urge to ask anyone to marry him before. But ever since they had split up, he had been falling more and more in love with Miranda.

He loved the way she looked – but that went without saying. She was absolutely his type. Curvy. Funny. Beautiful eyes that crinkled at the edges. Gorgeous feet. Sexy. And he loved her spirit. He had a feeling he would get on well with her son, Jack. He sounded like a male version of his mother. Generous.

What about Lucy? Cross that bridge when I come to it again. Or blow it out of the water. Whatever.

He carried on thinking about Miranda as he listened to Annie Lennox on his iPod. 'Song for a Vampire'. She was a legend, Annie Lennox. A brilliant songwriter and singer. Campaigner. She was great. Thanks, Mum, for introducing her to me. And for Joan Armatrading, Joni Mitchell and Joan Baez. Although they weren't for all seasons – unlike The Annie Lennox. He dozed off and woke as the seatbelt sign went on.

CHAPTER TWENTY-TWO

Heat in another country is subtly different. The temperature can read exactly the same, but if you were blindfolded, you would still know you were not at home. Maybe it's the smell, Alex thought, as he stepped off the plane into a wave of warmth and on to Spanish soil. Britain was essentially a soggy little island with occasional bouts of dryness, while Spain was part of a gigantic land mass. Its southern end had a massive bladder of water off its coast, but it was essentially a dry country with occasional bouts of damp.

On the plane, Samantha had told him about the travel arrangements. She would be going in the taxi with him to their destination, and Troy would be renting a car. 'I know it's tedious,' she said, 'but we're going to have to stick together while Troy sorts out all the paperwork at Hertz. I've suggested he get what they term a compact car because it's more useful. It's nippy in town and easier to manoeuvre round little country roads.'

Alex thought it would be funny seeing Urk in a small car, and wasn't disappointed. It was a snug fit. With the sun visor down, all you could see was an enormous shape, like Sugar Loaf Mountain.

'Fuck me. Let's hope you don't have to get in 'ere as well, Sam,' said Troy, as he fiddled with the buttons and dials.

'Samantha,' she said, as she always did.

'You'll 'ave to sit in the back if you do.'

'I'd imagine it's more likely you'll be travelling solo,' she said, 'and if you're now okay with everything, I think we should make a move. I can see the cab outside. You follow us. Any problems, ring me on the local phone.'

'Cool,' said Alex. 'You really are very efficient. Two local phones already.'

'Charged and everything,' she said, smiling as they got into the back of the taxi.

'I never thought to ask … do you speak Spanish?' asked Samantha, conversationally, as they drove away from the airport and past the sort of nondescript buildings found on the outskirts of most cities. One giant edifice screamed 'MUEBLES' at them.

'Rudimentary. And random,' he said, 'like I know that *muebles* means furniture – but that's from a previous trip to Bilbao rather than learning it in GCSE Spanish. The school was obsessed with conversational Spanish, so I can generally talk about what I had for breakfast and where I'll be going for my holidays. Oh, and I can do swear words and offensive phrases. Like … if you were twice as clever, you'd still be stupid.'

'Which is?' She raised her eyebrows.

'*Si fueras el doble de inteligente, aun serias estupido,*' he said promptly, then added, 'And another phrase, which my mates and I translated into Spanish, which isn't exactly swearing or offensive unless you think *Monty Python and the Holy Grail* is offensive – *Tu madre era un hamster y tu padre olia a bayas de sauco.*'

'From the only word I understood there, it's the line about your mother being a hamster and your father smelling of blackberries.'

'Elderberries,' he corrected.

'Out of interest, what's "fuck off"?' she asked.

He leant closer and murmured: '*Vete a tomar por culo.*'

'*Vetiatomar porculo,*' she repeated quietly, and then louder, 'In English it's much more effective. Shorter. Easier.'

'And you can make it even shorter by saying "c-off", which has the benefit of sounding palatable in polite society.'

She smiled, and turned to look out of the window as they got closer to the centre of Alicante.

'I'm not sure what I expected, but it's pretty built up, isn't it?' he said.

'And there's a big hill behind it,' said Samantha. 'Here. If you want to know anything else.'

She handed him a guidebook to the city and its environs, which he flicked through.

'Where the hell do we start?' he asked.

'Hmm. The worst thing is, they'll know we're here before we even start looking for them,' she said, wriggling on the sticky plastic upholstery.

They found a small hotel with a sea view, which Troy and Samantha declared they were happy with, security wise, and went to eat at a local restaurant.

Alex's flying companion, Bob Hewlett, had gone straight to the hospital, where he found Katie wearing a pale blue hospital gown, sitting in bed playing 'Froggy Jump' on her iPhone. There was the sound of the frog falling and an 'Ow', as Bob leant forward to give her a deep, satisfying kiss. 'Hello, you,' he said, with the melting smile that always made her heart leap. 'You really are a pesky pillock, aren't you?'

'Oi. You can't come over here calling me a pillock,' she said. 'You've got to be nice to me. My head hurts,' she added, in an itsy-bitsy voice.

'Well, you shouldn't go round falling off piers, should you?' he said lovingly, pulling a chair up to her bed. 'Now, tell me exactly what happened from the top. And it had better not have anything to do with that rusty knave you were having dinner with.'

'Rusty knave,' she repeated, and gave him another kiss. 'That's why I love you so much. No one else uses words like you do.'

'Or you,' he added.

'Anyway,' she said, 'no, it didn't have anything to do with the rusty knave. Did you bring me some grapes, by the way?'

'I came straight from the ruddy airport, you ungrateful bint. I have Marmite,' he declared.

'And that is why I love you.' She kissed him again.

'And I've brought you a Georgette Heyer novel.'

'And that is why I love you.' She kissed him yet again.

'And some M&Ms.'

'And that is why I love you.' Another kiss.

'And I'm now tempted to carry on and on telling you – singly – the things I've brought. But I know what you want, what you *really* want, is these.'

He rummaged in his bag, and with a chirrup of delight, she climbed out of bed and went off to change into her favourite soft white pyjamas with navy blue spots. While she was away, he put the rest of the stuff on top of the locker.

'Howzat?' she asked, slipping back under the thin sheet.

'Stunning. You look beautiful. Scrumptious. Like a goddess. A young filly. Like Red Rum in a pair of pyjamas,' he said.

'You were doing so well until then,' she said sadly.

He smiled.

'I can't tell you how lovely it is that you're here,' she said. 'Thank you. And how brilliant was it that you could get a seat on the first plane out? Was it packed?'

'Not really. Three-quarters full. I sat next to a man who I thought at first was going to be a bit of a smelly aphid, with dreads down to here,' he sketched a line about chest high, 'but then he took out the *Guardian*.'

'So you knew immediately that he was a good middle-class chappie, and you're now bosom buddies.'

'Hardly that. But, yes, he was all right. In fact, he smelt very clean. And then I was following him off the plane and he had the biggest bodyguard you've ever seen.'

'How do you know it wasn't his bum chum?'

'You really do have a way with words.' He rolled his eyes. 'It was obviously his bodyguard because he hardly spoke to him. And, rather oddly, this girl who was sitting about three rows back also seemed to know him.'

'Oooh. A story. Seemed to know the bodyguard? Or seemed to know the bloke you were next to?'

'Both. As in all three travelling together.'

'A *ménage à trois*. Club 18–30, I bet.'

He shook his head. 'Anyway, apart from that, an uninteresting flight,' he said.

'Do you want to see my scar?' she said brightly.

'Not really.' He made a face. 'But you'll wear me down until I do, so let's get it over and done with.'

It was very small – an inch or so long above her left ear.

'Tidy.' He nodded.

'I know. I keep thinking about how if it wasn't for the fact that the guy I was with was in the army and knew to get me here fast ...' She clocked his look. 'Stop it. You would have been brilliant too. Better, in fact. Much better. And much hunkier. And everything.' He smiled. 'But, seriously, if it wasn't for him and the doctors getting me straight in and then into surgery ...' She shuddered. 'It's rather repulsive thinking about brain swelling, isn't it? I imagine it like a pulsating thing out of *Doctor Who*. Growing all purple and veiny and tight. Urgh—' She broke off and they both made yurk faces at each other. Then she laughed.

'Bodies. They're incredible, aren't they? And humans – thank God for all those people who experimented years ago and discovered you had to do a spot of trepanning to let the brain have a bit of air. It's a bugger about not being able to go home for two weeks, though,' she ended.

'I thought about that, and after we've checked what you can and can't do, we can just consider it to be an unscheduled holiday. I've handed over the jobs I had booked in, and cleared the decks. And if you weren't lying to me, your diary is blinding in its empty white pages, so you don't have anything to cancel. Even if I do have to go home for any reason, I'm sure your mum or dad would love to come out.'

'Well, let's hope you don't have to leave – and that if you do, it's Dad who comes out. He's a lot more motherly than Mum. If *she* comes out, she'll spend all her time wandering off and doing water-colours of the port or taking flamenco lessons. I'd merely be the repository of her paints and castanets,' she said dismissively.

* * *

Before she had been kidnapped, Miranda Blake would have considered herself to be sunny-natured – a glass-half-full kind of a person. When her children had had the biggest nits in the world, she had decided that it made them easier to comb out. When she had broken her ankle in a freak accident involving a fake rubber toe and a set of steps, she had used it as an excuse to buy a lot of funky flat shoes. Even the discovery of Nigel's affair – which had been a huge blow to her ego – was useful for the divorce.

But here she was, wearing an orange caftan, her hair standing out like an explosion in an Etch-a-sketch factory, on her second day of enforced bed rest, and she could feel herself going into a downward spiral.

The more she tried to stop thinking about the what-ifs, the more depressed she got. She wondered if it would be easier if she didn't have children, since it was the thought of them worrying about her that was driving her insane.

She wondered if she had told them enough that she loved them. She worried what effect it would have on them if the worst came to the worst. And then she was off again on what the worst was if it came to it. Death was almost the best solution in some of the scenarios she was creating in her head.

She had roamed around the room so much that she was wearing holes in the area near the window. Things *would* be happening, at least she knew that.

And meanwhile, without a razor, her legs were getting prickly. And dry from the excess of sun and the lack of moisturiser. She rubbed a patch of skin and a cloud of dandruff floated off. When she got out of this place … if she got out of this place – Stop it! she admonished herself. *When* she got out of here, she was going to start waxing her legs again. Why had she stopped? Oh, yes, in-grown hairs. But there was pleasure to be had in squeezing them out. Looking on the bright side. And she had also stopped because you had to let the hair grow long between appointments, so you only had about five days before they started emerging again. Five days of legs out … and then they had to be hidden under trousers, particularly if there were children about, with the honesty serum coursing through their veins.

'Mummy, your legs are like that picture of the big fly on the wall at school – in magnificentstation,' Jack had told her one afternoon, as he was sitting on the floor playing with his fire engine.

She wondered if he and Lucy knew what had happened to her. Surely they would.

She looked at her watch. Pointless. It was ten minutes since she had last looked at it.

If it hadn't been for the overwhelming fear, she would have shouted that she was bored.

She looked at her watch again. Right. She was taking it off.

And she was back to the window.

It had been a nice, sunny day, and now it was dark, with ghostly clouds floating past the moon. She couldn't see the stars and the moon now without thinking back to the conversation she had had with Jon Wallis about the highwayman's moon. He must have thought she was such a gullible twit. She rubbed her eyes to ward off the tears that were now permanently lodged close to the ducts, like massive watery balloons. She needed some moisturiser. She hadn't felt this dry since she had overdone the Dead Sea mud pack and brought herself out in scales.

The locks on the door began to make a noise. It must be dinner time, she thought. Food was now the highlight of her day. Or perhaps it was just the chance to speak to someone and stop her brain going into meltdown.

She stood in the middle of the room and Lola came in.

They had taken to speaking to each other in a very clipped and formal manner.

'Good evening, Lola,' she said, with her teeth clenched. It was difficult to be pleasant to someone who had been watching you for weeks and had probably seen you surreptitiously pick your nose.

'Miranda.' Lola set down the plate and spoon.

'Paella. Nice,' Miranda said. 'I have very dry skin. Could you get me some body lotion?' And then she added belligerently, 'Please.'

Lola was feeling much more sanguine about Miranda's obvious attractions, now that they were less obvious. 'I'll see,' she said.

'And can I have a razor?'

Lola merely laughed, shook her head and left.

'And a radio?' Miranda shouted, as the door closed.

If she had had much of an appetite, she would have enjoyed the paella. It was chewy, packed full of ingredients and a glorious yellow. She made her way through it as though it was cardboard, then ate the apple, which was tasteless, but juicy.

She was back at the window when the door was unlocked and Jon Wallis walked in. 'Just to let you know,' he said, 'that we are communicating with David Miller, and he does seem to be giving your predicament some thought. We're hoping that the delivery of "your" thumb and part of "your" ear, courtesy of the local hospital, will result in a speedy resolution.' He smiled.

'Well, that will be nice for you, won't it? And did you want me to come and visit you in jail afterwards?'

'Come on, Miranda,' he said patronisingly. 'You know that isn't going to happen. You obviously have no idea who is involved in this operation, and how many of us there are. Mr Miller cannot protect all of his relatives, friends, business partners, workforce, if he reneges on a deal. And it's not as though we're asking him for much after all. Like a good marriage, it's a bit of give and take.'

'What the fuck …' she let the word hang for a minute, enjoying it '… do you know about marriage?'

He thought fleetingly of his parents, then said, 'Yes. You have a point. Anyway, I came to tell you some good news. We know that your boyfriend has landed on Spanish soil with his little bodyguard, and they're staying at a hotel near the coast.'

Her pulse quickened and her heart lifted. He was here. Alex, with his leaf-green eyes and gorgeous smile, had come for her.

'And, of course, you're thinking of rescues and the like. But let me disabuse you of that notion. The bigger likelihood is that we'll take him, too. Now it might be that we let you go after we grab him. So that's the good news for us. You've worked very well as a lure, so thank you for that. And for being so damned easy.' He chuckled.

'Glad to have helped,' she said facetiously, turning away to look out of the window, where she could see the Milky Way. The world was still turning, the stars were still coming out, while her life was becoming more and more like a bad melodrama.

'Now, I just need to take a lock of your hair, like so,' he said, grabbing it and cutting off a piece with some scissors, 'and we're done here. Enjoy your evening.'

He was out of the door, while Miranda was still spitting feathers. What the hell did he want with a lock of her hair?

Who wrote *The Rape of the Lock*? she thought randomly.

Outside the room, Jon put the hair carefully into an envelope he had in his pocket, and handed it to Lola.

'I wouldn't worry about getting an exact match,' he said. 'We'll be doing the alleged handover in the middle of the night. We just need him to think it's her.'

While Miranda paced the room, having added worrying about Alex to the long list of anxieties, her ex-husband was also having a worrying day. He had been bailed to appear before magistrates on a charge of breaking and entering, which was bad enough. But, now, the rest of his world was about to collapse spectacularly and he didn't feel it was entirely his fault.

If only he hadn't got involved with Andrew Flyte.

If only he hadn't got his daughter together with Andrew Flyte.

It was all Flyte's fault. But Nigel was going to get the blame.

CHAPTER TWENTY-THREE

There are days you can pinpoint as being pivotal days of your life. When you're a child, you think you'll always remember the first day you went to big school, the day you got your GCSE results, the day you won the egg and spoon race wearing your new navy blue sports pants, possibly the day that you finally had more stationery than everyone else, including a rubber shaped like a hedgehog, which came apart in segments.

But then you grow up – become almost as old as the teachers you thought were *ancient* – and those are not the days that stick out like the blip of a heart-monitor graph.

If Lucy had had to paste her top childhood memories on to a page, she would choose the day that she had become best friends with the coolest girl in the school and had a sleepover, with her pet rabbit at the bottom of the bed; the day she'd skived off with her mum and gone shopping in Oxford; and the day she'd had her first proper kiss. A boy called Graham, who had thick hair, soft dusky skin and the sweetest smile.

Those were her best days. The worst ones were all to do with being sent to Coventry, sitting on her own while the others talked about how to pluck their eyebrows and whether they had gone 'all the way' with boys.

But everything paled into insignificance compared to Tuesday.

It was the day she had discovered that her father and her boyfriend were involved in what she knew as a Ponzi scheme, and that they had lost an inordinate – almost incomprehensible – amount of money, including substantial sums of her own and her mother's. She did not need to hear her father's convoluted explanation as to what had gone on. How at the beginning it had all been above board. How they had tried to get more people involved by giving too much interest, when their investments – 'They were copper-bottomed, pumpkin, but it was the global crash' – had collapsed. How they were robbing Peter to pay Paul until it had spiralled out of control. And how they owed millions and millions of pounds. She felt sick to her stomach when she thought of how, only a few months ago, Andrew had been bragging about putting a deposit on a house in the South of France.

The whole sorry story had come out when her father had had to explain to her why he was going to be appearing in court on a charge of breaking and entering. And he blamed her mother for not having found the books he claimed could have saved him.

As if, she felt like saying. It would have been like waving a small cork at an overflow pipe.

Tuesday was the day Lucy discovered that her father, her wonderful strong father, was possibly a weak man. And that was not a nice feeling.

It was also the day she had an email from Jack, asking whether he should get on the next plane home, and a phone call from her mother's friend Amanda, asking why Miranda had not turned up to work.

All in all, Tuesday was the sort of day Lucy wanted to opt out of. She wanted someone to come along and sort it all out, for it to be made better. Or be a dream, like in a bad book or TV series.

Meanwhile, she had a deal at work that was proving complicated and needed her full attention.

Not so much an *annus horribilis* as a *dies horribilis*.

She chewed a fingernail and then quickly fired off an email to Jack.

> Yes. Get on a plane. You'll never forgive yourself if something happens and you're miles away. The man who is involved in trying to rescue Mum says he is fairly confident that all will be okay. But obviously, he can't be 100 per cent certain. And you can always go back out again. Xxxx

She'd decided to leave the news about Dad until he got home. No point in worrying him about that.

Amanda was more difficult. How to tell her that Mum wouldn't be at work for a bit, without spilling the beans? Eventually, she sent her a text: **Sorry. Should have phoned. Mum in hospital – nothing serious. But concussion, broken fingers and lost mobile. She got someone to call me. Don't know when clear to fly. Will let you know. Xxx**.

That should give her a bit of leeway.

As for her father … well. How was she going to help?

She assumed that the people who had put the burglar alarm in would have reset it, or done whatever they had to do to secure the property, so she couldn't go and rootle through the boxes – and, anyway, hadn't her mother told her they weren't there?

Lucy shook her head and got down to her work. It was difficult enough with her mother being kidnapped. She still couldn't get over that bombshell.

'What did we do before Google?' Lola asked Jon, in the area of his house that he referred to as the office – it was a big room with three computers and a safe hidden behind one of the paintings.

'With relation to what?' he asked, busy writing an email.

'In terms of finding things. Like the hair place I'm going to today. All you have to do is type in "hair" and "Alicante", and you get a selection of places.'

'As I said, don't go to too much trouble sorting out this wig. As long as it's vaguely the right colour. So, we're going to arrange the meeting with Alex for tonight. Should be able to sort things by then,' he said, his eyes still on his computer.

'How are we going to make sure the bodyguards don't follow him?' she enquired hesitantly. He'd been very tetchy and twitchy recently.

He looked up at her, his blue eyes boring into hers, and she felt her pulse race. She so wanted him to look at her like she had seen him look at Miranda Blake and Katie Fisher. In that way he had, where you just knew he was debating how he could get you into bed. The silver dress she had worn to the party on the yacht had failed, she thought, because he was too concerned with the arrangements for the kidnap. And then Katie had tried to get her claws into him. She had spotted the signs, and was plotting against her when her plans were rendered immaterial by Katie's tumble into the marina.

And as for Miranda, well, she wasn't sure what was happening there, but she had done as much as she could to make certain there was nothing with which Miranda could keep herself looking attractive. It wasn't like she was in her twenties with natural dewy skin and sleek hair. By the time you reached your fourth decade, you needed help. And Lola had bought the cheapest, nastiest shampoo, almost designed to strip the hair of its natural shine.

Jon answered the question she had posed: 'You can leave the mechanics of it to me, Lola. The fewer people who know what's happening, the better. Suffice it to say, there won't be any interference from them.' He returned to his computer and threw a comment over his shoulder at her. 'And as for what we did before Google, we used a phone directory. A large and cumbersome thing that doubled up as a very effective way for men to prove how butch they were by ripping them in half. A sad loss to the world.'

She smiled, appeased, and wondered if she could get away with wearing something pretty this evening to try to tempt him. It was all well and good having a plethora of qualifications in martial arts, but she wanted Jon Wallis. She had wanted him since he had employed her. But he had insisted that she dress to blend in. Didn't want her to stand out from the crowd. Mousy, he had said. Well, she was damned if she was going to be mousy this evening. She clicked her computer closed.

'Have you deleted your history and encrypted your files?' he asked, without looking up.

'Of course,' she said, standing up and wiping her hands on her trousers to get rid of the thin sheen of sweat. 'I'm going into town. I shouldn't be too long. I'll see you later.'

'Rendezvous here at twenty hundred hours,' he said, 'assuming I get the right response.'

'And if not?' she asked, raising her eyebrows.

'Sorry. I should have said we rendezvous here at twenty hundred hours, full stop. I *will* get the right response.'

That's why I find him so bloody sexy, she thought. Confidence. If she was going to write a manual for men, it would have only one instruction: 'Be confident.' Although misplaced confidence was a total turn-off. Bragging sucks. Maybe the manual would need expanding.

She got into the old white Seat and drove out along the bumpy road. She knew the state of the road was a deterrent to prying visitors, but every time she left, she did wonder if the car would make it back in one piece. It squeaked and groaned over the ruts.

The sun was still belting out heat, and she turned up the fan as she drove towards the city, through the shadows cast by trees and buildings. When she arrived, she parked, took a breath and braced herself. Heat was bouncing off the pavements. This really was the worst time of the day to be walking about in the asphalt jungle, she thought. It was oppressive. How did anyone get any work done when it was this hot? She walked past three men in fluorescent clothing who were digging up the road. One man, using a jack-hammer to break up the tarmac, was pouring sweat in rivulets. Mind you, she thought, at least he doesn't have to worry about the *policía* every time he goes home. Or have nightmares about the dead.

That was why she liked working for Jon. There had been no killings since he had taken over. He had started negotiations with other gangs. It was almost gentlemanly.

Right. What was she going to wear tonight?

* * *

287

The conversation with his father had not been pleasant, but Alex had explained in a reasonable tone why he had made the decision to fly to Spain in direct contravention of his wishes. Eventually his father had admitted to a grudging respect.

'I suppose I should have thought first about what I would have done under the circumstances – if it had been my, erm, paramour who had been taken. And I would, perhaps, have done exactly the same thing. But man to man, can I ask you to be beyond careful? Apparently, the operation is imminent. I can't say any more than that.'

On Monday night, Alex had gone to bed early, racking his brains and wondering what he was going to do until he had fallen exhausted into a dream-free sleep.

On Tuesday, he got a message. It was an instruction to meet at a certain time and place along the coast. He was to arrive on foot and without his bodyguards, or they would shoot Miranda. There was no number.

Alex was pretty clued up about how technology worked, but he could not see how someone could send a text with no number on it. He showed it to Samantha and Troy.

'Well, they can fuck off, the fuckin' fuckers. I'm fuckin' comin' with you,' said Troy. And then noticed Samantha's face and added, 'S'cuse the fuckin' language.'

'Wouldn't expect anything else, Troy,' she said. 'But it does state quite categorically that Miranda is in trouble if we turn up too.'

'Not if we fuckin' take 'em down first,' he said, and sat back, arms crossed, his gigantic thighs splaying out in his cargo pants.

'We don't know how many of them there are,' said Samantha, reasonably. 'Tell you what, we need to look at this area in detail. Let's go to my room and check it out.'

Alex was always interested in girls' bedrooms, and even though he was in the middle of an adrenalin rush, he still noticed that it smelt different. It was also impeccable. The suitcase was zipped up and by the window. He wondered where she had stashed the gun – assuming she had one. And all the rest of the stuff – assuming she had the rest of the stuff.

Samantha clicked on the computer and typed in the details. All three peered at the screen, with Troy's giant head casting a shadow on it.

'Right,' she said, having zoomed in and out and taken a look at the place from various different angles. 'Obviously they're not thick.' Troy shuffled slightly, his trainers squeaking. 'There's not much for us to hide behind. We also don't know which direction they'll be coming from. But we can have two cars to cover that.'

'What if they come by sea?' asked Troy.

Alex and Samantha both nodded.

'Good point. But I don't think they would. It would have to be an RIB to land there, and that would be an easy target,' Samantha said. 'You could easily puncture a dinghy and then that's them taken down. No. It'll be by car.'

The three of them sat in front of the computer, trying to plan for all eventualities, none of them entertaining for a moment the possibility that Alex would not go.

All afternoon, Samantha coached him, a crash course in what he had to do and say in the situations he might find himself in. The fall-back position was that they would have to rely on a small tracking bug she had brought over from England.

'A thousand and one uses for dreadlocks,' he said, his nerves jangling as Samantha worked to make the bug almost undetectable in his hair.

Finally, they were ready.

It was a clear night, with a waning moon. In his heightened state of alertness, Alex was able to appreciate the seriously cool figure that Samantha cut, in her tight black trousers and polo neck. Troy looked like an enormous black hole.

'Are we all ready?' she asked.

And they made their way to the designated area.

Unfortunately Troy had made the mistake of drinking from the sealed bottle of water in his room.

The most hateful thing about the room that Miranda was being held in was the lighting, she had decided. It was high in the ceiling and made everything flat. It was also giving her a headache. She didn't like the fact that it was controlled from outside, so there was a period between dinner and them coming to collect the plate and check up on her when it was gloomy.

She was also fed up of wearing the orange caftan and not being able to shave her legs – while being aware that those really were the least of her worries. And she had noticed in the hideous mirror that her eyebrows were getting shaggy. Stray hairs were emerging all over the place. How could they do that in just four days? The lack of sunlight and moisturiser had dried her skin so that she could see nothing but wrinkles and blemishes. At long last she was coming to the end of her tears, which had achieved nothing except to aggravate her throbbing headache and make her even uglier, with red blotches and a scaly nose. And she had washed the same pair of pants over and over again. If only she had put on something comfortable that Saturday night, instead of the most ridiculous thong in the world, which made her crotch feel as if it was being cupped by a cake slice. She would have gone commando, but for not knowing when the door would be opened. It was hard being brave when you had no pants on.

Also, she had begun to wonder if they were spying on her. A friend of Nigel's was obsessed with forwarding emails warning of one thing or another. She had been sent one recently, which she had deleted as yet another scare story she didn't need, about how you could tell whether there was a two-way mirror in your hotel or changing room. It was something about putting your fingernail on the mirror, and if there was a gap between the reflections, it was a proper mirror. If your fingernail looked like it was touching the one in the mirror … or was it the other way round?

She went and put her finger on the mirror again. There was a gap. But what did that prove? And it was probably all bollocks anyway. Like that one about people jumping into your car at multi-storey car parks. Or pretending to be injured in the road. There was probably one incident in a million. If you believed all that guff you'd never leave your house. You'd have to live in one of those gated communities and conduct all your business through a large plastic tube connected to the outside world. Or a small plastic tube – otherwise you'd have teams of gymnastic burglars swarming up it.

She tried to pluck some of the new eyebrow hairs that were growing outside the restricted area. It was exhausting. Her fingers had no strength. Instead she squeezed a small spot, which had arrived by the side of her nose.

When she had watched films with people who were imprisoned, they always did exercises to keep themselves fit. She sat on the floor in her orange caftan and did a sit-up, then lay down and did a press-up. She felt both idiotic and annoyed at how hard she found it. Cross-legged now, she bit at the skin on the side of her thumb, which was beginning to bleed through over-abuse. She transferred her attention to her ring finger.

She drew a ragged breath and tried to keep positive. Things will be happening, she said to herself. I will be released. It was a mantra she had found herself saying over and over again, as if by saying it enough times, she would make it happen.

Eventually she got on to the bed and stared at the ceiling, not even moving when she heard the door lock clang.

Voices could be heard and then footsteps came into the room, hesitantly at first, and then faster towards where she lay.

Her eyes flew open – she was expecting an attack – and there was Alex.

CHAPTER TWENTY-FOUR

At the age of eight and three-quarters – when every month had been important, and she had desperately wanted to be older – Miranda had almost drowned in the sea off the coast of Italy. She had been facing the beach, transfixed by a small silver fish wriggling in the brine near her feet, as the wave behind her hoovered up the water ready to throw a sucker punch at the back of her head. Miranda had been bending for a closer look and was thrown face down into the sand and pebbles under a ton of sea. Gasping for air, she struggled up and was knocked down again. And just when it was about to happen once more, her father had come striding into the waves and bodily picked her up, as she was choking and coughing, with snot running from her nose. She was wrapped in his hard embrace and instantly knew that she would survive.

That was how it felt being held by Alex. His strong arms around her, his murmured words of endearment in her ears. She was home. Nothing could touch her now. His hand tilted her face up to him, her lips were caught by his and every nerve tingled as he clasped her to him with a searing kiss. Then, as she felt herself falling into a cloud of pleasure, she felt him relax his grip. 'My darling,' he whispered, 'I don't think they'll let us stay together. But let me say really quickly … it won't be long. I love you.'

He didn't manage to say any more because, at that moment, Lola came in with Jon Wallis, who was wearing a khaki shirt and trousers and a sardonic look on his face.

'How very touching,' he said, 'but I hope you've said all you need to say, because obviously we can't allow you two to enjoy your stay here. We had a slight issue with your accommodation, Alex, but it's now been sorted. If you could follow me? And don't try anything,' he added, in a weary voice. 'It really would be most irritating if we had to kill one of you now, after all this effort.'

Lola – who was wearing a strange flamenco-type dress and, in Miranda's opinion, far too much makeup – picked up the dinner tray, which had not been removed earlier, and left, with a faint smile.

Miranda's heart was racing with a mixture of lust, excitement and fear. Energised, she walked round and round the room, chewing her bottom lip and racking her brain. Could she do anything to help him? It wasn't long before she realised that she was now in a worse position: while it was utterly fantastic that Alex was there, she was now terrified on his behalf. She wondered if they might rough him up. She imagined him clenching his jaw, determined not to make a sound. She imagined a knife being held at his throat. To his eye.

And there she was, worrying about her woolly eyebrows and hairy legs.

I promise, she prayed vehemently, that if you get us out of this alive, I'll never shave my legs again. Then she had second thoughts and tried to think of a promise that was sincere, profound, doable and didn't involve turning into a yeti.

Suddenly the lights were turned off from outside and, unusually, even the small strip of luminescence over the bathroom mirror went out. That wasn't normal, she thought. Do they want to have me bump into things all night as a penance for seeing Alex? Or has something started to happen already?

It had.

Earlier that evening, Lola had dressed in a red-gold wig, put on a new dress she had bought in town and set off to the rendezvous in a car with Jorge and Jon. Seven men in two almost identical cars had met them on the outskirts of Alicante, and final details had been dealt with before they drove the last mile to the designated spot.

Jon had been the one to go and meet Alex and make sure there was no one with him, before pointing out 'Miranda' in the back of the car.

Lola had waved to Alex from the dimly lit interior. 'Like a lamb to slaughter,' she said dismissively, and Jorge had laughed.

Meanwhile, Samantha was trying desperately to get through to Troy on the walkie-talkie, unaware that he was in a deep, drug-induced sleep at the wheel of his car, dreaming of green cats and a friendly chicken gizzard called Susan.

The tracking device bleeped as she followed the three cars, leaving a street's distance. They stayed together through most of the city, then raced through a series of red lights and split up.

Samantha gave up pressing the button on her two-way radio and shouting Troy's name, concentrating instead on following the blip as it went out of Alicante and began to head for the

hills. Having studied the map for a long time before she had
come out, she had a clear memory of this being a single road
with no junctions for about ten kilometres so she was able to hold
back.

She drove decisively and confidently, taking her eyes off the road
only once to answer a call on the mobile she had bought at the
airport. At one point, she was concerned about a vehicle behind
her, but it overtook her on a blind bend and she could see an old
man at the wheel, a cigarette in his mouth, before it raced off into
the dark.

The TomTom showed that the car she was tailing had turned off
the highway on to a small farm track. She pulled off the road and
got out, pulling down her balaclava and putting on a pair of gloves
with the fingertips free. She removed the slim box she had hidden
under the spare tyre. After 'tooling up', as Troy would have put it,
she began to run alongside the ditch that shadowed the rutted road
and arrived at the perimeter fence of the large house only a short
while after Alex and his captors.

Samantha could hear barking. She cocked her head to listen.
Big dogs. Dobermans or mastiffs. She took an ultrasonic whistle
from one of her pockets and blew. They were silent. Right.
That would work long enough for her to get into the house, she
hoped.

She ducked out of sight again as she heard another car approach.
She could see three men in what looked like one of the vehicles
down at the rendezvous. One more to come, then. She didn't have
to wait long. As the third car slowed towards the gate, she slipped
behind and, running low, held on to the bumper.

And then the house went dark.

Samantha could hear the men asking, *'Que pasa?'* but she knew exactly what was happening. All she had to do was follow the tracker to make sure Alex was where he was supposed to be … and that the dogs didn't attack her. She had been told that they were all bark and no bite but, in her experience, nothing that breathed and had legs was ever predictable.

Her eyes adjusted to the night, and she scurried round the corner to find a door she could jemmy open. Pausing periodically to listen to the sounds of disoriented people trying frantically to locate the fuse box, she made her way upstairs and slipped quietly into the first room on the right, locking it behind her. She felt her way along the wall and came to a handle, which she surreptitiously opened.

She heard Alex pad softly over, as she quietly locked the door. Then he was beside her.

'We're to stay here until it's over,' she murmured in his ear. She could feel him nodding.

'Is Miranda going to be okay?' he whispered.

'She's safe,' he heard her say, and then relaxed, sliding down the wall to sit with his knees up and wait for the dénouement.

Within a few minutes, they heard cars arriving and the lights suddenly blazed on, startling them even though they were anticipating it. Immediately there was a cacophony of people shouting, the sound of guns being fired, doors banging, dogs barking and running footsteps advancing and receding.

It was all over remarkably quickly.

There was a rap on the door, and a voice said in heavily accented English: 'Mees Kane? Ees Comisario Juan Diego Tela from the Cuerpo Nacional de Policía. It ees safe to come out now. And I 'ave Mees Miranda Blay safe here.'

'Alex? Samantha? Are you all right?' Miranda asked from outside.

Samantha had already unbolted the first door and could feel Alex's impatience as she unlocked the second.

'We're fine,' he almost shouted. 'Just a minute. We're here. We're here.'

And then, for the second time that day, he was holding Miranda in his arms. She was crying into his chest and he was kissing the top of her head until she subsided enough to lift her chin. 'Hello, beautiful,' he said, smiling at her. 'I told you we'd be all right.'

She raised her drenched blue eyes to his and his breath caught. 'Fuck, you are so beautiful, Miranda. I love you. I've been so worried about you.'

'And it's been horrible for me, too, I'll have you know,' she said, trying to grasp what he was saying – and what was happening. 'I've been so worried about *you*. I was pacing about thinking that you were being sliced into small pieces. And then the lights went out and—'

He hugged her so hard that she couldn't speak, and bent down to kiss her again, his soft lips pressing on hers with increasing urgency.

'Ahem,' coughed Samantha, loudly. She gestured to Comisario Tela. 'This gentleman would like to have a quick word with you, Miranda. Tomorrow, we'll all go down to the police station and give our statements. Alex?' She signalled that he should follow her out of the room.

Alex gave Miranda a final, brief kiss and said, 'See you in a minute,' with a lingering smile as he left. Outside the house, he was only vaguely surprised to find his father talking to another police officer. 'Hi, Dad,' he said, giving his father a manly clap on the shoulders. 'Good work.'

'Yes, it all went very well,' said David Miller, looking pleased. His grey suit, white shirt and pink tie looked incongruous among the sea of uniforms and next to Samantha's snug-fitting black top and trousers. 'This is Comisario Principal Gonzalez, by the way.'

There were handshakes, and then, in flawless English, Señor Gonzalez said to Samantha, 'I assume that you have all the requisite documentation for your equipment?'

'I most certainly do. Do you need me to bring it to the station tomorrow?'

'Indeed. Now, if you'll excuse me, I have work to do.' He almost clicked his heels before striding off.

Alex watched him go, and gazed thoughtfully at the police officers who were milling around, bringing out evidence in plastic bags and making notes. 'I'm still confused as to what exactly happened,' he said. 'I mean, how come you're here, Dad? And why did we bother about all that tailing and stuff?'

Samantha exchanged a look with David, who said, 'Put it this way, the reason Samantha was here was to make sure that you weren't taken hostage again. And obviously, with so many men – and a woman – bristling with guns, that would have been a very real risk. As for the rest of it, well, Señor Gonzalez says he was told that all the members of the gang would be here at this time and presumably he was also told that you and Miranda were hostages. As I mentioned when you came to see me that first time, the police have been thoroughly infiltrated, and with any plan, we needed to give the gang no time to disperse.'

'So who told Señor Gonzalez?'

'That's the part I myself don't understand. All he told me was that the gang had a very deep "sleeper", as it were. And that this "sleeper" was activated for whatever reason. Anyway, Gonzalez was given my number by this person and I phoned Samantha to tell her she'd be getting a sizeable amount of back-up. Until that time, I was extremely annoyed that you'd all risked your own lives – and Miranda's.'

'I'm sure I have lots of other questions, but the final one for the moment … How the hell did you get here so quickly?'

David Miller drew his eyebrows together. 'You really can't think much of me, Alex, if you honestly reckon I'd have stayed in England while you were gadding about in Alicante.'

Alex gave his father a wry smile. 'You activated the private plane for me. Nice one. Actually, I've had another thought. Where's Urk?'

'Urk?' his father echoed.

Samantha looked concerned. 'Yes. Where is Ur— Troy? If you're all sorted here, I think I'll go back to the rendezvous area.'

'That's fine.' David Miller raised his hand to send her on her way, then turned back to Alex. 'You know, deep down, I didn't blame you for coming out here. If you see the woman you … love …' he said carefully '… in danger, then obviously you would go to help. I would have done the same.'

'So who was this mole, then?' said Alex.

'I don't suppose it really matters any more. The main thing is that we've now taken this gang off the streets. They'll go down for a long time. Or, at least, I hope they'll go down for a long time – or long enough to make sure the hotel is established and that we have enough security to stop them ever getting a foothold again. It's a shame this hasn't been in the papers – can you imagine the price of the shares tomorrow?'

Alex shook his head, and caught a flash of orange at the top of the steps leading into the house.

Miranda was trying to feel confident and as though it was perfectly normal to be scooting about in an orange caftan and a pair of black lace-up boots that she had found in one of the rooms. More than anything else, she wanted to speak to Lucy and Jack – and battling with that was the desire to be once more in the safety of Alex's arms. Now that the immediate aftermath of the rescue had subsided, she felt absurdly shy as she walked towards him – and it wasn't just that the breeze was revealing a little more leg than she liked ... or that she was wearing the same skimpy thong she had been sporting for days.

With a small skip, she was locked into a warm embrace, and he was turning her towards a striking, silver-haired man, whom he introduced as his father. 'How lovely to meet you, Miranda. The architect of my nemesis's downfall. Nemesis and his cronies, that is.' He reached out to take her hand.

'How do you do?' she said, rather formally, 'The thing is, do you by any chance have a mobile I can use to call my daughter to tell her the good news?'

David silently handed her his phone and she rang Lucy, who promptly burst into tears and could barely speak for sobbing and hiccupping.

When the call ended, Miranda looked confused.

'What?' asked Alex.

She shook her head, pursing her lips and making a strange sound. 'I think I've been in captivity too long and have lost the ability to comprehend. Something about losing my money.'

It was lucky she didn't see David Miller's face as she said that, because he looked like thunder.

CHAPTER TWENTY-FIVE

'They've got your age wrong, Mum,' said Lucy, as she folded up the *Mail on Sunday* and handed it back to Miranda, who had been reading about the allegations against her ex-husband over a late breakfast in the sitting room.

She put down her coffee cup on the side table and shook open the newspaper again. 'There's nothing nicer than being in your own home,' she said, 'with your own bed, your own sheets, your own razor, your own food in the fridge. A choice of clothes and shoes. And a coffee shop around the corner that does nice cheese and onion tarts.' She ran her eye down the page. 'Oh, yes. They seem to have added a couple of years. It's the thin end of the wedge,' she said darkly. 'Before you know it, they'll be saying we've lost all of our money and I'm going out with a toy boy. Now, let's have a shufti at the horoscopes.' She looked up and saw Lucy's face. 'Oh, Lucy, I'm sorry,' she said. 'Honestly, I'm sorry. I was making a joke about the money because it really isn't important. I mean it. After I'd been stuck in a room for days on end with nothing to do, I realised that the most important things in the world are you and Jack. The two most treasured people I have. The thought that I might not see you again was almost unbearable. I kept thinking, Did I tell them enough how much I loved them? Really. Truly,' she eiterated. 'And in fact … just in case I get kidnapped again on the way to the coffee pot, come here and give me a hug and let me tell you all over again.'

Lucy, who was sure that she would feel guilty for all eternity for persuading her mother to invest in Andrew's business, tried to lighten up and rolled her eyes heavenwards in an exaggerated manner.

'Mum, if this experience has turned you into one of those yukky touchy-feely people, I'll personally have you taken somewhere secure for a lobotomy and electric-shock treatment.'

Miranda pointed to a spot next to her on the sofa and Lucy tutted, but went over and was unwillingly cuddled. 'Mum, I do love you,' she said, 'but this is strictly the last time. Enough already.' She wriggled away from her mother's embrace and went to stand by the window. 'How are we looking, horoscope wise?' she asked.

Miranda took up the paper again and crossed her legs, admiring their smoothness before addressing herself to the question. 'Well, apparently the winds of change are blowing through for me. And you … let me see … you're going to be full of energy and enthusiasm for a new project, it says.'

'That's why I like horoscopes. You can make them fit anything.'

'Do you have a new project on the go, then?' Miranda licked her finger and gathered up the croissant crumbs from her plate.

'Pah. My new project is to kill Andrew and then start saving again. All my money …' She added, in a humble voice, 'And yours, obviously. Sorry.'

'Hey, I'm old enough to make my own decisions.' Miranda got up and poured another cup of coffee. 'It was greed on my part. I should have looked into it more. There ain't no such thing as a free lunch. They were such big returns, I forgot the basic rules c investment.'

'But it was my fault,' Lucy stressed.

'All I can say, then, is that you're bloody lucky I got stuck in a small room with nothing to do and made a promise to myself that I would not ... What's that expression they have in America? ... that I wouldn't sweat the small stuff.'

'Fuck of a lot of money, Mum.'

'Language,' said Miranda, without thinking.

'Muuum!'

'Whoops. Old habits die hard. Anyway, the point is that we've lost it. We can't get it back.'

There was silence, and the sound of the radio drifted through from the kitchen. Michael Ball's *Sunday Brunch*.

'I *so* missed noise in that airtight room. If I'd had a radio I don't think I'd have felt so mad. That and a pair of tweezers. And dental floss. And a razor. And another pair of pants. And—'

'Do you think Jack's still asleep?' Lucy gestured upstairs.

'Jetlag, probably. Why don't you go and check he's breathing? But let him sleep on – we're not out to lunch until one.'

She watched her daughter leave the room and thought back to her arrival at the airport. Jack ... his big, beaming smile ... She had burst into tears and said over and over, 'Your hair's got so long.'

She had hugged Lucy so tightly that her daughter had been forced to gasp, 'Mum, you're literally suffocating me.'

The three of them had crab-walked away from Arrivals, hugging, as Alex followed, carrying what he had said was an inordinate amount of luggage for a week's holiday. He had walked them back

Lucy's car, then waved them off with the briefest of kisses and a meaningful look at Miranda.

The four of them had had dinner together, and Alex and Jack had immediately found common ground with eco-tourism, fish stocks, surfing and esoteric indie bands. But Miranda had known that Lucy still found it difficult.

Jack eventually surfaced and the three of them sauntered through the trees of Holland Park, past dog-walkers and children playing football, to a small pub where they met Alex and ordered four roasts and a bottle of wine. Lucy watched her mother and Alex flirting, trying not to be too obvious about it. She couldn't get over the age difference ... The idea of them in bed together repulsed her. Mind you, the idea of her parents in bed together was repulsive too, so she couldn't use that as a yardstick. Snap out of it, she admonished herself, remembering the rash promises she had made to be nicer to her mother if she was delivered home safe and sound.

Alex and Miranda had gone off on a flight of fancy.

'A friend of mine was telling me about Egbert, the first king of England,' said Alex, 'and I'm now wondering if eggs were named after him. You know, like we say Egbert Nobacon ...'

'Hmm. I think the egg was named before him. The chicken was named after him,' Miranda suggested.

'What – so his name was Egbert Chicken? That's a seriously shit name for a king. And Cumberland was named after the sausage, wasn't it?'

'No. Bangor was named after the sausage,' Miranda said promptly.

'Mum, that is genuinely mildly amusing,' said Jack.

'Oi, you. Don't talk wise to your mother,' said Alex, in a *j.*
American accent.

Yuk, thought Lucy.

'Do you have to do anything special to get hair like that?' she
asked – sounding abrupt even to her ears.

'Yup,' he said. 'Rub on a mixture of porridge, scorpion saliva and
jelly every hour for three days and then alternate Septembers.'

She actually smiled at that.

'What flavour jelly?' asked Jack.

'Goosehairy jelly, of course,' came the swift response.

'Not straw-like-berry jelly?' asked Miranda.

Jack nodded in appreciation.

'Or electrical-currant jelly?' Lucy suggested.

'Nice one, Lucy,' said Alex, and for the first time they smiled at
each other.

Miranda felt the thaw, and as they moved on to other topics, she
guarded that moment. Maybe this was the start.

'Do you miss having bodyguards?' asked Jack.

'Abso-bloody-lutely not,' replied Alex. 'I must confess that
having Samantha at the beginning …'

Miranda's 'Oi,' made him clarify.

'Having Samantha as my *bodyguard* was pretty cool at the beginning. A little bit of a rock god, a little bit of a roll god. But then it
became a bore having someone around all the time. And I never got
the hang of knowing whether to include or exclude her in things
like cups of tea. It got easier in some ways when Urk arrived on the
scene. Because it was – well, if I had to make three cups of tea then,
percentage wise, they were getting a better deal, so I stopped
offering.'

..d she was a lesbian,' said Jack, smirking.

'Yup. Stunning. What a waste.'

'Hey! What am I? Chopped liver?' Miranda asked, giving Alex a karate chop on his biceps.

He beamed back at her, his green eyes alight with mischief. 'You know what you are. Don't make me say it.'

She looked horrified and confused in equal measure, 'Well, I won't make you, since I have no idea what you're on about. Help. Help,' she said feebly.

'You,' he said portentously, 'are very lucky to be here after possibly one of the most eventful summer holidays ever – and, yes, if it wasn't for me, it wouldn't have happened in the first place. But all's well that ends well, as some bloke once said.'

'Phew,' she said. 'I wondered what on earth you were going to say, there.'

He gave her a cheeky look that implied he had been about to say something else. 'You back at work tomorrow?' he asked.

'Yes. And I'll have a much better story than I normally do after a week's holiday … because, of course, I'm now a qualified sailor and will no doubt be head of the fleet before the end of the year.'

They waited for her to mention the kidnapping, and she eventually said, with raised eyebrows, 'What?'

Alex's lips twitched. 'And nothing else exciting happened on your holidays?'

'Nope. Can't think of anything. Oh, yes – I bought a new red dress. I'll show it to you later. And I have a really nice orange caftan. Now. Does anyone want pudding or shall we get the bill?'

They all shook their heads, and she added, 'And, yes, of course I'll be telling them all about my experiences at the hands of the dastardly drugs gang, now that we have nothing to fear. Or I assume we have nothing to fear?' she asked Alex.

'No. Just my dad,' he said unthinkingly.

'Your dad?' Miranda echoed.

He shook his head. 'Oh, nothing. No. It's nothing.'

Aha, thought Lucy. Trouble in Paradise.

Miranda kept her counsel until they got back to the house. When they were curled up together on her sofa, the late-afternoon light beginning to fade, she broached the subject. 'What's with your father then – and why do we have him to fear?' she asked into his chest, one hand caressing his arm.

He shifted until he could look at her properly. 'I love you. Nothing can change that. But in the past ... well, he's been targeted because he's rich, and he worries about me being targeted for the same reason. So, you know, out in Alicante wasn't the best time for you to reveal to my dad that you'd got no money.'

'What?' she squeaked. 'For a start, I didn't say I hadn't any money. I said I'd lost money. And for another thing, I'm not some penniless gold-digger who's out to rip you off. I have sufficient funds to get me through, thank you very much – and I think you'll find I also now have a job. *And* I bloody love you, too. So blah.' She stuck out her tongue at him.

He chuckled. 'And your daughter worries about the age difference between us. I haven't stuck my tongue out at anyone since I was about eight.'

'Neither have I. It was very liberating,' she said huskily, thrilling to his hand, which was now exploring her body.

He stared at her, stroked her soft hair and looked deep into her blue eyes, as his own darkened with desire. 'I think you need perating from your clothes, that's what I think,' he said. Slipping off the sofa, he leant over, picked her up and strode off to the bedroom. 'Anyway, we'll get round my dad. I'm going to marry you,' he said firmly. 'I guarantee he'll be head over heels in love with you before we go on honeymoon.'

He felt her feeble protestations against his heart and pressed her closer. 'Now, stop fighting. Or I'll throw out your razors and force you to have hairy legs for the rest of your life.'

'You wouldn't dare.' She smiled against his chest before she was laid carefully down on the crisp sheets, and the afternoon slid, golden and oily, into evening, and the highwayman's moon glinted in the sky.

A fortnight later, Miranda took Jack to the airport. She felt very different now about him being so far from home. Before her ridiculous summer holiday, she had been sanguine about his adventures. Now she knew she was going to have nightmares, but as Alex – lovely, gorgeous Alex – had said, while stretched supine alongside her in his bedroom, you can only live your own life. 'After all, you would have been much safer if you'd stayed here in Britain rather than trotting about in dangerous bits of Spain. And your mother would have told you it was safer to stay with Nigel. Hmm …' He ran his fingers along her collar-bone, and tilted up her chin for a long kiss. 'Which do you think would have been better in the long run? Actually, don't answer that, because it would have been much, much, much better if we'd been together all summer, rather than snatching happiness from the jaws of … erm …' he nuzzled her neck '… unhappiness?'

'From the jaws of Captain Jon Wallis and his goons,' she gasped, getting goose bumps.

'Yup. From them. Only I think I would never have discov
quite how much I love you if it hadn't been for them. Marry me,'
demanded, his arm sliding round her and pulling her close.

She looked into his leaf-green eyes, smiled and said, 'Maybe.'

Captain Jon Wallis drove his black BMW up the dusty drive to the
house overlooking Lake Garda in the north of Italy and pressed a
button that opened the garage door. He parked the car, grabbed his
small leather holdall, got out and stretched. It had been a long day.

Striding into the sunlight, he admired the line of cypress trees
that stretched behind a hill to the west and the cluster of olive trees
in the distance. He turned to the house and went up the steps,
taking them two at a time.

A young woman with dark hair and almond eyes opened the
door and gave him an enormous smile.

'Signor Jackson. Welcome back. We 'ave missed you. You must
be tired after the drive. I 'ave set out ze wine and ze *antipasti* by ze
pool.'

'Giovanna. You're a sight for sore eyes. It's good to be back. I'm
going to have a quick shower, and I'll be down. Has anybody rung?'

'Everybody,' she said dramatically. 'And I've written zem down
for you in ze library.'

'*Grazia, bella*, I'll be right out,' he said, and bounded up the
stairs, dropping his bag on the bed.